THE INFERNAL TOWER

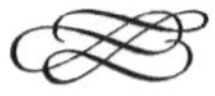

ADAM KARAOGUZ

Jacket art: Matthew Revert

ISBN: 979-8-9936782-1-4

❀ Formatted with Vellum

To Christine,

You are a woman to love.

BOOK I

SUMMONS

CHAPTER 1

Over the Indian Ocean

THE PLANE WAS DYING.

Slowly, but inexorably.

Nicholas had to hand it to the saboteurs. He'd personally checked the Gulfstream G550, and his engineers had given it a meticulous pre-flight inspection, vigilant for precisely this kind of threat. Men and women he'd known and trusted with his life in other contexts.

Could one of them have betrayed him?

Perhaps. But he doubted it. Someone had finally broken through his intricate safeguards.

He scratched his gray beard absently. Nicholas had planned for something like this. He just hadn't expected it right now. Maybe no one ever did. You always thought you had more time.

For the past hour, he'd watched the aircraft's oil quantity tick down and the engine temperature creep up. At this rate, the Rolls-Royce turbofan engines would fail within the hour. He'd logged the oil consumption of this aircraft over hundreds of flight hours, and this flight was a dramatic departure from the norm. What stood out was how the burn rate remained stable until he was hours into the journey—long past the last contingency airfields. Now, he was miles from anything, over an angry ocean, with daylight four long hours away.

Nicholas chuckled, mouth set in a grim mask. So much work left to do.

At least he'd prepared for this. However unlikely he'd deemed it.

He did the calculations in his head, mapping time, distance, and speed. The nearest search aircraft were out of Guam—hours away. The closest maritime vessels were even farther. A shipping channel lay ahead, but the odds of them spotting a matchbox-sized plane in the oceanic vastness were slim.

He pulled out his flask, took a nip. The battered metal had been a gift from his father, who had carried it through places with names like Guadalcanal, Tarawa, and Belleau Wood. Nicholas had taken it with him to Beirut. The air in the cockpit was cold and dry. Outside, nothing but a black void stretching to the horizon.

He dialed the satellite phone. She picked up on the second ring.

"Nicky." Sleep-heavy voice.

"They got me, my dear."

"What? What do you mean? How?"

He could picture her now—thick, gray-white plaits askew as she sat up and flicked on a light. Even now, she'd be summoning aides, working on contingencies.

She was silent for a long moment. "Who do you think it was? LC? Hopf?"

"Does it matter, J?"

"It matters to me."

Nicholas sighed. “Our enemies are circling. What we’ve discovered will be used—for good or for ill. Both, I suppose. Put the succession plan in motion. It’s time for the next generation to take up the torch.”

“You’re happy with the list as it stands?” She was already multitasking, speaking to her assistants in clipped directives: “Eric—call Admiral Sindri. Kathy—get Anders at Hapag-Lloyd, see what’s in the area.”

“I am. And even if I weren’t, we’re out of time. The world needs to know what we’ve found.”

“You still want to go through with the protocol?”

“It’s more important than ever. They have to be ready for what’s coming.” Nicholas exhaled, a rueful smile tugging at his lips. “Funny. I just finished recording the video for the finalists. The one they’ll see when they get through Treachery.”

“Funny is not the word I’d use.” She sighed. “There’s an Indian destroyer about sixteen hours from you at top speed. If you turn to two-seven-three magnetic now, we can—”

“Thank you, my dear. I’m lucky we found each other. I’m grateful for the time we had.”

“I’ll be seeing you in a few days, Nicky. Don’t talk like that.” Muffled aside: “Let’s get a satellite tasked—call Dr. Green at NGA. She owes us.”

“I have a few last calls to make. Then I’ll call you back. Just in case.”

“Don’t be long.”

Nicholas hesitated. “I was thinking about where we met. The light in the afternoon. Sangre Grande. If I could live in any memory, I think it would be there. The music, the people, the food.”

“Don’t forget the rum,” she murmured.

Even with the poor signal quality, Nicholas could hear

the quaver in her voice. He chuckled. "A lot of good ideas came from afternoon rum."

"In vino veritas."

A long pause. She was about to speak again when he broke the silence.

"I love you, J."

"I love you too, Nicky. I'll see you soon."

"That's my girl."

He ended the call.

Over the next hour, Nicholas made two more calls, each lasting less than a minute. In between, he continued troubleshooting the slow seepage of aircraft fluids.

Nothing worked.

The plane was going down.

He never called her back.

CHAPTER 2

San Francisco, California
Roz

LIKE A WRAITH, Roz drifted.

His birthday found him haunting misty San Francisco streets like some bitter specter, wondering how it had all gone sideways. The fog was rare for March—it usually held off until summer. He skirted a rust-pitted chain-link fence, ducked through a twisted opening, past the stench of old piss and broken bottles beneath weathered concrete bridge struts.

The dog trotted alongside, dodging glass with the dainty ease of a ballerina, tongue lolling in a stupid grin.

Roz wore clothing he'd scavenged from Goodwill three

weeks ago. They hadn't left his body since. His scent had long since transcended the funk of a week in the field with a SEAL platoon, evolving into something more robust. A bouquet of rank survival. His charcoal-and-gray mane was wild and unkempt, encroaching over an aquiline nose broken more than once.

He vaulted a dented guardrail at the base of the bridge. And just like that, he was at the stairs.

The maintenance walkway beneath the western span of the Bay Bridge wasn't well-known, even among locals. City workers tried to keep access restricted—locking the battered steel door—but someone always pried it open.

Roz ascended the corroded stairs.

Above him, muffled through thick asphalt and support beams, cars slammed by in both directions. It was only a few minutes' walk to where he wanted to be—a quarter of the way across the span. His favorite place to smoke a joint and zone out.

To forget.

There was a time, not long ago, when he'd walked to the center of the span and considered jumping. A fitting end for a Frogman—returning to the ocean that had birthed him.

Those days had passed.

Mostly.

He still found himself drawn here.

According to Wikipedia, the drop from the center of the span to the water was 220 feet. Depending on tidal variance. At normal acceleration, it was nearly a four-second freefall.

Eighty-one miles per hour at impact.

Not enough to reach terminal velocity.

But respectable.

Years ago, he'd known a man who'd jumped from a helicopter too early and lived. Brian "BB" Bretton. Roz's SEAL platoon had been helo-casting—jumping from an MH-60

Black Hawk into the ocean, chasing down the inflatable rubber boat they'd just cut loose. Nighttime. Raining.

Frogman weather.

A crew member cut the boat loose too early. Instead of ten or fifteen feet above the water, they hovered closer to two hundred. BB and "Starvin'" Marvin Walters jumped right after it. By the third flap of his arms, BB knew they were in trouble.

He survived.

Starvin' wasn't so lucky.

The dog whined.

"I told you already. I don't trust the shelters. We're better off on our—" Roz stopped mid-step.

A woman stood at the edge.

His edge.

Outside the guardrail.

The edge where he'd spent hours making his peace.

She faced north, toward Alcatraz Island. Bay gusts ripped perpendicular across the walkway, ruffling his hair. He glanced down. Her purse lay abandoned on the corrugated deck.

In the dim afternoon light filtering through the girders, her dark brown skin contrasted sharply against a crimson cotton sundress.

Her lips moved. A phrase repeated over and over.

"Hey."

She started, gripping the railing, rusted by decades of salt air and neglect. "Stay back! Don't try to talk me out of it!"

Roz exhaled. "Calm down, lady. I'm not here to talk you out of it. This is my spot. You gonna be long?"

She gawked at him. Shock and annoyance battled for supremacy. Annoyance won. "Be long? Find your own damn spot!"

Roz shrugged. "What's your name?"

"Doreen."

"Doreen, listen. I'd like a little solitude, so either get on with it or come back later."

She wagged a finger at him. "No! You do not get to do that. Coming in here, hurrying me up. Wait your turn. I'll jump when I'm good and ready."

The dog whined again, his paw rasping over the red guardrail.

Roz sighed. "I know, I know. I don't think she should do it either. Seems like a nice lady. Doesn't really want to jump."

"You don't know me. You don't know a damn thing about me. The things I've been through. Things I've seen."

She turned away, staring down at the whitecaps below. Her hair came loose, swirling about in sinuous patterns. Her yellow scarf danced in the wind.

Roz stooped and picked up the purse. "I wouldn't trust me either. People give out trust too easily, if you ask me." He rifled through the interior. "Anything good in here?"

"Hands off, stank ass!"

Her phone rang.

Roz pulled it out, checked the caller ID. "Uh-oh. Tracy is calling. Should I answer?"

"No!" Doreen lunged for him.

Roz stepped back, dodging her swipe. The dog panted, tongue cocked to the side.

"You could stay with her, keep her company," Roz suggested.

The dog barked, put a paw on his thigh.

"Fine, fine, I'll answer. Geez. Manners. Hello? This is Feroz. Roz. Mehran. Rhymes with Tehran. Who's this?" He looked at Doreen. "She's…indisposed." A pause. "We're under the Bay Bridge. West side, by Spear Street. Know where that is? Cool. Hang on." He covered the receiver. "Tracy. She wants to talk."

Doreen sagged, took the phone. Murmured. Wiped her face with her scarf.

At last, she ended the call and glared at him. "She wants you to stay with me until she gets here."

Roz groaned. "Great. Just great, Doreen."

He found a pack of cigarettes in her purse. Helped himself. "You're really screwing up my afternoon."

Cupped his hands around the lighter. Couldn't get it to catch.

Doreen gestured to the right side of his neck, where a mass of mottled scar tissue stretched from his collarbone to his ear. "What happened?"

Roz was persistent, finally coaxed a flame. He exhaled, watching the smoke vanish into the wind. "Bad day at the office."

Silence stretched between them.

Then: "You shouldn't do it either."

Roz glanced up. "Do what?"

"Jump."

He exhaled another plume of smoke. "I'm not. You thought jumping from here would be fatal?" He gestured down. "This is only a hundred feet. We're not at the center of the span. You're making me nervous, Doreen. Come have one of your smokes."

She laughed shakily. "*I'm* making *you* nervous?" She turned to climb back over—just as a gust of wind hit the walkway.

The railing gave.

She screamed.

Roz lunged. His fingers caught her scarf, but she slipped through his grasp.

He vaulted the rusting steel and stared over the edge. No trace of the woman. Roz moved to climb back over the railing.

The dog growled.

Roz sighed. "Seriously? Do I have to?"

The mutt held his ground, let out a bark.

Roz's pulse began to build.

Fuck.

"You're really not fun to be around, you know that?" He exhaled, turned back toward the edge.

Exhaled.

Stepped off into space.

AS HE FELL, he crossed his arms and legs, eyes on the horizon to keep his body vertical. Muscle memory. Doreen wouldn't have thought to do the same.

Then—impact.

A brutal shock, like always. The Pacific swallowed him whole.

Roz kicked, pulling his way to the surface. His jacket, waterlogged and heavy, had to go. He shrugged out of it and scanned the waves. A muffled cry. A flash of red to the east.

He swam toward her.

Doreen was flailing, barely keeping her head above water. One of her arms struck him full in the face as he moved in to grab her from behind. Pain flared. Copper flooded his mouth. A split lip, maybe.

Didn't matter.

She was panicked, latching onto him in blind desperation.

"Okay, okay," Roz murmured, soothing.

He took a bearing on the shore and started kicking, scissoring his legs. Doreen sobbed, shivering against his side.

The tide was moving in. Good. Otherwise, he wasn't sure he had the strength to get them both to land.

Still felt like forever.

Through the choppy water, he spotted a familiar Chevy Silverado parked near the base of the bridge. Hark.

Doreen had calmed now, the survival instinct giving way to exhaustion. She let him tow her.

"You know, I once swam five and a half miles in the Pacific," Roz said, mostly to keep her from going into shock. "Didn't want to. Some mean bastards made me do it. Called themselves instructors. I thought about every moment of my life on that swim. Twice."

Doreen coughed, sputtering. "Sounds horrible."

"I don't recommend it."

They were getting closer now. He could feel the pull of the tide shifting. Closer to slack tide.

"Hey," Roz said. "You didn't really want to jump, did you?"

She was quiet. He figured she wouldn't answer.

Then: "Not really. I just want things to be different. It hurts. All of it. I can't stand it." She craned her neck to look at him. "Why didn't you jump?"

Roz hesitated. Then sighed.

"My daughter." The words surprised even him.

"I couldn't leave her with that. Seemed too selfish. Even for me."

Doreen nodded. "Good reason."

They hit the rocks, Roz staggering onto solid ground, jelly-legged.

On the faded asphalt above, a woman hovered, wiry and restless. Tracy, probably.

The dog had somehow made it back to shore ahead of them. Resourceful mutt.

Roz guided Doreen up the uneven beach, then collapsed onto the sun-warmed pavement.

Diogenes, always opportunistic, seized the moment to lick his face.

"Back, foul beast," Roz grunted, pushing him away with a damp hand.

A shadow loomed.

"He has a name, you know."

Roz squinted up at Hark, who stood there, arms crossed. "He's still just 'dog' to me."

"Diogenes," Hark corrected. The dog wagged his tail, bounding over for attention. "You starting a swim club, amigo?"

Roz groaned. "Doreen slipped. And I needed a bath." He wiped his face, squinting at his friend. "How'd you find me?"

Hark smirked. "I know your haunts. You're not as unpredictable as you think." He scratched the dog's flank. "Happy birthday, by the way."

"Didn't think you'd remember."

"Ides of March. How could I forget? We threw you a rager in Rota after that trip to Gardez, remember? Welcome to middle age."

Roz snorted. "Nothing welcoming about it."

Doreen approached, Tabitha trailing.

"Thank you," she said softly. "I can barely swim and—"

Roz shook his head, flecks of saltwater flying from his beard. "Don't thank me. The dog made me do it. Thank him."

Doreen hesitated, then crouched and scratched behind the dog's ears. "Thank you, Diogenes."

Hark grinned. "The cool one. Of Sinope."

Doreen chuckled weakly. "Well, thank you, uh, Diogenes, sweet boy."

She and Tracy walked off, arms linked.

Hark turned to Roz. "You know you're late for court, right?"

Roz closed his eyes. "Thought it was next Monday."

Hark shook his head. "Come on. Sophie's waiting. I'll give you a ride and some dry clothes."

Roz looked down at his sodden clothing.

"But I just did laundry."

"THIS PLACE LOOKS LIKE HELL." Hark drove slowly and carefully, every now and then turning his head to look at the scenery. Needles littered the gutters, mixed with discarded fast-food wrappers, and assorted plastic containers. They passed bedraggled, strung-out humans of every stripe. "I heard there are addicts here that literally have flesh rotting on them. Zombie-apocalypse stuff. Or *Escape From New York*."

Roz refused the offer of fresh clothing but consented to sit on an old towel. "Places we've been overseas didn't look this bad." He waved languidly to a swarthy Hispanic guy he recognized as they passed. Hector the Collector, a fellow vet. Marine. Tents dotted the sides of the avenue, and temporary encampments had sprung up in vacant lots. With the windows down, the sharp tang of feces intruded into the truck cab. A massive, two-story-high fire raged one block over, black smoke pluming into the clear-blue California sky. "Kurt Russell is around here somewhere, filming the final movie in the trilogy. *Snake Pliskin: Escape from San Francisco.*"

Hark laughed. "I figured you'd have a starring role in that." His face turned serious. "When are you going to come stay with me out in the hills? I've got a room with your name on it."

Roz shook his head. "Bad enough that you saddled me with this wretched animal." He gestured to the backseat, where the dog sat, swiveling his head back and forth between them as if watching a tennis match. "I refuse to burden you any more than I already have."

"Diogenes doesn't need much," Hark responded, sipping coffee from a travel mug. "And have some respect—you're talking about a two-time Canine Medal of Courage winner. This hound has been in more TICs than we have."

Roz rolled his eyes. "Just because he's been in a few Troops In Contact, he lifts his leg to pee like the rest of us." The apocalyptic-looking city blocks slowly gave way to taller buildings as they entered the downtown proper.

"Sophie texted. Said Colleen and her lawyers were there. Bella too. Lucky for you, the court is running late, but your case should be up in the next hour."

"Lucky?" Roz closed his eyes. "How's things with you and Sophie?"

"Good. She helps me run the non-profit in her spare time, when she's not doing pro bono work representing joes like you in court." When he got out of the military, Hark built an organization devoted to helping veterans transition from the service. He only grew busier as time passed. "I need to talk to you about something," Hark said.

Never a good sign.

"Two somethings, actually. First, the bad news. Sophie can't represent you anymore. Pressure from her boss. She's in the window to make partner this year. They told her she'll get fired if she keeps you as a client. Your radioactive half-life hasn't quite decayed yet."

Roz shrugged. "Sounds about right."

"Now for the good news. You remember that guy we saved in Baghdad? Before…I went on R&R?"

Charitable of the Texan to phrase it that way. Not *before you went to prison for murder and your life imploded like a sub at crush depth*. "Berenger." Roz felt for his smokes, but his pack was a sodden mess he'd dumped on the rocks.

"Yeah. Nicholas Berenger," Hark responded. "Actually, his foundation's headquarters is right...there." Hark pointed between a pair of larger skyscrapers. "The old Pacific Bell building." Unlike the newer structures, it was hewn of concrete and stone, with intricate Art Deco flourishes on the exterior. Built in a different time.

Roz grunted. "What about him?"

"Dude was in a plane crash in the Indian Ocean six months ago. Solo flight. Anyway, his assistant reached out. Remember that woman at the airport when we dropped him off?"

Vague recollections came back. Tall, whitish hair, elegant. "Yeah, so?"

"Well, old Nicky had a last will and testament. He named little old you and I—" Hark gestured with his hand at the two of them, "—to be part of a selection process when he died."

"Selection? I'm done with selections, Hark. I'm more in the *deselection* phase of life right now, if you catch my drift. Besides, it sounds suspicious."

Hark met his eyes for a moment. "At a certain point, you're gonna have to trust something again. I'd be happy with almost anything at this point. This thing sounds interesting. It might be *challenging*." When they deployed together, they used to do all sorts of stuff in the name of the all-sacred *challenge*. Work ridiculous words into their portion of team mission briefings, crazy workouts in the gym, hilarious pranks on other unit members.

"You're invoking *challenge*?"

"Not yet," Hark replied with a sly smile. "Don't think I'll need to. I texted the woman in charge—Justine. The cougar at the plane, remember? The one that gave us the business cards. She's been trying to get ahold of you for the last week, but since your lifestyle is a bit...off the grid, she hasn't been able to find you. I told her to catch you outside the courthouse, to formally invite you to the selection thing."

"That won't be necessary."

"Don't say no just yet. Listen to what she has to say. Might be good for you. I've been prepping for a few weeks, getting a gear list together. Doing some research on the other candidates. And on Dante's *Inferno*."

"What does that have to do with anything?" Roz had read the first part of *The Divine Comedy* as a second class at the Naval Academy but couldn't remember much. That was the semester before his mom died, before he dropped out of the university. He remembered little from that time, curled up inside a bottle as he was then.

Hark shrugged. "On the invitation. See for yourself later." He pulled up to the courthouse and put his hazards on. "Want me to keep the hound?"

Roz shook his head. "You saddled me with this cursed canine. He can go in and fake it as my service dog. Besides, he's a bona fide war hero. I'm going to need that kind of credibility on my side in there."

Hark laughed. "You know where I live, Kemosabe." Roz opened the back door, and the dog bounded out, sniffing the concrete.

Roz gave him a sloppy salute as Hark drove away. Then he looked at the building, and his heart dropped into what felt like a buzzsaw in his guts. The dog gazed at him.

"Don't look at me—I don't have any answers."

CHAPTER 3

hree

Roz

"WHERE HAVE YOU BEEN?" Sophie hissed as Roz walked up, pulling him off to the side of the hall. People filed in and out of the courtroom. The second floor of the building was a blur of activity and noisy conversation. He wanted out of there immediately, at a bone-deep level.

"I'm sorry, Sophie. I got my days mixed up, and—"

She cut him off with an impatient wave of her hand. "Did Hark tell you?"

"About the selection thing?"

"No. That I can't represent you anymore." She wiped a wisp of brown hair out of her eyes. "My firm said I can't do pro bono work with you—you're too 'radioactive,' as they termed it. And I'm paying for full-time care for my mother—she has dementia."

Roz knew her story. Trailer-park girl from Oklahoma made good. He nodded. "I understand. I don't expect you to risk that for me."

She said nothing as they walked down the aisle. His stomach did a little lurch when he saw them standing with their lawyer. He noted the way Colleen flicked her eyes over him, the open contempt and disgust at what he'd become. He swallowed and put on a watery smile for his daughter. Bella's tween features reflected a mix of confusion and sadness. She wore a blue dress, her hair back in a ponytail. Already eleven, where did the time go? The dog sat and observed the goings on in the courtroom with enviable poise and composure. *Well, he's not the one with something on the line, is he?*

He barely had time to get behind the table when the judge spoke. "Mr. Mehran, thank you for gracing us with your presence today." She looked like one of the old *amehs,* the aunts that used to gather in the park near his family home outside of Shiraz in Iran, to talk and eat.

"My apologies, Your Honor," Roz stammered, before Sophie shut him up with a glance.

"You have missed two prior hearings in this matter before the court," the judge intoned. "Your former wife, Colleen Winston, is pursuing sole custody of your daughter, Bella Winston, with no visitation rights."

Roz winced as he heard her name read aloud. She didn't even have his last name anymore.

"Is it correct that you remain an unhoused person as of today?"

Roz swallowed. "I...yes, I don't have a place right now."

The judge nodded, making a note on a pad. "Your counsel has informed me she can no longer represent you. Is that correct?"

"Yes, Your Honor."

"And are you still intending to contest custody of your

daughter, or are you prepared to relinquish it fully to your ex-wife?"

He looked over at Colleen. She stared resolutely ahead. "I—I want to contest it."

The judge nodded again. "In light of your loss of counsel, I am granting you a stay of four weeks to seek new representation before I hear the final arguments in this matter. Mr. Mehran, I suggest you work on showing the court that you are improving your...situation in the meantime."

"Yes, Ma'am."

The gavel boomed, and strident echoes careened about the room. That was that.

Sophie looked at him as she slid her stuff into a leather bag. "I'm sorry, Roz. Really, I am. But if I lose this job, my mom is on the street."

He smiled faintly. "I get it. Thanks, Soph. For all that you've done for me. It was more than I deserve. See you around." Roz caught sight of Colleen and Bella heading downstairs. He followed.

A PLAYGROUND WITH WROUGHT-IRON FENCING squatted across the street from the municipal building, and that's where Roz caught up to his ex-wife and daughter. Colleen was on the phone and watched him approach, her face a mask of stone. The dog got comfortable under a tree outside the playground, panting contentedly.

"Dad!" Bella crashed into him. "What's that smell?" She wrinkled her nose, sniffing the dog as she kneeled to pet him. "It's not Diogenes."

"It's just these old clothes," he said, dropping to her level. "I've missed you so much, sweetheart. How are you?" She was so big. It felt like he was melting, staring at her. Flaking off and splintering into a million pieces. He wished his mother were here to see her grandchild. She'd always wanted a daughter—would have loved taking her shopping, braiding her hair. Even cooking.

"Mom got me a horse! I named her Starfire. We go riding almost every day after school—it's so fun!"

"I got you something."

Light bloomed in her eyes. "What is it, what is it!"

He knelt on the gravel, pulled a small box from his pocket. "It's a little waterlogged," he said ruefully.

Bella opened the sodden cardboard to find a golden necklace. The pendant was a bearded man astride a set of wings."

"It's Ahura Mazda. Lord of Wisdom and God of the Sky. He'll watch over you when you aren't with me."

"What's this?" Bella pointed at a watery slip of paper, the ink running but still legible. She squinted at the words, read them aloud in a halting voice. *"'Don't you know yet? It is your light that lights the world.' Rumi."*

She beamed. "I love it, Daddy." Bella hugged him, and Roz swallowed the lump in his throat, hugged back with his eyes closed. He tried to memorize every detail of the moment—the slant of the sun, the smell of the flowers at the playground's edge, the laughter of the nearby children. Finally, she broke the hug and hopped onto a swing. "Push me!"

Roz gave her a weak push. "That's great about the horse, honey. Really great." They'd always talked about getting her a horse back in their San Diego days. Colleen's family still had some land with a stable over the bay in Castro Valley. They'd only begrudgingly tolerated him, and no doubt loved to be proven correct in their estimation after Iraq.

"You should come visit. You can ride Papa's horse, Brown Jen. I'm sure he'd let you." Bella pumped her legs, going higher and higher into the air. Roz grimaced. There was no way in hell that Phillip Winston IV was going to allow Roz on the property, let alone ride his horse.

"Sure, honey, we can definitely—"

"Why don't you let me talk to Dad for a second, sweetheart?" Colleen smiled tightly at her daughter and gestured for Roz to come over.

"Okay!" She pumped herself even higher on the swing.

Roz had an ache in his side, like a cramp during a long ocean swim. He steeled himself and walked over. Colleen held her tongue until they were safely out of Bella's hearing.

"Jesus, Feroz, you can't even take a shower before your daughter's custody hearing?" Colleen shook her head in disgust. "Can you just, for one moment, look at yourself?"

He glanced away, watching people walk down the sidewalk outside the playground.

"You can't be a dad for Bella right now. Maybe never. Think about what is best for her, not for you. For once. Just once. Sign the papers." She stabbed a manicured hand toward him. "Then we'll be out of your life forever. You won't have to think about us. You showed how much you thought of us in Iraq. Or how little, I should say."

He turned away, as if he could hide from her words. "Coll,

she's the only family I have left. It might not look like it, but I'm trying to get it together."

Colleen gritted her teeth, her jawline flexing in and out like she was trying to resist the urge to take a bite out of him, Mike Tyson-style. "Don't fucking 'Coll' me." She exhaled sharply. "Fine. Fine. Fine. Of course. The judge will decide for you soon enough." She stalked off and collected their daughter from the swing set.

"Bye, Daddy!" Bella yelled with a big smile.

Roz waved back and clutched his stomach with his other hand. It ached like he got kicked in the side by a cranky mule. Colleen was right. He was a mess. She—

"Mr. Mehran?" A voice intruded on his ruminations. A twenty-something woman stood outside the playground. She wore business attire—skirt and blouse, but they didn't quite fit. Like she was a young woman trying to wear her mother's clothing.

"Yes?"

"I'm Kathy Woods. I work for Ms. Lipton—she requests a moment of your time."

He frowned. "Who?"

"Justine Lipton. From the Plek Foundation, Mr. Mehran."

Roz exhaled unevenly, watching Bella fade from sight with his former wife. He wondered if it would be the last time he saw her. "Fine. Lead the way."

KATHY LED ROZ TO A SIDE STREET, an urban canyon deep in the shadows of surrounding skyscrapers.

What a mess. Roz didn't know how he'd let things get this bad. If he'd just gotten a job when he got out of Leavenworth. But he hadn't been in any condition to do that. Still wasn't. It was like he was underwater, watching blurry shapes wave and gesture. Roz was certain they were yelling something important, but he wasn't able to make out what they were saying. He just couldn't get his shit together.

Outside a bodega, a black Cadillac CTS squatted heavily on its suspension, engine purring like a jungle cat. An Escalade idled quietly behind. A pair of men stood outside the car, conspicuous by the bagginess of their suits and athletic builds. They glanced his way, and their eyes kept moving, scanning the environment with a vigilance layered in nonchalance. One opened the door to the back of the CTS and bade him to enter with a gesture.

"I can keep an eye on your dog, sir," the other said, holding out a hand. Muscled and bearded, long hair tightly wound at the back of his head. Clear Special Operations type —he had the look. Roz's spider sense didn't mark him as a Frogman, though. He guessed ex-Ranger.

"Manbuns, huh?" Roz gestured at his choice of hairstyle. "What would the boys back at Regiment think?"

The man responded with a knowing smirk. "I expect they'd be jealous."

Roz gave a faint smile of his own and handed over the leash. Kathy got in the front as Roz slid into the back of the sedan.

The woman inside smiled and extended her hand. Firm and dry grip in a bony hand. She was tall and blonde, mid-sixties. "Mr. Mehran, Justine Lipton. We met—"

"At the Baghdad Airport. I remember."

She cocked her head, and her eyes searched his face. "You never called."

"Regrettably, I was detained. For a few years."

She smiled, revealing a bank of well-maintained dentistry. "Well, these things happen."

Roz laughed, a discordant bark that caused Kathy to start in the front seat. "You're funny, Justine. Is there a reason you're enduring my ripe smell to have this conversation?"

Justine cleared her throat. "Yes, well, you are a hard man to get ahold of. Thankfully, Mr. Harkness was able to put us onto your *scent*. My apologies. I couldn't resist the opening."

"Well played."

She took the compliment with the faintest of nods. "Did Mr. Harkness mention what this was about?"

"Something about Berenger, a plane crash, and a selection."

A curtain seemed to fall over her features. "Yes. Quite. Nicky—Dr. Berenger was lost at sea, after developing mechanical trouble on the way to our island facility."

"I am sorry for your loss, but I'm not sure what that has to do with me."

"Dr. Berenger was quite grateful for your efforts to intervene and get him out of a rather dangerous situation in Iraq. At great personal and career risk to yourself, I might add."

Roz shrugged and said nothing.

"He cultivated the Plek Foundation from the ground up, from profits in various industries over decades. He left very particular instructions for the determination of suitable stewards to lead it into the future."

Roz stared out the window, watching Manbuns play with the dog. "Do I look like C-suite material to you?"

"The leadership that Nicholas had in mind is not business oriented. Not primarily, anyway. It was, and remains, finding the *right* humans to guide the organization through the years to come."

"Does that list include convicted murderers?"

She regarded him squarely. "Did you murder Major Justin Vanders?"

He returned her stare for long moments before looking away. "Murder, no. We got into a fight that day, but I didn't kill him. I gave him a black eye and just choked his Massengale ass out."

"Massengale?"

"You know, *Once an Eagle*? The book? Never mind, it's not important. No one reads anymore."

Justine smoothed her skirt, picked a piece of lint from the material. "Well, what *is* important is that Nicholas saw something in you. Something of value. Some *propensity*. Whether you rise to that propensity is entirely up to you."

"So, what is this selection thing?"

"Kathy has an information packet with all the details, since you don't seem to have a cell phone or email. Briefly, it is an intense testing and evaluation period. The process is designed to assess your character and decision-making in uncertain and arduous environments. I believe you have taken part in similar events before."

He shrugged. "Once or twice."

"Nicholas was very clear about the people he wanted to guide Plek through the next decade, which is shaping up to be rather critical for humankind. Have you ever heard of the 'Great Filter' theory?"

Roz shook his head.

"It's one explanation for why we haven't found other intelligent life in the universe. It holds that life may be self-terminating after it progresses to a certain level of advancement. One of the primary missions of the foundation is to keep humankind from that sort of self-termination in the face of these rising exponential and existential risks."

Staring at her phone, Kathy cursed softly.

"What is it?" Justine asked.

Kathy held the phone out, and Roz watched Justine's face darken. Then the mask of neutrality slipped down once more. " No matter. We'll deal with it later." Justine faced him once more. "So, what say you, Mr. Mehran? If you complete the selection process in good standing, you stand to gain sizable financial resources for the custody dispute with your ex-wife."

Roz shook his head. "Not interested."

"May I ask why not?"

"I'm not really a joiner. Besides, this whole thing seems suspicious to me."

"How so?"

"You're going to be recording and monitoring the whole thing, right?"

Justine nodded.

"Seems like a gimmick. A reality show. In my experience, when something sounds too good to be true, that's the time to run the other way. No thanks."

"I assure you, that—"

Roz reached for the door handle.

"Wait," Justine said, reaching out a hand to stay his exit. "I hesitate to mention this, but if you're going to decline participation—and our protection—I feel it's only proper to inform you of some recent…developments."

"What kinds of developments?"

"Some of the selectees have found themselves…targeted," Kathy said from the front seat. "Targeted for recruitment by an external entity, and targeted for assassination. We don't know who is doing it, or how they're finding the names of selectees."

Justine added, "If you elect to take part, we can provide security. A place to stay, out of the elements, until selection begins."

He got out of the sedan without answering, letting the door shut. Heavy. Armored. By the heft, it could probably stop a fifty-caliber round.

"If you change your mind, here's my card." Kathy thrust it at him from the front seat.

He ignored it. Walked over to Manbuns.

"Fine animal. A Malinois saved my life once," the man said.

"Where?"

"Tagab Valley."

Roz nodded, taking the leash. "Dangerous neighborhood."

The man grinned. "It is. For Westerners."

CHAPTER 4

Roz

ROZ WOVE THROUGH SEVERAL LANES OF TRAFFIC on the street until he got to the sidewalk, ignoring the blaring horns. He wandered without a destination through the finance district. Later, he'd hit one of his usual bed-down locations, catch a few hours of sleep, maybe after he found a joint to smoke. Roz cursed, drawing an inquisitive glance from the dog and furtive looks from passersby, who hastened their pace down the boulevard. "Don't gimme that," he muttered to the dog. What a train wreck the morning had been. Four weeks. That's all the time he had to find a new lawyer. Less than that, really, when you thought about it. The lawyer had to get up to speed on the case. Call it three, then. He put the whiskey pint up to his mouth, downing the last in a gulp before heaving it in the general direction of a trash can. A nice, comfortable burn.

His stomach growled. Roz hadn't had much in the way of food lately.

A gaggle of suits streamed out of a trendy after-work cocktail joint, guffawing at something the suit in front said.

"What is that smell?" the man said loudly when they got to Roz. He had a beefy, frat-boy air about him. The group all gave the dog a wide berth, staring Roz down. "Oh, there it is."

Roz stopped and met each of their gazes in turn. It was clear it had been a three-martini afternoon for these boys. Maybe four.

"Someone needs to clean this town up. What a disgrace," said one.

"Can't even walk a block without smelling piss or stepping in a pile of human shit," said another.

Roz laughed and blew out a loud raspberry at the men.

"You got a problem, stinky?" the lead beefcake asked.

"You gonna help me solve it, big boy?"

The dog walked away, found a spot between a few rusty newspaper boxes that hadn't been filled in months, maybe years. Slid down with a bored grunt.

"Why don't you go over to Castro, bother some of the freaks there? Leave us good Americans alone. You're a leech. You're ruining this country. A cancer." Beefcake loomed over him. The others crowded into a loose semi-circle. Four of them.

"What'd you say? You're a great dancer?"

Beefcake paused a second. Even through his buzz, Roz imagined the impulse travel the synaptic gap—from thought to the faint slackening of the right shoulder. The right arm slid backward, movement caught in a receding tide of hesitation. Roz had time to get his left hand up to his ear, forming an elbow block. Beefcake's haymaker collided with Roz's elbow instead of his jaw and sent a shot of numbness through his arm. The man let out a shocked cry and recoiled. Roz snapped a kick to his balls, grinning as the others closed in. He blocked their punches until their combined mass took him down. Roz turtled into a ball on the filthy sidewalk and covered as much of his vital areas as he could as the men launched a flurry of kicks at him.

There it was.

The pain. For a moment, there was nothing but the pain. No custody battle. No dishonorable discharge. No ghosts of the past hovering over him like hungry ghouls.

Like watching a stop-motion video in jagged flashes, Roz saw Beefcake climb to his feet. "Broke my hand, you piece of trash." He launched a kick into Roz's side that stole his breath.

"Hey, you a vet?" His shirt had ridden up, and dimly, he heard one of the other men call out. "Yo—that's a Bone Frog tattoo. I recognize that from this charity golf thing I did last year. This guy's a vet. A Navy fucking SEAL."

They must have seen the tattoo on his side. Stupid decision when he'd first gotten his Trident. Roz looked up, saw that one of the men was keeping the others from pummeling him. He had a stupid-looking mustache like Hark's, and a bow tie for some ungodly reason. "Yeah. So what?"

"Hey, man. We didn't know." Beefcake cradled his hand, blood streaming down between the knuckles. "I'll tell you what. I won't press charges for this."

Roz slowly swiveled to a sitting position, his back against the weathered bricks of the bar front. He spat onto the sidewalk. Smiled a bloody smile at the men. "Mighty...charitable of you."

"Let's get out of here," Bow Tie said to the others. He spared a final glance Roz's way. "Thank you for your service," he called and hurried to catch up to the others.

"Thank you for your service," Roz muttered quietly. He looked over at the dog. "Thank you for your service, you mangy mutt."

The dog stared back from a Buddha-like repose.

"Some help you were. I thought Hark told you to look out for me."

The hound yawned, broke into a panting grin.

"Typical."

SILAS MARINO LEFT HIS HOUSE in the early morning darkness. Same as he did most days. It was the only time of day he could squeeze in a run. The rest of his waking hours were filled with coding and business work for Razoracle, the startup he founded with his wife and best friend. Luckily, that was the same person. It was a constant challenge—seemed like there was always a pull on his attention. Answer this email, take that phone call, meet with this representative, travel to that conference. His morning run was a non-negotiable, sacred ritual. It connected him to his body and prepared him for the daily insanity that followed, without fail. The predawn air held a salty chill coming off the bay as Silas slipped through the misty Palo Alto streets. No trace of the wildfires to the south. Winds must have shifted overnight. Silas wondered if he was ready. The Plek thing could be a chance to really make a dent in all the troubles that humanity faced. Physically, he was in the best shape of his life. Mentally, he was sharper. He picked out the next podcast from his list. *Dumpster Fire,* Episode 63. Silas always listened at 1.5 speed to maximize content intake in a timely fashion.

The host of *Dumpster Fire* came into his AirPods. "Our guests today are Brent Steinberg and Dan Scorpinski, cofounders of the Attunement Project, an organization whose stated aim is to 'publish research and analysis to help decision-makers and leaders toward the wisdom necessary to address the unique challenges of our time.' That's a mouthful. You talk a lot about global coordination challenges, catastrophic risks, and social technologies. Brent, can you unpack what this 'polycrisis' thing is for our listeners?"

"Yeah, Jon, thanks for having us on. There are many crises drawing increasing amounts of public attention—climate, the economy, social, border security, domestic and international politics, and energy. But there is also an invisible crisis unfolding within our own minds and cultures that is getting much less attention. This can be called the *meta-crisis,* which has to do with how humans relate to themselves and the larger world. The prefix 'meta' relates to the crisis above and behind the crisis, so to speak. While polycrisis refers to the symptoms we can see, the meta-crisis refers to the drivers of these symptoms. Our systems and societies are in trouble, but it is the *psyche*—the human dimension—that is in the direst of straits. That is, at least in the Western world."

Silas crossed Bellevue and continued southward, toward

the point. The geography there reminded him of the coastline from the movie *Goonies,* which he had first watched in high school. It would be a good place to watch the sun rise, do some yoga. His lanky body warming up, he sped up, referencing his watch to check that his pace and heart rate were where he wanted them. *The quantified self, what a time to be alive.*

The podcast host continued. "And, Dan, can you pick up that thread and explain what these components of the polycrisis are? Why should people be concerned about this?"

"Sure, Jon. There are other players in this space who define this differently, but I find the following framing helpful. First, there is a sense-making crisis. It's like the old Buffalo Springfield song: 'There's something happening here, what it is ain't exactly clear.' There is confusion at the level of understanding the world. *Every day,* people and experts are struggling to say things that are true, unable to comprehend the increasing complexity. Political and bureaucratic forms of power are failing to provide convincing rationale and justification for trust in their continued authority. Finally, and I would say, most important, there is a meaning crisis that Brent mentioned. Why should we do anything? We see widespread inauthenticity at the level of personal experience. Individuals from all walks of life are questioning the purpose of their existence, the goodness of the world, and the value of ethics, beauty, and truth."

"Wow, Dan, that's quite the take. Where can people go to learn more about this?"

Silas neared the one-lane bridge and checked both ways. No pedestrian lane—just a fifty-yard stretch of rusted metal. Exhibit No. 574 of America's aging infrastructure. The slow decay of high modernism, as James Scott would say. No cars in sight. He powered himself onto the cracked surface with a dynamic burst and started across.

Halfway there, powerful headlights washed the bridge from behind. Silas looked back. *Where the hell had that guy come from?*

A car barreled forward, engine roaring as it accelerated.

No time—get hit or jump.

Silas jumped.

It was about thirty feet to the hard-packed sand and stones of the river embankment. His right leg impacted first, then his side. Silas struggled to breathe. Pain surged up his leg. He tried to stand, found he couldn't. His left arm seemed off as well. Maybe dislocated. A flash of light, and Silas watched a car idle into the parking area below the bridge. Dark shape, a muscle car. It idled to a stop as the fog wafted across his vision in the predawn light. Driver must be coming to check on him. He crawled toward the headlights.

It looks like you've taken a hard fall, his AirPods reported what his watch read. Silas pawed at it, couldn't seem to press the button to respond. His vision narrowed. A shadowy figure strolled toward him. Framed by the car headlights, the sight resolved itself into a woman in black. She appeared to Silas to be some sort of dark angel—long, raven hair flowing and swirling in the light breeze over a black jacket. Something in her hand. Couldn't make out what it was.

Silas tried to speak, but only mumbled nonsensical syllables. He reached his uninjured arm upward. Cold crept in from the ragged stones and sand beneath him, and Silas shivered.

The woman beamed at him before slowly shaking her head. Her hair cascaded over bare shoulders and tautly muscled arms.

She raised an object he now realized was a piece of rubber, like an oven mitt.

Or a whoopee cushion.

"Wait, wait!" he yelled, too late. The woman knelt and gently placed the rubber over his face with both hands.

He begged, fought, scrabbled, flailed. Begged some more. Smothered by a whoopee cushion. Not how he imagined going out. Anxiety, anger, and fear came over him in successive waves. In the end, it didn't matter.

CHAPTER 5

Roz

A FEW BLOCKS INTO HIS WALK, he picked up the surveillance. It's hard to follow someone unobserved. Takes training and practice, and even then, it's a matter of time, location, and route variations to pick them up. Two disheveled men trailed behind him. They weren't street people, though, no matter how they tried to cloak themselves in secondhand store clothing. It's hard to fake the thousand-yard stare of weary resignation mixed with jittery intensity. Not easily, anyway. The dog saw them too—his big Malinois ears scoped like radar domes, tail straight, and a low growl at the bad vibes the situation presented. One of the men was squat and dense—built like a beer can. The other long and willowy, a weathered piece of beef jerky.

Naturally, Roz christened them Gimli and Legolas, a reference to the dwarf and elf from J.R.R. Tolkien's magnum opus. A glance across the street revealed harried commuters, eyes locked into their phones. No one wanted to make eye contact and risk an honest-to-goodness, unscripted interaction with a stranger. It was one thing if it was just the homeless folk like him, but lately it seemed no one wanted to talk, period.

Strange times, indeed.

Across the street, a woman matched Roz's shambling pace. Dressed for a backwoods hike—all North Face and Mountain Hardware. Roz frowned. Maybe they were going to follow him, figure out where he was sleeping. It didn't feel that way, though. It was that hinky feeling he got when the locals all seemed to vanish right before an ambush overseas. Felt like being on the mats, a jiujitsu blood choke closing in on his carotids—vision constricting before the lights dimmed out. Long-dormant survival patterns came online, tunneling through the whiskey haze. The self-loathing was temporarily banished to the murky recess of his skull.

Roz lit a cigarette and kept walking, crossing onto Harrison Street. *Lull them into complacency.* Bore them to death—always the goal with surveillance. If he took the maintenance walkway under the bridge, it would only invite a convenient place to target him, assuming that was their plan. Instead, he and the dog made their way up the bicycle on-ramp to the western span of the Oakland Bridge. Completed recently after a huge public outcry, the path allowed bicyclists to pedal from San Francisco to Oakland. The city had closed the southernmost lane on the span to create a bike path across the bay.

Roz wondered how they found him. The courthouse. It had to be. A gate in time and space he'd been forced to pass through, with public records of his presence there available to those who had the cyber-skills to see. He carried no electronics. That meant they watched the finance suits use him as a punching bag. Only one man followed up the ramp, dropping a football-field-length back. There was nowhere else for Roz to go unless he jumped. *Legolas.* He knew the others would be scrambling to load up in a vehicle, sprint ahead, and get into position ahead of his path.

The western span was a mile long. Traffic whisked by in the early evening rush hour. All the white-collar office drones heading back to their roosts for the day. And those were the lucky ones—the few that could afford to live within easy commuting distance of the city. Legolas kept the same distance between them as they crossed the bridge. The dog wanted to go after the man, but Roz talked him out of it. Cyclists swept past in singles and groups of two or three.

Once through the tunnel section on Yerba Buena Island, they made their move. A slight bend in the path screened their movement. Roz boosted the dog into the bushes to the right of the bike lane, then followed, up and over the guardrail. The duo slogged up the earthen slope, cutting back and to the west as they cut through the scrub brush above the tunnel they'd just walked through. The plants filled the air with a deep, mesquite scent. They increased their pace through a construction site and descended a steep hill into even more undergrowth. Now they were under the support columns of the bridge.

Their destination came into view. Century-old windows glinted in the late, fast-fading sun.

Roz was fleeing a winter rainstorm when he happened upon the old white house in the shadows of the bridge. Later, he snuck into a public library and did some research. The island was full of deep history. In the days before settlers, it was the site of a fishing village of the Ohlone tribe called Tuchayune. Early Spanish colonists named it "Isla Yerba Buena" after the spearmint-like plant growing on it. A "good herb." The military didn't establish a base there until after the Civil War, in 1870. In 1900, the Navy built Classic Revival-style dwellings for military officers posted to the Naval Training Station.

"Stop wiggling," Roz muttered as he climbed the rusting fire escape ladder, the dog on his shoulders like a sack of potatoes. The animal was well-versed in the tactic from climbing ladders to scale walls with operators overseas, but he grew skittish when Roz used it.

Maybe he was afraid of heights. Or my ability to climb.

His ribs ached from the ass-kicking by the finance guys. Flecks of rust fluttered down from the fire escape as they ascended—the salt air played havoc with metal. An old line from a Yeats poem came to mind: *Things fall apart, the center cannot hold.*

In 1963, World War II icon Admiral Chester Nimitz moved there with his wife, passing his days in what came to be called Nimitz House until the man died in 1966. The land went to the Coast Guard for a spell, and in 2007 fell under the jurisdiction of the City of San Francisco. The city had big plans for the place. They evicted longstanding residents from Yerba Buena and worked with developers to cash in on the unique locale. They did, however, offer to move them to nearby Treasure Island.

How very fucking magnanimous of them.

Over the decades, Nimitz House had fallen into disrepair and neglect, a relic of a different era.

At the ladder top, he opened the attic window and let the dog clamber in. He was about to follow when a sound reached him on the breeze—a murmur barely audible over the zooming traffic above. *Drone.* He looked up, but he couldn't see it. He went inside, bolted the window, and crept from window to window to watch the sight lines.

Sure enough, within a few minutes, Legolas arrived in a rush, down one of the service roads from the construction site. He lurked near the trees at the front of the house.

Waiting.

Before long, an unmarked silver Tahoe arrived. Out-of-state plates. North Face woman at the wheel. Gimli and another man piled out. Gimli moved toward the rear of the house, and the other man, mid-thirties, weightlifter, tribal tats, joined up with Legolas. The two advanced toward the front door. The woman stayed in the Tahoe.

Roz looked at the dog. "You mind giving me a hand here?"

The mutt stared back, poker-faced. A veritable sphinx.

"Look, you make me crazy, but I could really use the help."

The dog sneezed. Looked bored.

Roz sighed. "Let's go."

"Feroz! Rozzy!" one of the men called as they entered. Maybe Legolas, maybe Tats. Must have used a pick gun on the deadbolt. He didn't hear them force it open. "We just want to talk, Feroz," another voice said, pronouncing his name "ferrous," like the metal.

The dog went quiet, body crouched as he listened to the men. *Hunter mode.*

Roz watched them in the mirror from the shadows of the dining room. Legolas had a suppressed pistol at the low ready, while Tats produced a baton.

No good options.

The army had a battle drill for this called "react to the near ambush," in their wonderfully understated manner. Roz drew out a charcoal Benchmade tactical pen from his pocket. Made from Damascus steel, the tip was strong enough to break glass. His fingers fit in the knurled and filigreed contours as if born for them. One of the few items he'd managed not to lose over the years.

Better than nothing.

In the other hand, Roz held a faded baseball he'd found in a closet upstairs. One part of him idly wondered if it was a home-run souvenir from a game in the 1960s that Old Chester took his son, maybe his grandson to.

"This doesn't look like any conversation I want part of," Roz called out, stepping into the foyer, hands clasped behind him.

"Ah, so you *are* here. We need to have a conversation." Tats smirked. "You need to stay away from the Berenger thing. It's not good for your long-term health."

"And what if I say no?"

The man shrugged. "Doesn't matter much to me either way. We're gonna give you a medical excuse not to take part. Nothing terminal, mind you—the instructions were clear on that part. Someone likes you." He advanced toward Roz while Legolas circled to keep a clear line of fire.

"Conversation," Roz replied. "I don't think that word means what you think it does." He slapped his leg and pointed at Tats. "*Vuhrit.*"

At the Dutch command, the hound tensed and launched himself into movement—a meat missile seeking union with the flesh of an adversary. In a blur of fur and fury, the dog latched onto the man's arm, even as the man brought the baton down to strike.

Too slow, Tats.

Roz hurled the baseball, and it impacted high on Legolas' chest with a meaty slap. The lanky man rocked back with the unexpected impact, and Roz closed the distance, deflecting his pistol arm offline. Roz struck with the pen, targeting the brachial nerve in the shoulder. On the other side of the room, Tats screamed in a manner unbecoming of a bearded badass. But that's what a Military Working Canine could do to you.

Easy to be a Frogman on Friday, as they said during SEAL training.

The incisors and the jaw strength of the hound would

pulverize the meat on a forearm, crack bone, slice tendons and ligament as it thrashed up and down. Roz stripped Legolas of his pistol and smacked him with the muzzle until he lost consciousness.

Roz stood up and took a breath before firing two rounds into Tats' left knee. The burly man quit fighting the dog and curled in a ball. Something slammed into Roz's side, and he went down. *Gimli.* The pistol slipped from his fingers and Roz swiveled to counter the attack.

There was a nonverbal language transmitted through hands and feet when you grappled with another human. A flowing, intuitive back and forth communicated between partners. When you locked up grips, you got a sense of their abilities. That, coupled with Gimli's cauliflower ears and wildcat top fighting game, told Roz he was a wrestler. Probably collegiate. Maybe Division One. Lots of mat hours, judging by his body awareness. Roz shrimped out from underneath the man and scrambled to his feet, blocking strikes. Gimli stuck on him like a tick, working to take him back to the floor.

Damn, he was out of shape. Too many cigarettes.

Roz swept inside and blocked a punch before Gimli could land it. The two grappled before Roz caught him in a tripping *ouchi-gari*. Sometimes it was hard for wrestlers to defend the judo moves. Roz collapsed on top of him on the wood floor, worn and scratched by long decades of naval officer footfalls.

Gimli lunged for the pistol. The two fought before it went off, into Gimli's shoulder. The scrappy man roared in pain. Roz knelt on his back and searched him, silencer pressed to the nape of his neck. Roz used handcuffs he found on Gimli to cuff him to Tats by their wounded limbs so that they'd be more reluctant to move. Legolas was still out cold, but he cuffed him to Gimli's other leg anyway. The dog was reluctant to give up his bite on Tats, but Roz finally talked him off. He grabbed their cell phones and their pocket litter—cash, but no IDs. He kept one pistol and a spare magazine and hid the other in an empty tea-service drawer built into the wall of the dining room.

Roz slipped out the back door, into the trees, the dog at his side. He slunk up on the Tahoe's driver's side. Tried the door. Unlocked.

Rookie move.

"Hands," he said as he covered the woman inside with the pistol. She stared at him like he was a loose tiger but complied. A quick cuffing and search relieved her of a pistol and a cell phone, but no identification.

"Any chance you want to tell me what this is about?" he asked, squatting down to her level.

The woman stared up at the dog warily, who sat behind Roz. A lean, windburned face. Years of experience in the crow's feet, graying hair wrapped in a tight ponytail.

"Contract says we break your leg. Don't know the employer. Don't know why."

"Tats seemed to know."

She shrugged. "He's our team leader. He gets to know names, not us."

"What company do you work for?"

The woman was silent. He knew what it was like, not wanting to give up anything you didn't have to. Cultural taboo.

"We're a boutique firm. Mostly West Coast stuff."

Roz nodded. He found he didn't want to kill her. Even though she came here to hurt him. She had a job to do. He used to be the same. Hell, if things had played out a bit differently, he might have been in their little outfit.

"Any chance you want to give me the passcode to this?" He held up her phone to her face, and it unlocked before she could look away. "Never mind." Roz watched the frustration play across her features.

"Are the boys still alive?"

Roz sighed. "Against my better judgment. But I am taking your ride." He thought about sticking around and interrogating Tats, but he didn't know what kind of backup element this crew had, what their response time was.

"Figured as much. See you around." The ghost of a smile played over her face.

"I better not." Roz got in the Tahoe with the dog and drove off into the deepening twilight. East, and then south. *Traffic, traffic, traffic*. The highways were like clogged arteries, the cars oozing and pulsing blood. One number on the phone, the rest of the call log deleted. He memorized it before tossing all the devices out the window when they drove over the bridge.

Then, he pulled over to the side, put on the hazard lights.

The shakes came, like he knew they would, and he breathed his way through them. Roz stroked the dog's head while his body processed the encounter. "Good, boy. You saved me."

The dog kept his own counsel.

He always did.

CHAPTER 6

Roz

HE LIMPED UP THE GRAVEL DRIVE toward Hark's place outside Monterey. Mature cypresses, coastal oaks, and pines dotted the sides of the path. The house was a sun-bleached, alabaster, Spanish-style home, with solar panels on the burnt sienna roof tiles. The dog padded along beside him, smelling all the smells with that annoying, carefree air that he always seemed to possess. Roz ached in a dozen places from the altercation on the island and the fight in the city. He didn't recover like he used to. At least when he had something to focus on, it didn't hurt so much. Something like walking the four miles from the bus stop to Hark's.

After searching the SUV, he ditched it on a side street in Oakland. Not much to speak of—a few spare drones, operating funds, weapons. He got rid of all the electronics before he dumped it, kept a silenced pistol and the money. Roz was certain someone would scoop it up before the cops did. After checking out his fellow travelers on the San Francisco-to-Monterey airport shuttle, he fell into a deep slumber. The dog kept watch. In Monterey, there were plenty of homeless hiding in the nooks and crannies, in little copses of trees by the interstate. Hell, you could live on the beach if you wanted. It was cooler here, more of a breeze. He had everything he owned on him now. A battered Swiss army knife, the titanium pen, a quality set of clothing, an old toothbrush, stolen cash. Some would call it wealth, in the freedom it promised. Roz just called it Tuesday.

Hark opened the door before he could knock, faded paperback in one hand and the hint of a smile under the caterpillar-esque mustache. Roz spotted game cameras on the way up the drive and figured they triggered an alert on Hark's phone.

Transient vagabond approaching, beware.

Was "transient vagabond" repetitive? He pondered this mystery while trudging up the well-worn porch steps.

"Welcome, amigo, glad to see—" Hark's face darkened as he noticed the bruises on Roz's face, the stiff way he moved. "What happened?"

Roz filled him in as Hark gave him a quick once-over with his paramedic bag. "I pulled a number out of a phone on Yerba Buena. Grace Phillips. Didn't even bother to use a burner. Phillips took over as Milena's aide after Vanders... met his end. Now Milena is head of a defense company called Laughlin Carmichael. Looks like she's interested in my health again."

Hark said nothing as Sophie came out on the porch, holding a pair of local microbrews. Smashing Frog IPA. "Glad you could make it, stranger."

Roz took the offered beer with a smile. "Hey, Soph."

"I have a water bowl and a tennis ball with your name on

it, Diogenes," she said in a singsong voice, leading the hound around the side of the house. The two men sat down on the porch rocking chairs.

"Gorgeous spot of land, brother," Roz observed, taking stock of the area. "I still can't believe your uncle left it to you."

Hark nodded. "Yeah, no way I could come within a country mile of buying this today. Not without a few million lying around." He looked over at Roz. "Milena. Was that what made you change your mind?"

Roz was silent for a long while, rocking in the chair. "Doing this is my best chance to afford a lawyer," he said finally. "My only chance, really. Not to mention I can show the judge I'm not just wandering the streets all day long. Plus, fuck Milena. She'd have had better luck ordering me to go to selection."

Hark rocked in the chair, sipping his beer. "You could just get a regular type of job."

Roz stared at him. Seconds passed. The silence grew. He watched the Texan's normally stoic expression break. It started at his eyes and moved down to his lips. Hark started laughing, doubling over. "Damn, Kemosabe, I was just joking!"

"Funny man..." Roz replied. "What are you reading?"

"*The Inferno*. Didn't you see the invitation?"

"Didn't get that far."

Hark shook his head gently in what Roz referred to as his best "disappointed dad" impression. "Classic. Come on, I'll show you the war room." Hark got up and walked toward the barn.

"War room?" Roz hurried to catch up. The first floor of the barn reeked of manure and was filled with equine material—saddles, feed, blankets, and so on. The finished second floor—a large loft with repurposed wood walls—overlooked the horse stalls. A mosaic-like group of pictures and documents hung on the far wall. Gear and weaponry of various types lay on the large table in the middle of the room. "What is all this?" Roz asked finally.

"Let's start here." Hark tossed him a packet of papers. "Take it all in, and I'll come back in a bit. Need to get some shish kabobs on the grill for dinner. More beer in the fridge in the corner."

Roz sat down on the faded futon and read.

Mr. Harkness,

You may have seen recent media reports regarding the untimely demise of Dr. Nicholas Berenger. During his eventful life, he created revolutionary medical devices and served as the founder and leader of the Plek Foundation from its inception in 1999. This tragic event has left an irreplaceable hole in our hearts but filled us with a determination to carry on with his grand vision for our organization. The mission of the Plek Foundation is to shepherd humanity through this time, setting the conditions for future flourishing. Dr. Berenger left specific instructions regarding the method by which we will select the next set of leaders for the foundation. We call these individuals "stewards," because of their role as leaders and guides in this endeavor.

We are pleased to inform you that you have been chosen to take part in the selection process for stewardship of the foundation. If you accept our invitation, a follow-on document will inform you in greater detail of the process itself, how to prepare, and a short biography of the other selectees. We look forward to your response.

With greatest respect,

Ms. Justine Lipton—Acting Director, Plek Foundation

Under the signature, a quotation:

"The real problem of humanity is the following: We have Paleolithic emotions, medieval institutions and godlike technology." —Edward O. Wilson

Roz finished the beer and went in search of another before reading further. Two other documents stood out, amidst the rest.

Confirmed Selectees

1. Abeni Rutu, Esq.

Abeni is the proud daughter of Kenyan immigrants and earned a bachelor's at Yale and a JD at the University of Virginia. As the first woman of color to make junior partner at Bellows and Jenson, she pioneered a variety of initiatives targeted at climate engagement at the national and international levels. Abeni competed nationally in archery while at Yale, earning All-American status for two years.

2. Chief Master Sergeant Joshua Harkness

An accomplished United States Air Force pararescueman, Josh led a Combat Search and Rescue operation deep into the Kunar Valley in Afghanistan to recover a downed AH-64 crew. Under heavy fire, his team recovered both pilots, earning a Silver Star for his actions. After departing military service, Josh started an award-winning and much-sought-after non-profit focused on assisting veterans transition to civilian life after service.

3. Grady Corstead

Grady is a startup investor. Born and raised in New York, he also spearheaded the development and creation of several gaming apps which achieved a combined fifty-six-million-dollar valuation. An avid Muay Thai practitioner, Grady has amassed an amateur mixed martial arts record of 5-2, with three wins by knockout.

4. Gabrielle Corstead

A native of New York City, Gabrielle built a multi-million-dollar international fashion company—*The Liminal*. As its primary brand ambassador, Gabrielle amassed a following of over twenty-six million on various social media platforms and leveraged that reach to create changes in corporate and governmental policy, as well as raise awareness of critical issues around equity and justice.

5. Tabitha Winkel

Tabitha is an information security professional with expertise in fortified software systems. Her recent efforts have been instrumental in both offensive and defensive cyber operations. Tabitha earned her B.S. from Boise State University, where she graduated summa cum laude and received both the Byron Rogers and Sienna Marvin Outstanding Senior Awards. She earned her M.P.H. in information technology and security from the George Mason University School of Technology.

6. Tau Matamua

Tau is a native of Kaikoura, New Zealand. After a tour in the New Zealand military, he now serves the community and land as a *kaihao ika* and *rangatira* of the *Nagati Kuri hapu*.

Under his leadership, Tau led groundbreaking efforts to improve fishing concessions from the national government, as well as scale the tourism sustainably.

7. Silas Marino

Silas is the founder and CEO of Razoracle, a groundbreaking startup pioneering decentralized autonomous organizations, along with his wife, Cyren. In under four months, the company has already completed a fifteen-million-dollar, series-A funding round. Silas is also active in Thinking Children, a non-profit online school devoted to engaging Socratic wisdom traditions in underprivileged youth. When he's not writing code or involved in charitable endeavors, Silas is a competitive skydiver and wingsuit flier, making history in 2016 by landing a wingsuit *inside* a light aircraft.

8. Richard Danault

Richard has over two decades of business experience, beginning with work at McKinsey, and shifting into private equity. While working for Gravely Capital and the Dover Consulting Group, Richard was instrumental in the turnaround of five major distressed companies, cumulatively recovering over ten billion in capital. He currently serves as CEO of Danault Acquisitions.

9. Dr. Audrey Zhou

Audrey grew up in the shadow of oppression—her mother faced torture and persecution by the Chinese regime for her Christian faith before fleeing to Hong Kong in the 1990s. Drawn to service from a young age, she followed in her father's footsteps and became a Foreign Service officer within the U.S. State Department. In multiple arduous postings, Audrey spearheaded several community-changing initiatives in conflict zones. After recovering from a severe attack while abroad on a diplomatic mission, she currently teaches classics at Georgetown University's Walsh School of Foreign Service.

UNCONFIRMED SELECTEES

Feroz Mehran

Born in Iran just after the revolution, Feroz's family fled after political purges of the Ayatollah in 1988 and settled in the United States. As a Naval Special Warfare operator, he served his country with distinction in multiple areas of the world.

ONE OF THESE things is not like the others.

ROZ LOOKED up and saw pictures on the wall with names matching those on the document. He had nothing like the glowing accolades and accomplishments the others did. Roz turned his attention to the last sheet. It was spartan.

PREPARATION INSTRUCTIONS

Selection will test your capabilities to the fullest—your intelligence, creativity, teamwork, resilience, grit, strength, and above all, your *character*. We recommend you arrive at selection in a fit and rested condition—we require a medical physical administered by our doctors to ensure that no outstanding health condition will prevent you from participating. Prior to the commencement of selection, you must return the hold-harmless documentation, signed and notarized by a competent official.

There will be periodic stations for food and water during selection; however, if you'd prefer to eat/drink in between those, you may bring your own sustenance. The first part of Dante's *Divine Comedy—The Inferno*—will prove important, and we recommend a close reading of the work.

PROHIBITED Items

Flamethrowers (in particular the Boring Company model) and explosives are prohibited to be brought into the tower. You may not bring firearms and communications devices of any kind into the tower. However, crossbows, bows, and other projectile devices are permitted, in addition to hand-to-hand weapons. All personal gear will be inspected thoroughly prior to entering the tower for compliance with Plek Foundation policies.

HE HEARD Hark coming up the creaking stairs. "So? What do you think?"

"What does *The Inferno* have to do with any of this?" Roz walked over to the wall, filled with pictures, drawings, and various printouts. He gestured at it. "Look at this mess—I thought I was supposed to be the mentally unstable one."

Hark chuckled. "Just trying to wrap my head around the battlespace, amigo. My guess is that the testing will have something to do with all the stuff that Dante goes through. But who knows?"

Roz stared at the picture of the Plek Headquarters building, the one that Hark had pointed out when they'd met earlier in the week. "What do we know about the structure itself?"

"The old Pacific Bell building. Built in 1927. Forty-three stories tall—tallest building in the city until 1964. Used to be the nerve center for all telephone usage in the Bay Area. Fun fact—it was once visited by Winston Churchill."

"Looks like the building from *Ghostbusters*. Keymaster and Gatekeeper must be around here somewhere."

Hark squinted one eye, cocked it sideways. "Huh. Guess I can see that."

"You got the dog gear too?" Roz lifted a piece of desert-colored nylon in the air. A harness for the dog to wear, it was filled with pouches and pockets of various sizes.

"Of course, Kemosabe—can't let him go in without some tricks. Check this out—" Hark flipped a piece of velcroed nylon off to the side, revealing a camera lens. "HD camera. Improved battery life, durability, and signal range. Records footage locally on the device itself."

"Audio too?"

"Yep. And this one here is the 'low visibility' model. Not as obtrusive as some others, so I'm hoping we can slide it past the 'no communications' restrictions. Comes with a pair of smart watches so you can watch the feed from your wrist."

Roz shook his head. "You are one devious SOB, you know that? To be clear, I am not smuggling that in as a suppository."

"What's that Frogman expression?" Hark set the gear down, eyes twinkling with mirth.

"Oh, we have so many. Two is one, one is none; if you're wrong, stay wrong; never play cards with anyone named after a city..."

"If you ain't cheating, you ain't trying."

Roz nodded. "That too." His eyes fell to the end of the table. "Oh, no. No way. You couldn't. You didn't."

Hark grinned. "Oh, yes. I did. I did." Clearly he had been waiting for this.

Roz set his beer down and picked the object up with a reverence reserved for the holiest of the holy. The Aegis. His ballistic shield. Level Four-rated protection. The impact from the AK-47 round was still there on the bottom-right corner, a slight deformation of the material. He ran callused fingers over it. The logo of his old unit was faded but still legible on the outside face, spray-painted on in black and gray. A helmeted Odin, flanked by his trusty ravens, *Huginn* and *Muginn*. In the mythological story, they helped him keep tabs on Asgard by flying over the land and reporting back on what they'd seen. The mythic embodiment of modern-day intelligence, surveillance, and reconnaissance. Roz tore his eyes away from the shield to look at his friend with wonder. "How did you—"

"My methods are mysterious. Inscrutable. But effective."

"I figured NCIS would have locked up all my kit in some sort of *Raiders of the Lost Ark*-style facility, never to be seen again."

Hark nodded. "They would have. If they'd known about it. I still think it's weird as hell you use a shield, but I know how much it means to you."

"It saved my life more than once. How'd you get it out?"

"Not all your Frogman brothers turned their backs on you. Some of them helped me get it out."

Roz chuckled darkly. "You sure about that? Didn't get too many visitors in the brig."

"You know that a lot of guys received direct orders not to contact you. A few even went to captain's mast for trying."

Roz waved his hands dismissively. "Did that stop you?"

The sentence hung in the air like the fast-approaching Monterey Bay fog, as nightfall crept through the hills.

"Have some grace. Remember that? That thing humans used to extend one another a thousand years ago?"

"*I'm* the one who's supposed to have grace? Do you hear yourself? I got hung out to dry for something I didn't even do, by someone—" He set the shield down heavily on the table, running his fingers through his gnarled, matted hair.

Hark closed his eyes, breathing out. "You had a bad beat, amigo. Let's get you out of that hole, yeah?"

"Bad beat, my ass. I'm going for a walk."

Hark watched him leave. "Don't be gone too long, Kemosabe—we've got work to do!"

Roz let the slam of the door be his response.

CHAPTER 7

Audrey

SHE LIKED TO WALK to her eight AM class from the Rosslyn Metro stop across the Key Bridge, and up the stone stairs featured in the movie *The Exorcist*. It was a good thirty-minute walk, and she found that her thinking flowed well during that time, listening to jazz. Mostly classics, Davis and Coltrane. She did it every day she could, weather permitting. Gave her time to go over her lesson plan in her head; she hated talking in front of a group. Not the most ideal situation for a university professor. All the collective attention focused on her—the unspoken questions hanging in the air when she walked through the classroom door.

What happened to her?

Look at her face.

You know what they say—"if you can't do, teach."

That sort of thing. She didn't plan on teaching early-

Asian conflict to a group of eager undergrads in the Walsh School at Georgetown when she became a Foreign Service officer. But here she was. Audrey glimpsed herself in the window of a parked car and made sure her headscarf was in place.

On campus, she fit right in—there were women of several faith traditions who wore such coverings. Hers was for a more pragmatic rather than religious reason. The scarf covered about two-thirds of the scars. Unless she wanted to wear some kind of *Phantom of the Opera*-style mask, the other third stayed exposed to the world. She had considered it. The wind blew hard off the Potomac, and she was grateful to hit *The Exorcist* stairs and get a brief respite from the gale. At least it was clear, even if it was cold. She crested the top and turned to walk the last several blocks to her building on campus.

"Dr. Zhou? Is that you?" A man stood there, Starbucks in hand. Mid-forties, trim, dressed in business attire and a long coat. Those earmuff things that she always thought looked strange on men to ward off the chill.

"Do I know you?" Audrey paused for the slightest moment, then resumed walking. Her fingers found the pepper spray in her pocket. She mentally rehearsed spraying his face, sprinting for the nearest university call box, the first of which was just ahead on the shoveled sidewalk.

"Not yet," the man replied with what he no doubt imagined was a disarming smile. "May I walk with you?" He fell into step without waiting for her to reply.

"I am late for class, Mister...."

He gave her a little smile and a jaunty cock of his head. "Oliver Farbas, Esquire, from the offices of Korst, Ridger, and Lind. I represent a party who is interested in retaining your services for a rather sensitive matter."

She didn't recognize the name of the law firm, but then

again, she knew little about the legal world. "Does the party that you represent have a name?"

The wattage on his grin decreased slightly, replaced with something a bit more forced.

"Because of the sensitive nature of the matter, they would prefer not to bias your decision-making until you have had adequate time to consider the offer in its fullness."

"Offer? What offer?"

"Are you planning to attend the Plek Foundation event on Good Friday, in San Francisco?"

Her eyes narrowed as she stared at him. "How do you know about that?"

"It's public knowledge that Dr. Berenger disappeared in the Indian Ocean last year. The media have covered it breathlessly since it happened. The disposition of his estate is of ongoing interest to my client, and we have recently learned that you received an invitation to take part in the selection of future leadership for his foundation."

She took a deep breath. "Again, I ask you, what is the offer?"

"My employer is prepared to offer you significant assistance in completing the process competitively."

"Mr. Farbas, I don't have the slightest idea what you're talking about. Yes, I got an invitation. I'll probably go, just because I'm curious what it's about, and I can visit family for a few days." She frowned. "Why would I need help?"

"To be honest, Dr. Zhou, I am not entirely clear myself. I am not privy to all the details of this developing situation." He extended his arms to either side and offered a sheepish grin. "I should mention that besides the resources, the offer comes with a substantial compensation package. We need a little time with you to discuss what we're looking for. You could take care of your mother, get her the care that she needs."

How did he know about my mother's medical issues?

She considered pepper spraying him then, out of general principle. Then she remembered the cameras. And that he was in a law firm. Could get messy. Lawfare. Audrey exhaled instead, relaxed her grip on the spray. "I really need to get to my class, Mr. Farbas."

He nodded. "Fair enough." He extended a hand, gloved in black leather, holding an embossed business card. "Please call this number if you decide you'd like to work with us. I'd love to speak to you further about ways we can be of service. Good day, Ms. Zhou. Enjoy your work with the Ancients. Warring States period, right? *Besiege Wei to rescue Zhao* and all that good stuff. Cheers." He walked off, leaving her standing, holding the card in a faintly trembling hand.

ROZ WOKE WHEN THE DOG DID, to a soft creak on the stairs. The hound sprang to his feet. But it was just Hark, a pistol in his hand. Roz looked at the wall clock—castoff from some long-defunct Salinas factory. Four AM.

"Company, amigo," Hark said, handing him his phone.

On the screen, Roz watched a line of men walk slowly through the trees "How far?"

"North side of the property. Ten minutes, they keep this pace." Hark opened a large gun safe with a six-digit code, revealing a variety of firearms. "I got Sophie holed up in the master bedroom closet on my laptop, watching all the feeds, with my shotgun keeping her company. Lately we've been skeet shooting off the back deck after dinner, so she's pretty decent with it."

Hark offered him a suppressed pistol—an HK45 Compact Tactical, and several magazines. Hark held it for a moment as Roz reached for it. "You sure you're good, bro? You remember how to do this?"

Roz stared. "Some things you can't forget."

Hark let the pistol go.

"Do they have night vision?"

"Some of them, at least. Check the laser on that. Batteries should be good."

"Do we have night vision?"

Hark gave him a look. "What kind of operation do you think I'm running here?"

"Good. What's the plan?"

"I'm taking the barn roof. Best sight lines on the avenues of approach. Gonna try to pick a few of 'em off, get the long guns out of play. You and Diogenes circle around behind them. They won't be expecting you."

Roz grinned, chambered a round in the pistol, then released the magazine to top it off with an extra round. "I'm letting the pararescueman take the sniper rifle? I'm never gonna live this down, am I?"

"If you live," Hark replied. "My guns, my rules, amigo."

"Fair enough." Roz found the Aegis leaning against the wall. "Didn't think we were getting into action so quick, old girl, but here we are."

"Here's a headset and a Motorola radio. Sophie, can you hear me?"

"Got you, baby," came the response as Roz slid the earpiece in. "Looks like they split in two. One group is coming from the north, the other swinging east. Three in each."

Hark shined a red lens headlamp on the wall. "Overhead imagery of the property. Head south from the barn, pick up this little ridge." He traced it with a callused finger. "It'll take you right across the path of that eastern group."

Roz nodded. "Got it."

"Oh—last thing. Floodlights on motion sensors. Those will start kicking on when these yahoos expose themselves to cross the backyard."

"Until they shoot them out, you mean."

"Yeah. That's your time to hit 'em."

"You know, I don't tell you how to do the medic stuff, do I? I'm hearing a lot of micromanaging going on right now. Is this what they taught you in the Air Force?"

Hark ignored the jibe, slid an extra box of ammo into a jacket pocket. "Catch you on the flip side, amigo. Good hunting."

"Likewise."

Cool and clear outside the barn. Cicadas sang. Light wind from the north, just enough to feel on his cheek. The night vision goggles attached to his head with a catcher's-mitt-style piece of nylon webbing, and the optics painted the dark woods in green tones. No moon. Good night for a capture/kill mission. The trail was easy to find, winding through the pines and the citrus of the bushes. Roz exhaled. *In for four, hold, out for four, hold.* Dio panted with excitement, snuffling around the trail excitedly.

"I'm in position, darlin'. How's it looking over there?"

"I'm still moving," Roz replied. "Oh, was that for Sophie?"

"Very funny," Sophie replied. "Still two groups. One of them is all bunched up together. They're messing with a bag on the ground."

"Shit. These guys have drones. I forgot to mention that."

"That would have been nice to know, say, before I got up here all exposed on this roof."

"Put a tarp over you. It'll look like you're just a pile of roofing material."

Sophie chimed in. "Yep. They just launched something."

After a minute or so, Roz heard it. A soft buzzing. Probably another quad copter. Thankfully, the trees would keep him out of sight. He crept carefully now. No more jokes. Thoughts drifted back to SEAL sniper school, sneaking up on the instructors every week on graded tests. As a city boy, those were some of the toughest lessons to learn. Luckily, one of the instructors took pity on him and worked with him on nights and weekends, until Roz figured out the finer points of stalking.

"Oh no," Sophie came over the communications net. "They just found one of the cameras. I lost the feed. The one over by the garden, Hark."

"Copy."

Close. Roz caught the scent of Copenhagen chewing tobacco. Sickly-sweet wintergreen flavor. Plenty of his teammates had dipped that brand over the years. As if to confirm the odor, he heard loud whispers from the shadows in front of him. Fifteen, maybe twenty yards in front.

"—just need to go. These cocksuckers are sleeping. We have to hit 'em now. 'Specially if the motion sensor on that camera wakes them up."

The argument continued as Roz picked his way through the undergrowth, sliding each foot back and forth to push twigs off to the side before slowly adding weight and planting in the mossy earth.

"I'm fittin' to go hot here, Kemosabe. Hope you're in position."

Roz keyed his handset twice in acknowledgement. Hark would know what that meant, even if Sophie didn't.

The dog was in full hunter mode, skulking through the deadfall, nostrils questing. Ahead, lights burst on, and Roz tilted his head to stare out from under the goggles with his naked eyes. Pistol at the low ready, braced on the side of the Aegis. Spare mag in his left hand, arm through the shield strap, holding it over his upper body and midsection.

"Somebody take those things out," a woman called from the shadows in front of him.

He recognized the voice. The woman from Yerba Buena. *That's what mercy got you.* Gunfire rang out—the thin crack of 5.56-millimeter rounds, speeding toward the floodlights of the house. Roz hoped Sophie was behind something thick. He slapped his thigh softly with the pistol and pointed. The dog saw the nonverbal command and exploded into motion. Roz waited a beat. He heard the deeper boom of Hark's sniper rifle, trying to hide in the noise of lighter-pitched carbine rounds. Roz aimed at a rifle-toting invader. He settled the laser sight of the pistol on the back of the man's head and exhaled deeply. Pulled the trigger. Roz kept shooting as the man went down. Humans can be hard to kill, especially with pistol rounds. Looked like he might have gotten lucky with a central nervous system hit to the back of the head.

Lights out.

Roz swiveled to the next target while a man mewled in agony. Incoming rounds panged into the shield.

The woman.

He fired at her muzzle blast.

. . .

Phut phut phut phut slide lock mag seat tap tug rack target phut phut.

Darted to the left, behind trees. Panicked yelling and gunfire wafted on the breeze from the other side of Hark's house. Roz flanked the group. Following the sound of the dog, Roz located him and his target, wrestling in the bushes. He put three rounds into the man's face. Called the dog off. Damn hound never wanted to let go once he got his teeth in something. Leading with his pistol, he searched for the woman. It didn't take long. Arterial bleed, upper left thigh. Her chest frothed; she was nearly bled out. He watched it bubble through the night vision. Roz wished she hadn't come. Wished she'd let go of the job. She'd tried to put a tourniquet on, but the location of the wound site made it nearly impossible to do herself. Watched her features, pale with the loss of blood. She tried to say something. He couldn't make it out. Then she went still, eyes staring into the middle distance.

"Sophie, I only got two of 'em. Last one got inside. Sophie?" The borderline panic in Hark's voice was not something Roz had heard before from the Texan. But then again, Roz had never seen one of Hark's loved ones in danger.

No response on the radio.

"On it." Roz sprinted for the back door, the dog close on his heels.

Entered fast, glided toward the stairs.

Boom of a shotgun, and the man clattered down the steps into a boneless sprawl. Roz put rounds into him until he stopped moving. Until he heard the rattle, saw the final shiver and shake. It was Gimli. "Soph? You good up there?"

A pause, then a shaky voice husked out. "Yes. Yes. Thanks, Roz."

"Tango down, Hark. Soph's okay."

"Thank you, Kemosabe." Relief palpable in his voice. "I'm coming down."

"Think anyone called the cops?" Roz asked when Hark joined them.

"Doubt it. I know my neighbors pretty well." He held Soph in a tight embrace. Hark held up his phone in a free hand. "Police scanner is clean right now."

"The woman from Yerba Buena was here. And that's Gimli there on the stairs. The others are probably in the group you took out." Lips tight, Roz shook his head. "I put you both in danger by letting them live. I'm sorry."

Hark shook his head back. "Nothing to apologize for. You gave them a chance. Until they gave you no choice." He looked at his girlfriend more closely. "You gonna be okay, babe?"

Sophie was shaking, crying silently. Hark shushed her, picked her up in his arms and carried her into the study.

Roz shut the door softly behind them, then prepared to carry Gimli out of the house.

Lots of work to do before the sun came up.

CHAPTER 8

Milena

SHE SWIVELED THE PEN with her right hand.

Down, down, flip.

Down, down, flip.

An old habit from her cadet days at the Air Force Academy. She'd been to enough corporate mindfulness retreats to understand she flipped the pen on her knuckles as a form of meditation. To still her racing mind and prepare herself for the ordeal to come. Whatever it was. Milena used to do it in squadron pre-flight briefings, too, after she commissioned.

She kicked off her heels and padded to the window, staring down into what seemed like endless rows of office-park buildings. Tysons Corner. Corporate hub in Washington, D.C., for so much of America's economic power. All of that which directly fed the military power. The building was just down the road from her old digs at the Pentagon, where she'd retired a few months ago in a ceremony that rivalled her wedding in pomp and circumstance, including the overly exaggerated and verbose stories of her prowess and competence on operations they couldn't even speak openly of. Wet, melting flakes slid down the thick, floor-to-ceiling glass. What the weather channel called a "wintry mix." No answers for her out there, in the slush. No solutions to the dead ends and obstacles that seemed to pile up in her path. The slowly accumulating dread at the prospect of failure.

Failure.

Her eyes swept over the precise rows of plaques and photographs lining the walls of her corporate suite. Pictures of Milena with celebrities and politicians interspersed here and there—at dinners, fundraisers, and USO tours overseas. The one she loved the most was a mounted shell casing from an AGM-176 Griffin missile, used to end the life of a notorious Boko Haram leader after an eighteen-month manhunt. One of her subordinates had tried to calculate the cost to the U.S. taxpayer of each strike they took, from initial finding until the death of the terrorist. The aviation fuel alone was over several million dollars. She cut him off, then. Sent him to exercise in the well-appointed base gym before he added in the cost of all the man-hours of intelligence analysis. Not to mention the direct-action raids to collect intel before and after.

"General?" A voice cracked through her musings.

"Yes?"

"Were you following our discussion?" Grace Phillips, her longtime aide, leaned on the side of a leather sofa, legs crossed, a sheaf of papers in hand. Aggressively short black hair. Stylishly understated dress.

"About?"

"Berenger's succession plan, Ma'am." Barrett answered, in an unhurried bass rumble. Barrett Jensen was a recent addition to her team. She'd seen good things out of him so far. A stellar career as an Army infantry captain, cut short by allegations of detainee abuse. Big exposé in the Gray Lady. Played linebacker at Howard University before commissioning. The man still had the compact, tightly muscled moves of a panther. He paced back and forth on the carpet, looking sharp in a well-tailored suit.

"What specifically?" She saw the look that passed between them. Milena knew it well. She'd given it to others enough times while serving on a senior officer's staff. The well-disguised annoyance at bringing the leader up to speed because they weren't paying attention.

"We're gaming out options," Grace said. "Figuring out if we need to use the asset."

Milena walked back over, sat behind the massive desk. It had belonged to her predecessor—a bald and portly former admiral ousted by the board when she retired from active duty, as they'd promised. Now it was hers, and she had to deliver on her end of the bargain. "And what are you thinking?"

"There's probably a transition point, if we don't think the odds are breaking our way." Grace finally gave in and sat on the sofa. Grace had been a career civil affairs officer before Milena had snatched her up to be her aide. She had come with Milena through promotion to major general, and now to the corporate world. Lots of miles. Lots of hard decisions. Lots of influencing, socializing ideas, and preparing the battlespace for future moves.

Barrett sat down next to Grace. "The inclusion of Harkness and Mehran threw some of the predictive modeling into a tailspin."

Milena kept her features composed, as she knew they were both examining her. *Calm breeds calm.* Grace had wanted to eliminate Mehran from the start, rather than simply take him out of contention with an injury. But something gave Milena pause. She couldn't say why, exactly.

Nostalgia? Guilt?

She didn't do guilt. Milena cocked her head to the side. "How so?"

"They're strong candidates, say what you will about Mehran's mental state. The professor at Georgetown could pose problems as well."

"Tell me about the professor."

"Audrey Zhou. Thirty-six years old. Father was a diplomat. Mother was an NGO-type in Hong Kong, before the turnover back to the motherland. Zhou did eight years as a Foreign Service officer before calling it quits."

Milena pursed her lips. "Where was she posted?"

"Somalia—when the embassy was in Nairobi *and* in Mog, and Pakistan. That's where she had the incident."

"Don't make me play twenty questions with you," Milena said, sliding her shoes back on. "I have a lunch meeting with a supplier. I have to convince them not to drop us when our contract is up. What incident?"

"An acid attack on an NGO visit outside of Islamabad. It left her with heavy facial scarring, and she lost the use of one of her eyes," Barrett answered. "She left State after that. Been at Georgetown ever since."

"And what does our illustrious AI prediction engine say?" Milena stood and smoothed her blouse, picking up some stray hairs. She ran her fingers over bun of her hair, ensuring it was still tight.

Grayer every year. "We're paying enough for it."

Grace nodded. "It all depends on the alliances that form during the event. If the twins solidify their relationship with Matamua, they'll be in a commanding position."

Milena paused at the door. Turned to face them. "We have a few tricks up our sleeve before we put the asset in play. If it doesn't look like our people will prevail and become the stewards, we can put them in motion."

JUSTINE STEPPED OUT OF THE CAR in front of 140 Montgomery Street and strode into the lobby. No matter how many times she did it, she had to pause and admire the intricate carvings in the stone and terra-cotta facing of the building. So much beauty back then, layered into the very architecture. A different era. Kathy and Manbuns followed in her wake. She breezed through the lobby of the Plek Foundation headquarters, past the ceiling fresco, with its unicorns, griffins, and all manner of fanciful creatures. They gazed down in a sort of benevolent air. Must have been nice, back when people had the attention span to admire such things. When society made beautiful things just because. Before it succumbed to such extractive, nihilistic instrumentalism.

Nicky had gotten a deal on the building from a real estate investor right after the 2008 financial crash. The basement featured the timbers of an old storeship from the 1850s, the *Byron.* In one six-month period in 1849, over five hundred ships sailed into San Francisco Bay, disgorging humans of all colors and stripes, all chasing after one thing.

Gold.

They abandoned the vessels in their haste, and the city slowly grew over them. The early designers of the skyscraper had simply built around it, leaving it as a monument to the city's past. She wondered what they would make of the structural alterations the foundation had recently made to the building.

Justine strode into the third-floor operations center three minutes before the six PM update meeting to find a flurry of activity and spirited conversation. She brushed off the light accumulation of rain she'd gotten on her coat and draped it on the table. A piece of elegant style amongst empty Starbucks cups and assorted food containers from upscale eating spots. Justine took her seat and one of her assistants, Hazel, handed her a folder.

"Two things. Both bad. One selection related, one not."

"Give me the non-selection one first."

"Kate Veil is missing."

Justine regarded her. "Missing, as in, she's on a bender in Vegas?"

Hazel swallowed heavily. "Not that kind of missing, although that's not a bad guess with Kate. Missing as in, we have no communications with her. She's not using her phones or emails. Vanished."

"Okay. That's a mystery for later on. What's the selection-related one?"

"Silas Marino is dead."

Justine quickly skimmed through the folder, scanning the contents, before meeting her eyes. "How?"

Hazel brushed her hair out of her face. "Took a fall off a bridge on his morning run. Autopsy and toxicology are still pending."

Justine exhaled. "He was the favorite. In the predictive modeling. Wasn't he?"

Hazel nodded. "Dmitri will get into the details of that in his section of the brief."

"You're just full of good news, today, aren't you?"

Hazel gave her a pained smile as the rest of the group gathered. The operations center itself was huge. Built in the old worker cafeteria, they'd created an enormous circle of tables, with over two dozen workstations. In the center, pillars with three triangular rows of flatscreen televisions, so everyone around the circle could view the same thing. At present, all four input spots displayed a football match from England, with the sound off. Serving table stood around the periphery of the room, stocked with snacks for the long hours ahead.

"How are the selectees we have sequestered?" Justine asked.

"We have the Corsteads and Matamua on the Carmel estate. Winkel and Rutu up north at the farmhouse. They seem to be fine."

"What about Zhou?"

"Flew in this morning, staying at her mother's place in the city. She may have been approached by LC in Georgetown."

Justine shrugged. "Who knows if she'll be safe there? If they gave her an offer, they would likely wait to see how she responds. It's the ones who don't get offers that you have to worry about. They seem to take the terminal option with those. This makes three who died under questionable circumstances."

Some of the staff exchanged glances. *Terminal option?* one mouthed and made a face. Justine noted it without remarking. "Next?"

"What about Mehran—is he coming?" Hazel asked.

"We don't know," Kathy answered from behind. She'd entered after Justine and handed her a steaming cup of tea.

"He is...undecided at present," Justine replied.

"And the remaining selectee—what is his status?"

"Just confirmed this morning, Ma'am. He'll get into the city tonight," Hazel answered.

"Danault?"

"Correct. No sign he's been contacted by anyone."

"So, we're looking at a final pool of between eight and nine?"

"Depends on if they all stay alive until Friday, but that's the tentative range we are seeing, yes," Hazel responded.

Justine sighed. It should be much higher. Nicholas wanted more, which was why he'd given her a larger pool of contenders. But your adversaries always get a vote, whether they be human or environmental. That was one of his go-to phrases whenever the foundation encountered obstacles. Which was frequent.

"Alright, let's get a protective detail to watch Dr. Zhou, ensure she stays among the living. Anything else on personnel?" She scanned the assembled room of her team. Head shakes or no responses. "Talk to me about LC."

Hazel nodded. "Yes, Ma'am. Laughlin-Carmichael is the product of the merger of Laughlin Chemical and Carmichael Aerospace in 1993. This was in response to the infamous 'Last Supper' gathering with Deputy Secretary of Defense Perry the same year. The pairing proved resilient to the stressors and cannibalistic nature of the defense industry in the late '90s. This is 'peace dividend' stuff, fall of the Berlin wall, all that jazz," Hazel continued, sipping a cold brew through a straw. "It was a bad time not to have 'Boeing' or 'Lockheed Martin' in your name, although those two giants grew out of the same 'eat-or-be-eaten' environment."

"Given that background, what does LC sell today?" Justine asked.

"Their core business has shifted over the decades," Hazel said, flipping through her briefing book. "Chemical augmentation for battlefield soldiers. Amphetamine-based drugs they sold to the government to support long-duration operations. In the last ten years, they have expanded the neuroscience section—cognitive enhancements for the human operator."

"Huh," Justine said, biting the stem of her eyeglasses as she read the briefing document. "How long has that part been going on?"

"It looks like a new CEO and several board members came in about ten months ago and initiated pursuit of that line of effort. A retired U.S. Air Force general…Milena Janek took the helm."

"All right, thank you, Hazel. Let's move on to the venue."

All eyes shifted to the chubby guy in the trucker hat. "We are about ninety-six percent ready, as of this meeting." He sat in a wheelchair. The wheels had playing cards in the spokes that clicked as he maneuvered it to the front. "We're waiting on one shipment from Florida, which will augment some of the middle circles."

What was his name? D something? Dmitri, that's what it was.

"And the timeline?" Justine asked, flipping through a diagram and running a finger down it.

"We expect the shipment in and deployed by late tonight. The tentative plan is to run a full rehearsal tomorrow morning, pending your approval."

"And what do the modeling simulations look like?"

"Stochastic analysis shows a range from one to three participants will finish, with varying confidence levels. It's difficult to run the scenario engine without a final list to pull psych profiles from. The Marino murder throws all the existing extrapolations in the trash. We will have to start the modeling from scratch. Run it with and without Mehran," Dmitri answered.

"No one said it was murder," Hazel said. "The police are still investigating."

"Yeah, okay, sure. But it sure is quacking like a duck, isn't it?" Dmitri flipped a few pages in his book.

Hazel said nothing.

"Assume Mehran is part of the group, for nine total selection participants," Justine offered.

"Nine Little Indians. Cool. Which brings me to my next point. I don't think we can make the Good Friday start in two days. The tower itself will be ready, but the software won't be completely secure."

Justine regarded him over her tea. A flowery smell in the wafts of steam. "How so?"

"We have some vulnerabilities I'm not comfortable with in the monitoring and control system. There is a potential for exploitation if we don't take the time to further harden the infrastructure."

"Aren't you a circle runner?" Kathy interjected.

"Yeah," Dmitri replied, moving his hat and scratching the poofy auburn mane underneath. "Rena and I are each in charge of alternate circles as the selectees ascend."

"Why don't we hear from an IT person?" Kathy responded with a glacial smile. "Jarvis?"

A slender, thirty-something man stood up from the back. He had long, thin sideburns and a very well-groomed mustache. "Although Dmitri is correct—there are some backlogged pieces of tech to ensure the tower is completely secure. However, our department has put in place mitigation safeguards in the interim, to ensure a timely launch. They will cover the exploitable segments for the duration of the event."

Justine was silent for long moments, considering. "Nicholas—Dr. Berenger's wishes were that we execute the selection in keeping with the timeline established for *The Inferno*. That means a Good Friday entrance, and an Easter exit. Do we really want to consider delaying the process an entire year?"

Dmitri exhaled. "Yes, if it's the only way to ensure that it will be completely safe."

"That's not accurate—" Jarvis raised a hand, and Kathy began to respond, but Justine cut them all off.

"Safe comes from the French '*sauf*' and the Latin '*salvus.*' It means 'free from danger or risk.' Nothing about what this foundation is about is free from danger or risk. We exist to shepherd humankind through this time of transition." Justine looked at each of them. "We will have to take some risk here, ladies and gentlemen. Let's make things as tight as we can, but we will continue with the Good Friday commencement of selection." She stood up. "Thank you all." As she walked off toward her office, Justine hoped she projected more confidence to the group than she felt.

CHAPTER 9

Audrey

AUDREY TOOK THE RED-EYE—a direct flight from Dulles to San Francisco, winging her way across the slumbering center of the country, fighting the jet stream the entire time. She fled the sunrise westward at several hundred miles per hour. The land below looked cold and lifeless. The cities beamed pale shades of yellow. She still didn't know what to make of the unnerving run-in with the lawyer back at Georgetown. It left her with a troubled feeling in her stomach, a sour pit that threatened to flare up at every glance from a stranger, or loud noise. The encounter brought back memories she thought she'd left behind when her career as a Foreign Service officer had ended.

She rode the BART in a narcoleptic haze, trying to lose herself in a David Sedaris book, but she couldn't get into it, couldn't focus. She kept reading the same sentences over and over again, without understanding what they said. The compartment stank of body odor. A man yelled at the map on the wall of the BART, flecks of spittle flying through the air. Everyone pretended he wasn't there, Audrey included. She contented herself with staring at the old neighborhoods flashing by until the train ground to a halt at her mother's stop. She ignored the stares of the other riders, the curiosity in their glances at her ruined face behind the scarf. Since it was around her mother's mid-morning nap time, she let herself in, creeping on stockinged feet to drop her bag in the guest room. Audrey was surprised when her mother called from behind the closed door of the bedroom.

"Chen-Yi," came her voice, a little hoarser, a little softer than she remembered. She sounded tired. Maybe a cold. Audrey peeled the door open with a creak and found her mother sitting up in bed. The television was on, but muted, showing some old game shows from the 1970s and '80s. *Let's Make A Deal* was ending and *Match Game* just beginning.

"Mom, are you ever going to call me by my name?"

"Audrey is your American name, but you are my baby, and you'll always be my Chen-Yi. My little rose."

"More like Charred Rose, now." Sometimes Audrey's evil eye would water, and she had to dab it with something. She did so now, as she regarded her mother's frail frame, lost in a sweaty tangle beneath the sheets.

"I thought you were done with such sad talk."

"It's real talk, Mom. I have to look in the mirror. I can only do it with one eye, but I have to look all the same. Doesn't do any good to sugarcoat it."

"You can't let that *Húndàn* stay in your head anymore. Stop carrying him. Like the monks and the woman."

"Language, Mother," she said. Audrey smiled faintly at the reference. It was one of her father's favorite parables. Two Buddhist monks were crossing a stream. A woman asked one of them to carry her over, so he obliged. After they crossed, and the woman went off her own way, the pair travelled in uneasy silence. Finally, the other monk blurted out, "I can't believe you carried her! You know our faith forbids the touch of a woman."

To which the first monk replied, "I put the woman down minutes ago, but you're still carrying her."

Her mother gestured to the corner, where a Chinese spear sat with a pile of other items. "I think you should take that when you go."

Audrey walked over to the spear and picked it up. As a child, she'd trained in *wushu*—Chinese martial arts—both back home in China, and once they'd moved to the States. The spear was always her favorite of the various implements they studied. She tested the balance, and the honed edge of the spear point. Her mother had spent some money on this. She nodded. "Fine. Are you okay? You look thinner than normal."

Her mother's face froze a twitch before her features smoothed into a placid smile.

That's when Audrey knew something was wrong, even before she drew another breath. "Cancer is back, Chen-Yi."

"No." She felt her stomach drop and a sweaty film build on her skin. Audrey sat down on the bed. She forced herself to breathe, slowly and deeply.

"It's no matter. They said it could after the first time, remember? All the years at the dry-cleaning business. When it's time, it's time. I will see your father sooner than we thought." He had passed away shortly after they'd resettled in the States when she was a child.

Audrey crossed her arms and wiped her eyes. Now both eyes were weeping, not just the ruined one.

"Doctor papers are in other room. If you want to see. What do you want to have for dinner tonight?"

"I'm not feeling hungry right this second, Mom."

"Maybe we get the Thai takeout. You like that."

"Mom! Are you going to do chemo? What did they say?"

"This is unnecessary, Chen-Yi. The...prognosis...is not favorable."

"Prognosis." Audrey breathed out. She wouldn't go to selection. She'd make an appointment with her mother's doctor, first thing tomorrow. Figure out a treatment plan that would work. She'd—

"I have made my decision, Chen-Yi. You must honor it."

"But—"

"No but. And don't even think about not going to selection. That is your path. Now, let us have a nice dinner and watch a movie. How about Jackie Chan?"

Audrey smiled, wiping a tear from her good eye. "Ha. Still have your sense of humor. Are you in pain?"

Her mother smiled, that bright radiant smile, full of joy and fullness. "No, Chen-Yi. Decay and death part of life. I am dying. But everyone is dying. Even you. Don't forget that."

"I'll live long enough to get the takeout. You want the usual?"

"Extra egg rolls," her mother replied. "Why not?"

MILENA SWIRLED HER RIESLING GLASS and smiled at the woman speaking. *Jordyn Richards, State Department Counter Threat Finance and Sanctions,* read her name tag. Mid-thirties, bony bleach-blonde, droning on about preschools in the area. The loose semi-circle of half a dozen women commiserated on the lack of good options. Got to get those little rug rats ready for college early, and a life spent climbing over each other reaching for the brass ring. Milena allowed herself a glance around the atrium at the several hundred other people filling the room. Cocktail hour at the Conrad Hotel, smack-dab in the epicenter of Washington, D.C. The Women in Defense Annual Awards Gala was the last place she wanted to be right now. Sometimes she wished she was still flying jets. Her eyes lingered on the interior architecture of the building, imagining the composition of the support material. From twenty thousand feet, the structure would look like a stick figure without the arms, with a sleek, glassy façade. Right around ten stories tall, concrete and rebar material. She'd go with a pair of GBU-38s, the Joint Direct Attack Munition guided by a coordinate given to her by either the Joint Operations Center or a guy on the ground. Ripple fire one of the munitions on top of the other. The most likely target would be ground level on the north side, at the lobby and main entrance. If her wingman could—

"—General Janek, might I have a quick word?" The voice pulled her from the musing like a splash of cold water. Her heart tripped when she saw who it was.

"Reginald, of course." She allowed the man to lead her to an unoccupied part of the atrium. Reginald Simon, senior vice president of Mergers and Acquisitions for Northrup Grumman. He was, for lack of a better term, a corporate assassin. A man whose very *raison d'être* was scooping up scrappy, upstart companies like Laughlin Carmichael for a late breakfast snack.

"Please, call me Milena," she replied.

"Very well," he smiled at her, revealing a small gap in his front teeth. "I've been hearing some rumblings, Milena. That Laughlin Carmichael is looking for another round of funding for several of your product lines. That *Project Wayfarer* is failing. Imploding, in fact." He wore some vaguely offensive product in his hair that she couldn't quite identify.

She resisted the urge to either wrinkle her nose at the scent or show her feelings about his conversational gambit.

Son of a bitch.

She should have known it would get out, eventually. Milena kept a poised nonchalance to her face and body language as she improvised a response. "We're still on track to meet the majority of our milestone deadlines. Not planning to seek additional investors at this time."

"Come now, Milena," said Reginald, looking around at the gathering and gesturing languidly with a hand adorned with a West Point ring. "It's just *us girls* here. If LC needs a capital infusion, you need only let me know." A business card appeared as if by magic in his hand. Maybe he had a spring system rigged in his suit sleeve. "My personal cell is on here. Say the word. We can work out the details later." And with that, he was gone, a shark swimming on toward his next prey.

She swallowed heavily and exhaled, smoothing her silk blouse. No one should know *Project Wayfarer* was in shambles. No one outside her vetted circle of consiglieres, that is. Her flagship initiative was in a medical hold after two experimental subjects—both former Rangers with stellar records—died from cerebral aneurysms. Wayfarer was going to be the next big thing in Special Operations—a way to take existing operators and augment their perception, cognition, and reaction speed. Next-generation *Jason Bourne*-type stuff.

After some initially promising trials, her scientists had run into a veritable brick wall of setbacks and obstacles.

Her eyes flicked down at the card and surveyed the crowd. Milena met a few stares that swiftly looked back at their conversations.

Back off, bitches.

She slid the card into a pocket of her handbag as her husband ambled up.

"There you are. Brought you a drink, but I see that you have one already." Tim was still lanky after all these years—captain of the water polo team at Air Force when she was a freshman. They married when she commissioned from the Colorado Springs school and went out into the force as a couple. A C-17 pilot, Tim ended up getting out after a decade at major, while she got F-16s and her prospects for command were greater.

Milena glanced at the bags under his eyes as though noticing them for the first time. Which she was. The business with Plek was sucking up all available bandwidth. "I'll take it." She downed the remains of her drink and accepted his. Liquid courage for the speech. "Everything okay? You have that look on your face. The same look you got when Henry got in trouble for egging the neighbor's house."

A tired smile from her husband. "It's nothing. Well, not nothing. But not before your speech. Tell you later." He gave the faintest eye flick toward the retreating Reginald. "Grumman nosing around?"

She nodded. "Bastards smell blood in the water."

"You know what I'm going to say, don't you?"

Milena gave him a faint smile. "How much runway do I have left?"

"Sounds like not enough for your taste," Tim responded. He sipped his neat whiskey, then nodded his head at the other side of the ballroom. "There's Congressman Kellogg. Didn't you want to pull his ear?"

"Good eye, *Elrond,*" she said, leaning over to kiss him on the cheek. He loved it when she called him by his call sign.

"Go get 'em, *Goon,*" he said with a grin. She had to admit she didn't mind hearing her old call sign, either. From the soccer field to the battlefield, it had served her well.

Milena squared her shoulders and pushed off. Felt the eyes watching her.

Always someone watching in this town.

Congressman Kellogg held court with a pair of lawyers from a K Street firm and a hedge fund manager, telling a story that had the trio enraptured. She slowed to a stop and adopted a similar pose of engrossed interest, plastering a smile on her face.

"So, then the HASC chair says, 'Tell him to take his amendment and go sell crazy somewhere else.'" The group all laughed in unison, and Milena saw Kellogg's eyes notice her.

"Milena! Excuse me, *General* Janek. Great to see you."

"You too, Congressman. Please, call me Milena. I haven't been a general for a year now."

"I'm sure the Air Force misses you." Kellogg grabbed a drink from the table and took it down expertly. "You're speaking tonight, aren't you?" The hungry eyes of the group swiveled her way.

"That's right. Guest of honor for NDIA." The National Defense Industrial Association was the parent organization of Women in Defense. Creating the organization was a relatively painless way to show that the industrial complex was hip to changing societal norms.

Girl power, am I right, ladies?

"Your story is so inspirational. To survive what you did," one woman gushed.

"I don't know how you led that task force under those conditions. And that horrible, murderous man," said another.

Milena gave them a smile. She had a smile that could charm an ill-tempered cobra, something that had taken her decades to perfect. "Bless your heart, ladies. You're too kind. Congressman, could I pull your ear for a moment, before the cocktail hour concludes?"

"Certainly, Milena. Lead the way."

She took him out into a side hallway near the kitchen, where she hoped to minimize prying ears. Just had to watch out for the waitstaff. "Did I hear you killed the Gibbons Act?" Benjamin Gibbons was a former senator, and the Gibbons Act provided funding for up-and-coming Defense companies. The intent was to spur innovation and early adoption of new technology for the emerging competition with China. Not the big boys—the scrappy little upstarts, like LC. Cutting down on the flash-to-bang of the procurement process, to get equipment to the warfighter faster.

Kellogg favored her with a reptilian stare. "Kill is such a brutish word. The act is on hold. For now. It will move from committee when I see some progress from a few companies on several key national security issues."

Milena tamped down the incandescent jet of rage that surged through her. She'd been working with an old classmate. Off the books, of course. One-on-one CEO coaching. The woman played poker semi-professionally and had been teaching her about subconscious "leaks." Microexpressions that could telegraph thoughts and feelings. Right now, she wanted to drive the tip of one of her elegant yet uncomfortable high heels right into his balls. She could picture the stance, windup, and execution. Just like a corner kick. Milena imagined him absorbing the blow with a little surprised *oof*, and keeling over, like a listing battleship. No, Kellogg was more like a cruiser or a frigate—he didn't rate battleship status. She put on her most inquisitive, *please mansplain what's going on* face.

"And what might those key issues be, Congressman? I told you we're working on the prototype now, and it should be ready for an initial round of testing by the fall. We are close to a viable—"

He slurped the remains of his drink, waving at a passing waitstaff member for another. "I don't want to hear *close* anymore, Milena. *Close* was last year. I want to see something that works, not PowerPoint slides that brief well. Even if they look *so good* when you brief them." Kellogg's eyes flicked suggestively to her legs, and then back upward.

Milena nodded, exhaling as though she was giving the matter some thought. Next time, she'd engineer a recording, or a witness, and nail his ass. "Thank you for your patience, Congressman. When we speak again, the circumstances will have changed. Count on it."

The slimeball actually winked at her and gave her a gentle squeeze on the elbow. "Thatta girl. I look forward to it. Can't wait to hear your speech." He walked off, no doubt in search of more alcohol and female attention.

Fine. This would still work. If the runway was running out, she had two options. She could jettison weight or add thrust. She wasn't ready to do the former, so the latter would have to suffice.

CHAPTER 10

Roz—Good Friday, 3 PM

THE DAY HAD FINALLY COME. They'd spent a week preparing. After the attack, they stayed vigilant, but Milena didn't send anyone else against them. Roz got comfortable with the gear, read *The Inferno*. They gamed out possible scenarios that might wait for them in the Plek building. He got proper rest. Roz forgot what that felt like, after sleeping with one eye open for so long. *Peace.* He trained with the Aegis and had a few other tricks up his sleeve. They packed water bottles and backpacking-friendly protein options—jerky, bars, and trail mix. Hark found an antique Navy enlisted cutlass at an old Army surplus store outside Salinas, got it sharpened up.

After presenting themselves for inspection, a Plek employee ushered them into an elevator for a ride to the fifth floor. The dog camera and smart watches made it through without pinging the radar of the inspectors.

A young man in a suit greeted them as they exited and directed the pair to a room at the end of the hall. An old conference room, with wood-paneled walls and intricate, art deco molding on the ceiling. Judging by the photos that Hark had on his Carrie-from-*Homeland* conspiracy-theorist wall display, several of the other selectees had already arrived.

"What the hell is this? We can bring animals? Nobody said anything about that! What are you doing with that shield—going jousting?" a gravelly voice boomed from behind them. A hefty, meaty man sprawled in a chair at the massive conference table in the room's center.

The dog eyed the man, picking up on his aggressive tone and non-verbals.

Roz shrugged. "No one objected downstairs. What, you wanted to bring your falcon?"

The man frowned. A Realtree-brand crossbow case sat at his feet, and a swollen Rambo knife bulged on his belt.

Danault, that was his name. He'd put on a few pounds since the last picture they'd found of him. Looked like a long-lost Baldwin brother.

Danault squinted. "It's you. I wondered if you were gonna show up when I saw your name on the invite. What did they call you on MSNBC? The Butcher of Baghdad? Everyone, we've got a real-life celebrity with us here. Nice shield—you doing some kind of Renaissance Faire cosplay?"

Heat bloomed on Roz's face, but he ignored the insults.

Not worth it. Keep moving.

A blonde woman with piercing eyes sat at the other end of the conference table, a spread of cards in front of her. She gazed at him. "Don't listen to that. I just met him five minutes ago and I can tell he's a blowhard already. Feroz, right?"

"I go by Roz. Gabrielle, is it?"

She smiled. "Guilty. That's my brother, Grady, if you

couldn't tell from the resemblance." She gestured to a lean twenty-something wearing an expensive-looking leather harness on his chest, holding half a dozen throwing axes.

"This unironic mustache-wearing Southern gentleman is Hark." Roz pointed at the Texan, who gave her a curt nod. "He'll probably want to compare notes on the axes with your brother."

"And who is this?" She leaned over, and the dog backed up a few steps, watching her carefully.

"He's a little skittish," Roz explained.

"Too bad. Dogs normally love me." The woman shrugged. "I'm going to do a card draw for you two. I'm doing it for all the selectees."

Roz gestured at Hark. "Ooh ooh, do Mr. Nasty Stache here first."

She looked over at Hark as she shuffled the deck. She flipped one. "Interesting."

"What is it?"

"Death."

Hark grunted. "I don't believe in tarot."

"Ah, but tarot believes in you, Mr. Nasty Stache." Gabrielle replied with the trace of a smile. "Death can mean many things. Usually, it means a costly loss."

She flipped the next card. Roz leaned over and looked. The card had a Roman numeral sixteen written on the face. Two people fell from what appeared to be a burning building.

"The Tower. *A structure must suddenly and violently come down. Chaos and distress, making room for something new to be built.*"

Roz smirked. "I'll buy the chaos bit. Not quite sure about the rest, though."

Gabrielle sidled up and put her arm on a slab of a man who looked to be a Pacific Islander. He looked like a distant cousin to the Rock. "This is Tau. Matamua." She affected a Kiwi accent. "He's from down undeh."

Roz gave him a polite tip of a nonexistent cap. His eyes fell on a handheld weapon on the table. Inscribed with intricate designs and a carved notch on the edge. "I dig the club."

The man grunted. "My *wahaika*."

"See you around, Roz." Gabrielle turned away from him and stroked Tau's cheek, murmuring something into his ear.

Roz glanced outside and saw a woman in a green scarf talking to Justine. He left Hark and pushed out the doors onto a good-sized balcony, whipped by the wind at this height. Roz fought an unpleasant feeling in the pit of his stomach as he recalled the bridge incident with Doreen. Alabaster wisps of light mist floated between the skyscrapers.

"—Stage four lung cancer," he heard the woman in the scarf say. "Thing is, she never smoked. She worked in a dry-cleaning place for years, around some nasty chemicals."

"I'm sorry. Is there anything—" Justine replied, eyeing Roz as he walked over to look down at the street below.

"She's been to three different oncologists. Same outlook. It won't be long now."

"Would you like to withdraw from the selection process and return home to be with her?" Justine asked.

The woman had a backpack of her own, with flags from several countries in the Middle East and Africa.

This is the professor?

She turned, and Roz saw her face for the first time. The entire right side was a mass of scars and burns. She met his eyes, and some instinct told him she was sizing him up for a reaction.

"And that is why I don't use off-brand exfoliators. They leave a nasty mark. Is that what happened to you?" Roz pulled down the collar of his shirt, revealing his own set of scars.

He heard Justine's sharp intake of breath, but he kept his eyes locked on the woman. Roz watched the emotions on her face flicker and oscillate, anger, sadness, anger, and finally settling on amusement.

She rolled her eyes. "That's cute." Turning to Justine, she said, "I'll go home when it's done, Ms. Lipton. My mother is adamant that I participate." The woman's gaze returned to Roz. "I'm Audrey."

"Roz."

"What happened to you?"

"IED."

Audrey nodded. "Bet you're a real hit with the ladies, with lines like that."

"I apologize. You're not getting my best work right now. I'm a little gassy, and just a touch nervous—don't know if I'm on foot or horse."

She turned her back on him, faced Justine. "Ms. Lipton, what's that flag?" Audrey asked, pointing up toward the top of the building. It was huge—hard to tell exactly how big at this distance. It flicked and fluttered on a stanchion in the building breeze from the west.

"A bit of the past that we like to keep alive. Back when it was the tallest building in the city, our roof served as the official city storm-warning station. That flag communicates to the citizenry bad weather is coming."

"Is there?" Audrey asked, looking out to the south. The weather seemed clear. "A storm coming, that is."

Justine gave her the ghost of a smile and a slight twist of her eyebrows. "It's already here, my dear."

JUSTINE LOOKED THROUGH THE WINDOWS into the boardroom at the assembled selectees. "Four PM. It appears as though we have a quorum. Time to begin."

They followed her inside. The rest of the group took seats around the conference table. Justine walked to the podium at the head of the table and waited for them to settle into their chairs.

A small, blue-haired woman hurried over from the bathroom and took her seat. That would be Tabitha Winkel, if Hark's intel packet was correct.

"You nine have come here at the express request of the late Dr. Berenger. His final wish was to provide all of you the opportunity to earn a position of leadership. Leadership over the foundation he built over the course of a lifetime of service and sacrifice. The moment has come for that opportunity. Now is the time, if you'd like to change your mind. You may walk out the door now. But if you decide to stay, we will begin the selection. Does anyone desire to depart?"

She looked them all in the eye, one by one.

None made a move to stand.

"No? I'm glad to hear it. Or not hear it, rather." She

walked over and slowly closed the massive double doors. They married together with a final sounding *thunk*.

Nowhere to go, now.

The lights dimmed, and automatic shades whirred downward to keep even the day from encroaching.

The group looked at one another, an awkward silence broken only by the dog's panting and occasional stray whine. A large screen descended from the ceiling, and a projector clicked on at the back of the boardroom. A video began to play. It opened with scenes of violence—political riots in the United States, Europe, Africa, South America. Environmental degradation, trash-filled oceans. Social media feeds filled with vitriol. Then cable news talking heads monologuing darkly. Flotillas of yachts filled with opulence and splendor, contrasted with scenes of squalor in a Brazilian *favela*.

Then a British-accented voice-over began. "The polycrisis. A confluence of social, economic, political, environmental, epistemological, and technological crises. We have never had so many ways to destroy ourselves than at this very moment. Whether through nuclear, chemical, or biological weapons, artificial intelligence, or a runaway economic model dependent on infinite growth on a finite planet. Collectively as a species, we are at a decisive point unlike any other in humankind's history. The word *decision* comes from the Indo-European, *caedere*, to cut or to strike. Now is a time when our collective decisions—when we cut away other alternatives for action or inaction—will have far-reaching consequences for the future. The market has abandoned efforts to solve these problems. Billionaires are building their bolt holes to wait out the collapse in places like New Zealand. The State—whatever State you choose—cannot respond effectively to the dynamism and interconnectedness of the problems. Senators can barely operate their iPhone, let alone understand artificial intelligence. Which leaves the Commons. The poor, sad, shriveled Commons. Networked associations of individuals and groups. All coming together in a decentralized manner to help humanity muddle through this evolutionary bottleneck. No other non-profit organization in the world is as organized, resourced, or possesses the multi-layered vision of the Plek Foundation. With the help of a massive donor base, in addition to a sizable endowment from Dr. Berenger himself, the foundation pursues several lines of effort. As a charitable organization, it collaborates with a network of other NGOs to provide essential human services in conflict prone regions of the world. Less known but just as important, the historical section canvasses the world, searching for ancient treasures and forgotten mysteries from our indigenous ancestors. Answers to where we go in the future can often be found in the murky reaches of our past. The pioneering R&D arm is working on a variety of initiatives. One involves a revolutionary nootropic compound and a bleeding edge combination audio/visual delivery mechanism, informally called the *Berenger Blend* by members of the foundation. The modality bypasses normal sensory-gating mechanisms in the brain to increase human perception to levels never before seen in the modern world. The charity, historical department, and R&D directorate align to work toward a more resilient environment for humanity."

Roz watched Gabrielle move her hand onto Tau's thigh. The Maori shifted a bit, but he clearly enjoyed the attention.

The voice continued. "None of this would be possible without the genius of Dr. Nicholas Berenger. From humble, hardscrabble roots, this son of a factory foreman and a waitress served as a platoon leader in Beirut before he returned stateside to complete a PhD in cognitive science. Several periods of solitude—at Esalen and other locales—informed his vision, and ultimately led to multiple patented bio-technological devices. Three are still in use in hospitals today. As the founder and CEO of Berenger Medical, he navigated the tempest of Wall Street in the 1980s to emerge triumphant. His early diversification into several current Fortune 100 publicly traded companies provided the backing behind many of the survivors of the dot-com bust in the early aughts. In the mid 2010s, Nicholas turned over the reins of his financial empire to focus his efforts completely on foundation initiatives. He withdrew from public events and devoted the remainder of his life to this mission."

"This would be the 'Howard Hughes' stage of his life," Danault muttered, as he twirled the Rambo knife between his hands.

"Shh," a dark-skinned, lithe woman said, without taking her eyes off the screen. Roz figured she must be Abeni Rutu, the Kenyan-born lawyer. Roz noted the bow next to her weathered pack on the floor.

"In September of last year, Nicholas piloted his personal plane from Dar Es Salaam, Tanzania. to a remote island—the hub for several of the foundation's projects. He never made it. After a weeks-long search involving three surface ships and seven planes from four nations, Nicholas was officially listed as lost at sea. His legal team began executing his last wishes. Your presence here today is one of the final steps in that process." The video faded to darkness. Silence.

Justine wiped an eye, exhaled sharply. "A little housekeeping before we begin. Please don the glasses in front of your name tags and direct your attention to the holographic projection at the center of the table. There, you will see a schematic of the circles of Hell, as described by Dante Alighieri."

The group watched the diagram materialize in the center of the table. People on both sides could see the same three-dimensional image, projected upward and downward by a series of lights and lasers. A side view of the building revealed the floors above them. Small icons moved on the levels, around other strange mechanisms. It slowly rotated counterclockwise, floating above the surface of the table.

"This, ladies and gentlemen, is Hell. These are the challenges which lay between you and assuming the duties as a steward of the Plek Foundation. They will test the depths of your character, your grit, and your ability to make decisions under pressure. We will take the total of your performance into consideration, prior to final scoring. In each circle of Hell, there are two authorized exit doors, painted crimson red. If you cannot continue for any physical, medical, or other reason, you may exit either of those doors to receive aid. But you may not reenter the tower once you step out. The consent forms you have all signed grant permission to ingest medicinal substances, to include chemicals such as ayahuasca and psilocybin. Are there questions about any of that?"

The doors to the conference room opened, and a team of medical personnel came in, pushing a cart full of equipment. They set up what looked like an IV station at one end of the table. The sharp tang of sterilizing astringent wafted over the group.

"Are you talking about microdosing or something like that?" Abeni asked. She had the faintest traces of a British accent.

"Something like that, Ms. Rutu. It's part of the process, assessing your conduct in altered states of consciousness." Justine stared at each of them. "It is not hyperbole to say that a great deal depends upon the selection of the proper stewards to replace Dr. Berenger. The risks facing our reality are at a critical inflection point. The confluence of crises requires humankind to grow up. Like a baby chick breaking free of an eggshell that can no longer support it. It requires us to remember the ancient wisdom of our deep history in order to properly steward our advanced technology." Justine gestured at the two women and one man in white who approached. "These nurses will administer a chemical cocktail under the supervision of our anesthesiologist, Dr. Kellogg."

"Give me an IV, Doc, I'm hungover," Danault said, winking at the doctor. She ignored him, lips tight, helped the nurses sterilize injection points on the arms of the selectees.

"We even retained a veterinarian to ensure we gave Diogenes the right amount," Justine said as a woman bent down to administer an injection to the dog. He accepted the needle without so much as a whimper.

Always the strong, silent type, the dog was.

"It is now four thirty-two PM on Good Friday. You must transit the nine levels of Dante's Hell and reach the chamber at the top before dawn on Easter Sunday morning. This gives you—"

"Thirty-eight hours and some change," Roz finished for her. He felt the drug begin to take effect. A placid contentment stole slowly over him, an ebbing and flowing not unlike an ocean surf. Roz reclined the chair and closed his eyes.

Let the darkness take him into oblivion.

BOOK II

SELECTION

CHAPTER 11

Roz—Good Friday, 8:30 PM

Midway in our life's journey,
I went astray from the straight road,
and woke to find myself alone in a dark wood.
How shall I say what wood that was!
I never saw such drear, so rank, so arduous a wilderness!
Its very memory gives a shape to fear.
Death could scarce be more bitter than that place!
But since it came to good,
I will recount all that I found revealed there by God's grace.
How I came to it, I cannot rightly say,
so drugged and loose with sleep,
and I become when I first wander there from the True Way.
Inferno, Canto I

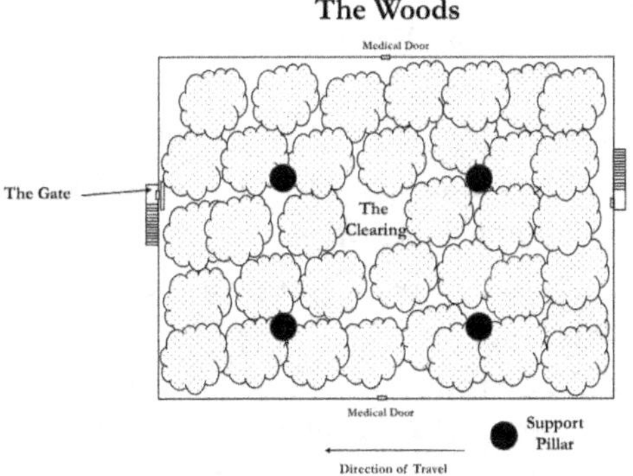

THE JANGLE OF THE DOG'S COLLAR rang like a rattlesnake tail, dragging Roz fitfully into consciousness. The hound shook himself and sneezed violently. Roz sat up. Humid and earthy. Dank. Groggy from the sedative. The next thing he noticed were the trees—vertical lines breaking up the shadowy light. They appeared real, but he could see traces of walls beyond. Walls painted to look like trees, but they were still walls when you looked closely. Lights off in the distance.

A woman moaned, somewhere off to his right. The dog froze, nostrils of his snout flaring in and out as he quested for some scent Roz couldn't detect. A low growl came from his throat. Roz pulled the Aegis from the exterior straps on his pack, tested its balance. Light and strong, as always. He could always trust in the shield. It had never let him down. Unlike people. Pulled the cutlass out with a rasping *shink*. Roz stiffened when a guttural call echoed through the woods, rebounding from the walls. A sound he hadn't heard in years. On a five-day safari out of Nairobi, he'd heard it at night—the roar of an enormous cat, out in the darkness. Back then, they had the relative safety of a large group of armed men. Here, he felt naked.

Roz scanned to his left. Hark kneeling, oriented toward the sound without speaking, an arrow nocked in the bow but not drawn.

"What is this? What the hell is this?" A voice stammered from a few yards away, drawing angry glances and shushing from some others. Sounded like Danault.

"We need to get out of here," Roz whispered to Hark. "Away from these people."

Hark nodded. The ground sloped upward in one direction, and down in the other. Dull light toward the high ground. Downhill was darker, full of shadows. They moved uphill, toward the traces of wall he'd seen. There wasn't much to go on, but better than nothing.

You pays your money, and you takes your chances.

The pair froze when the cat roared again. Different position this time. A howl answered from the other direction.

"Okay, book review," Hark whispered as they crept through the foliage. Plek had installed actual trees and bushes, judging by the humidity, spongy dirt beneath their feet, and the feel of the leaves. The dog slunk through the shadowed greenery to their right as Roz picked a careful path for Hark to follow.

They reached the wall. Roz bent over and found a speaker built into the concrete.

"Makes for a nice ambiance," Hark mused, as the sound of crickets and other nocturnal noise came from the device. "Which way, amigo?"

Roz looked down the wall in both directions. "Take the high ground or the high ground will take you." He started up the slope, Hark and the dog in trail.

It was quiet and deadly, when it came.

Out of the darkness, a furry mass slammed into Roz, knocking him to the ground. A feral musk filled his nostrils, and he scarcely had time to bring the shield up. Roz stabbed with the cutlass. He felt the impact when the dog latched onto one of the beast's legs, coming to his defense. The two animals became a rolling ball of fur and sharp-edged violence. Roz used the break to reset himself and stab into what he could now see was a powerfully built wolf. It bellowed as the cutlass slid into its ribs and snapped its teeth toward the sword. The animal bucked backward, and the sudden movement ripped the cutlass out of Roz's grip.

As quickly as it had arrived, it was gone, taking the sword with it as it slunk back into the foliage. In the distance, they heard yells and the snarl of another animal.

They caught their breath and Hark did a quick hand sweep of the dog to ensure he wasn't injured.

"That was a big fucking wolf," the Texan remarked quietly. "At least a hundred pounds, maybe more."

"Let's keep moving," Roz panted, out of breath. Hark nodded and took point. The lights they'd seen in the distance resolved themselves into electric sconces, flickering irregularly in a mimic of torchlight. Door up ahead, sound and movement in the trees to their left. Hark drew tension on his bow, but relaxed when a woman came into the light, walking stick in her hand. Her short blue hair made Roz think of *Sonic the Hedgehog*. He wasn't about to say that to her. Her shirt had a dark stain on it, but they couldn't tell if it was her blood or an animal's.

Winkel gave them a curt nod. Didn't seem to talk that much. The three of them and the dog came to a halt in the clearing in front of the door. It was massive, easily fifteen feet tall, made of some hardwood banded with iron strips. Letters etched deeply into the coarse wood in cursive script filled the surface, and the wavering sconce light made the words seem to dance in the dimness.

They looked at the engraving on the door.

Seven cursive words that darkened the mood of human and canine alike.

Cold tendrils snaked through Roz's midsection as he considered the script. Perhaps a premonition, a bone-deep inkling of things to come.

HECTOR SPRAYED A LINE OF PAINT on the weathered concrete below the freeway. The wind was picking up and messing with his aim. Across the trash-strewn way, two of his "tag bros," Jameon and Kayla, did the same. It was part of a larger, Banksy-style project they'd been working on off and on for weeks. His phone buzzed in his pocket. Setting the can of primal green down, he looked at the text. From a number that he didn't recognize. He usually got a lot of spam — mostly ads for Viagra knockoffs and increase-your-penis-size-type ads. But this one caught his attention.

Hector DeAngelo, would you like to earn $2,000?

It will involve a bit of mischief, but nothing you're not used to.

We've left you a down payment at a location nearby.

Are you interested in earning the full amount?

Text Y for yes and I will send the down payment location.

Fear wormed its way through his insides. Who the hell

was this and how did they get his number? Was it a trick? He'd never heard of cops pulling some kind of shit like this. First time for everything, though. He watched Kayla finish the shadows beneath the eye of the giant face, her own features lost in concentration. Two Gs would hit nice right now. Depending on how much work was involved, of course. *Fuck it.* Hector texted the Y. The response came immediately.

There is a trash can in the south-east corner of the bridge underpass.

From there, walk toward the wall directly behind it.

Look for the brick that says "Resist."

The down payment is behind it.

If you take it, we expect you to do the task.

Don't disappoint us.

You won't like the result.

Heart beating, he walked over to the trash, found the brick. It was as the text message said. Five hundred dollars in twenties, nicely rolled in a little plastic container. He thought about just keeping the money. It was easy enough to do. But he was a little creeped out that someone had his number. If they had that, what else did they know? His instincts, the reptilian intuition that had kept him mostly safe for two decades on the streets, said the person on the other end of the phone was not someone he should fuck with.

"What's that, Angel?" Jameon had stopped tagging and was looking his way. Kayla had paused as well, watching him bent over the wall. His phone vibrated in his hand, and his excitement took on a bit of a colder feeling as he read the words on the cracked screen.

Your friends can help if you so choose.

We will increase compensation.
But the task will slightly change.
Your call.
"Ya'll wanna make some green?" he called out.

CHAPTER 12

Roz—Good Friday, 10 PM

I am the way into the city of woe.
I am the way to a forsaken people.
I am the way into eternal sorrow.
Sacred justice moved my architect.
I was raised here by divine omnipotence,
primordial love and ultimate intellect.
Only those elements time cannot wear were made before me,
and beyond time, I stand.
Abandon all hope ye who enter here.
Inferno, Canto III

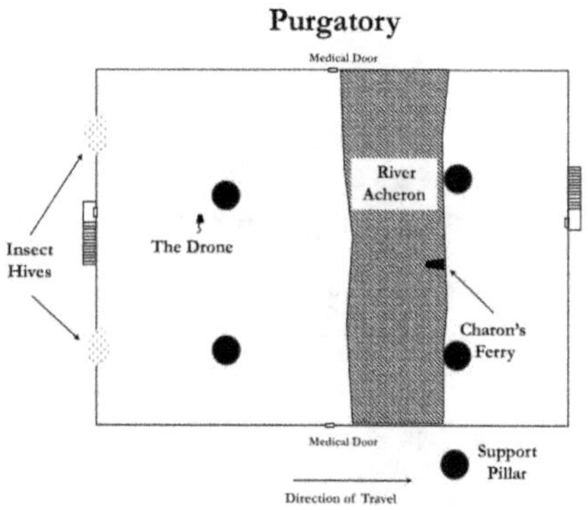

NO ONE SPOKE AS THEY PASSED THROUGH THE PORTAL. It led to a path ramping upward at a steep angle. Roz found himself in the front, Tabitha behind, and Hark bringing up the rear. The dog stayed by his side, as he always did. Too dumb to do anything else, Roz assumed.

If you're going to be dumb, you've got to be hard.

The Malinois was definitely hard, that was for sure. More of the flickering electric sconces bathed them in a dim, yellow glow. The air smelled of the charged ozone before a summer storm, and Roz felt that same sense of pregnant potential looking out to the next level.

They bunched up at the top. Roz estimated that they ascended at least three stories of height from the woods level. He peered into the gloom from the entrance of a large, open space. Most of the other selectees had beaten them to the level, moving with a purposeful urgency in the center. The area was flat and featureless, like a desert. Rough concrete floor. A medium-sized quadcopter drone flew above the selectees, trailing a banner. Occasionally, a yell or scream reached their ears across the expanse.

"This is Limbo?" Roz asked no one in particular.

"No. Purgatory," corrected Winkel without taking her

eyes off the drone. "According to Dante, this place houses the uncommitted—souls who refused to give themselves to either God or Satan." Then she looked out into the room. "The uncommitted chase a banner through the level, pursued and harried by wasps and other insects."

Hark pointed. "What's the deal with the water?"

"The river Acheron. Souls must pay a levy to Charon to use his boat for the crossing."

"What does he take?" asked Roz. "Isn't it usually coins or something on eyelids, if I'm remembering my *Boondock Saints?*"

"Usually," Tabitha replied. "I have no idea what *Boondock Saints* is."

They heard a metallic clanking behind them, then a deep, discordant humming. The dog yelped, hopped to the side.

The dog yelped, hopped to the side.

"Wasps," Hark reported, shrinking back from the wall.

"We need to move," Roz said as the humming grew in the small vestibule. They sprinted onto the main floor and found the air thick with more insects. Some were of the stinging variety, wasps, and bees, but they found plenty of June bugs, beetles, and stink bugs. The air was thickest with them near the walls, so the group slowly found themselves pulled to the middle of the cavernous space with the other selectees. A large moat bisected the level, blocking their path with a band of dark water. Above, the quadcopter circled at twenty feet, trailing a long black banner.

Roz watched another pair of selectees run up from the ramp. Danault and Zhou.

"Ow!" "Yah!" A succession of yells came from other selectees as the insects stung.

Roz watched Abeni shoot an arrow at the copter, but it flew wide. Grady threw an axe straight in the air. It sailed in a lazy arc without scoring a hit.

"We might have to swim for it, Kemosabe," Hark said, sizing up the inky liquid and swatting at a beetle. Others came to the same conclusion, Roz could see, as they fought off the insect apocalypse.

When the drone neared Roz, he heaved the Aegis. It spun and spun, end over end, smacked the drone.

Lucky shot.

Sparks flew, and angry metal rotors fragmented around them, and the others cheered. The copter, mortally wounded, gyrated in an off-balance fashion. It shrieked like a wounded animal and plummeted to the concrete. Roz retrieved the Aegis. Another few scars on its weathered face to burnish its legend.

Tabitha ran to the banner, yelled triumphantly. She pulled a credit card-sized device from the wreckage. "Thus, it is willed there, where what is willed can be done," she read aloud.

"What does that even mean?" Grady asked, stowing an axe.

"It's a thing Virgil says in *The Inferno* to get Charon to do what he wants. They're not happy that—ow, ow, ow!" Tabitha convulsed as a swarm of insects descended on her. Convulsed into a ball. Bees. A *thunk* came from under the floor after she said the words aloud. The water churned in the middle of the moat. A long mass rose from the depths, became a narrow walkway, water sluicing down as it shuddered to a stop.

The Corstead twins ran across, ignoring Tabitha. She lay contorted in agony on the ground. The others followed, heading for the door at the far side. Roz began to cross as well.

"Kemosabe!" Hark called. He knelt next to Tabitha and examined her. The dog whined and sniffed at the blue-haired woman.

"Let's go, Texas," Roz called. "She'll be fine."

"She's going into shock, numb nuts. Get your Persian ass over here and help me."

Roz sighed and came back, getting stung again for his efforts.

"Must be allergic—look, she's got an EpiPen right here." Hark pulled the kit out of Tabitha's cargo pocket and injected her, then assessed her vitals and prepped her to move. "Ready, one, two, three, up," Hark called to synchronize their movements. They lifted her unconscious body and carried it through the insects to the medical stairs. Roz pushed the door open and found two men and a woman wearing blue jumpsuits with the Plek logo on the front.

"We'll take it from here," the woman said as they passed Tabitha across.

Hark let the door close and gave Roz the Look.

Disappointed Hark.

Roz had been seeing more of him lately. "We're here to finish selection. Us. You and me. We're not here for anyone else." He straightened his pack and moved for the exit.

Hark shook his head and sighed, fell a step behind. "I see you've forgotten everything I tried to bang into your gourd in Iraq."

"Not everything. I remember the words to 'Deep in the Heart of Texas.'"

The Texan said nothing.

"This is a competition, Hark," Roz continued. "We have to survive. You may not like it, but we do. And I have to get to the end. I don't care how many bodies I need to hurdle on the way there."

"Winning and being a good human are not mutually exclusive. You *can* do both."

"That's debatable."

CHAPTER 13

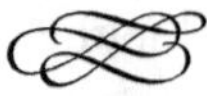

Roz—Good Friday, 11 PM

And I found I stood on the very brink of the valley called the Dolorous Abyss,

the desolate chasm where rolls the thunder of Hell's eternal cry,

so depthless deep and nebulous and dim that stare as I might into its frightful pit

it gave me back no feature and no bottom.

Death-pale, the poet spoke: "Now let us go into the blind world waiting here below us.

I will lead the way and you shall follow."

Inferno, Canto IV

Circle I: Limbo

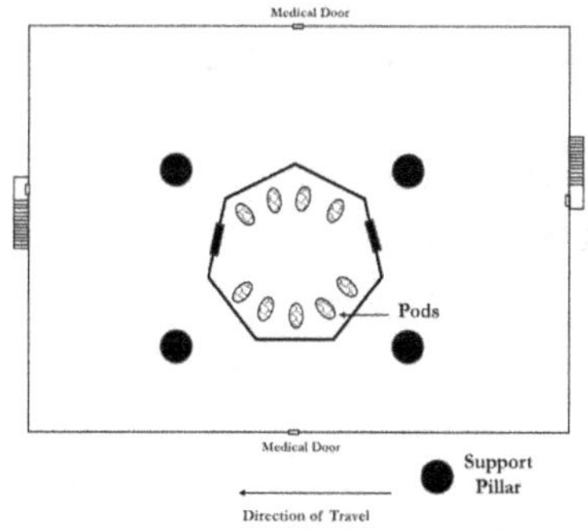

Medical Door

Pods

Medical Door

Support Pillar

Direction of Travel

ROZ STEWED.

Glared into the next circle from the entryway. Sometimes he forgot how much Hark liked to lecture. Roz wasn't going to let anything get between him and finishing. Artificial turf on the floor, the kind found in an athletic facility. The center of the wide space boasted a two-story-high, octagon-shaped castle. A building within the building. Parapets at each corner, where striped flags hung limply. Evenly distributed throughout the open area of the level, four massive support columns rose from floor to ceiling—the load-bearing ribs of the opened-up building interior. None of the other selectees was in sight. He looked down at the dog, who stared back up at him, panting with that mindless grin of his. "Looks peaceful enough."

"Yeah." Hark drawled out the word slowly. He was using a small pair of binoculars to scan the area. "Don't see anything that sticks out yet."

"You think they dosed us with something? Like in the water or something?"

"Why—you feel weird?" Hark looked over at him.

Roz shook his head. "Not really, but who knows? This

whole thing is weird. No sign of the others. They can't be that far ahead of us."

Hark exhaled as he stowed the binos. "Don't like the quiet, though."

"Only one way to find out," Roz said. He walked out toward the castle, shield at the ready. The dog trotted alongside. Hark followed a beat later.

They entered the castle, slow and careful. No ceiling. It was an open-air structure.

Found the interior ringed with large, egg-shaped objects. Nine of them. Gabrielle sat in one of the pods wearing thick gloves, a bulbous headset perched on her forehead.

"Where's blue-hair girl?" she asked as they approached.

Roz shrugged. "Allergic reaction to the bugs."

"How sad," Gabrielle replied absently, staring off into the distance. She shook her head. "Oh well." She pointed at a pair of open pods. "The instructions are inside—put the wireless headphones in and they can talk you through the process." She swung down the cover to the unit with a solid *thunk*.

"You ever use this stuff?" Hark asked, as they found two empty units next to one another.

"I walked around a VR simulation of Bin Laden's compound once—some company demo, but that's about it," Roz answered.

"My niece has an Oculus. I played *Beat Saber* with her a few times. It's like *Fruit Ninja* but three-D."

Roz grimaced. "I'm going to pretend I didn't hear you say that."

Hark laughed. "Aww, come on, where's your sense of adventure?"

Roz rolled his eyes and set up the collapsible dog bowl and some treats for the hound.

"Check out the statues. Recognize any of these?" Hark

pointed around the courtyard. Between each of the egg pods stood a marble bust of an ancient figure.

"That ugly dude over there has got to be Socrates," Roz said. "And that guy with a perm must be Marcus Aurelius." He pulled the earphones from the box at the base of the pod and slid them into his ears. Someone began speaking immediately.

"Mr. Mehran? Feroz?"

"Who's asking?" Roz replied as he took his backpack off.

"Ah—this is Dmitri. I will be your guide on a fantastic, fantabulous journey this evening. Please make yourself comfortable in the pod. You can leave your bag on the ground outside if you'd—"

"No thanks," Roz replied. He kept it in the pod as he sat down, scrunched between his legs. He didn't trust any of the others not to go through his bag. "Okay, what do you got for me, Dmitri?"

"Cool, cool, cool," Dmitri replied. "First things first. Chest belt—connect and tighten. The blood pressure cuff is on the right—slide it up above your elbow and snug it up."

"Is this for a polygraph?" Roz had been polyed a few times at organizations he'd worked in his career. The equipment was the same.

"Polygraph? Well, we will monitor vital signs during this test. Fidelity to any truth claims may or may not be a component of that. Next, see the gloves to your left—no, your other left."

Smooth, well-practiced answer.

"Fidelity to truth claims? Are you a lawyer, Dmitri?"

Dmitri ignored the jibe. "Real simple setup here. VR headset to your right. I would recommend putting the headset on first, then the gloves. Easier that way."

Roz did as he recommended, flexing his hands. The

gloves were a deep blue, with black and red cables snaking from the end. "Fred Savage would be jealous."

"Who?"

"You know? Fred Savage—in *The Wizard*?"

"Umm," Dmitri said. You could hear his fingers clacking keys in staccato tones in the background. "Oh! *The Wizard*! Nineteen eighty-nine. I was only NEGATIVE ELEVEN years old when that came out."

Roz laughed, sliding the goggles onto his forehead. He looked over at the dog, sitting peacefully at his feet. "*Blijf.*" Dutch for stay. Hark was ready over in his pod. "I was nine when I first watched it. My first taste of America."

"Catch you on the flip side, Texas." Hark gave him a lazy wave as he slid his hatch down.

"Okay, when you're ready, slide the pod door down and... there you go. Enjoy the ride, my friend. Sequence launching in five, four, three, two, and...we're off."

At first, there was nothing. Silence and blackness. Then, a succession of tones alternated back and forth, and a blinking halo floated across his field of view. For the next hour, the program ran him through a battery of questions. It seemed like an hour—he couldn't tell without looking at his watch. The questions were a combination of IQ and psychological assessments. One question was particularly annoying. A three-by-three field of dots swam across his vision, looking like a tic-tac-toe board.

"Please touch each dot only once with a straight line, making four straight lines. Draw the line with your finger," a voice instructed. "You have three tries."

Roz experimented with finger pinching and swiping. The way it worked was fairly intuitive. His first try was going around the edges of the dots. Failure. The second was even worse—like playing tic-tac-toe and getting a stalemate. He closed his eyes and thought. It had to be a trick. Brute-force tactics weren't working.

Think.

He opened his eyes and reread the directions, then did a quick visualization. "Son of a bitch," he muttered. He etched in a pattern. The dots dissolved with no sign of whether it was a correct answer, replaced by another puzzle. He was getting bored and ready to get out of there. Then Dmitri came back into his ears.

"Roz, please describe the circumstances in which you left your birth country and emigrated to the United States."

"Is this really necessary?" Roz asked.

"Part of the selection process is getting a comprehensive understanding of the individual. The 'complete human,' if you will."

"Fine." He exhaled and let a long silence grow before he spoke again. "My mother and I were living with my uncle. No one else would have us around, so—"

"Could you clarify why that was the case?"

"Why does this matter?"

"Please, Mr. Mehran."

"Because my mom was sleeping with an oil exec, and he left the country when Khomeini flew in. Our neighbors couldn't handle an unwed mother around, so we had to move. My uncle took us in." He wanted to rip the goggles off, and all the monitoring equipment.

Technical difficulties, please stand by.

"And what happened in 1988 that caused you to leave?"

Roz could still picture it. One of those flashbulb memories that would never go away fully. Indelibly seared. The way the soft morning light fell on the pockmarked walnut table in the kitchen of his uncle's house in Shiraz. Roz had just gotten up and padded downstairs, excited for the day to begin. His uncle

Reza was hard on him most of the time, but he had a soft side, and on this morning cuffed him on the head affectionately as Roz slid into a chair at the table. Breakfast was a time when Reza could talk, and Roz asked him questions about the world. Reza was a fierce supporter of the Tudeh Party, that of their deposed prime minister, Mohammad Mossadegh. A book-seller, he owned a few stores and ran a mail-order service for hard-to-find volumes. Roz piled a plate high with *sangak* and omelet, part of the spread that Reza's wife, Nivar, always filled the morning meal with. His own mother was still in bed, sleeping off a night partying in the city. Roz remembered the last thing his uncle said to him when the VAJA officers came and broke down the door. The *Vezarat-e Ettela'at Jomhuri-ye Eslami-ye Iran,* the Ayatollah's intelligence service, dragged him out of the house, for unspecified seditions against the new state.

"Stand up for what is right, Feroz, or nothing will change!" Look where that had gotten him. In her rage and grief, Nivar—never a huge fan of his mother anyway—kicked them out. Although it made little sense, Roz thought she blamed them for what happened to her husband. He never saw his uncle again.

"So, my mom wrote to some friends in America, asked to come stay with them. They agreed, sponsored us. Found her opportunities for work." Roz shifted in the seat. "Is this thing almost done? I have to take a leak."

"Almost, Mr. Mehran, just a few more questions. How were you able to get a nomination to the Naval Academy?"

Roz laughed. "Funny story. I got approached by someone who said they were representing a guy in Texas. They found out I was interested in applying to Annapolis. Wanted to do me a favor. Offered to connect me to the right people to get my congressman's nomination."

"Who was this person representing?"

"They didn't say right away. But I did some digging. This

was the nineties, so it wasn't like you could Google anything. But I figured it out—it wasn't my biological father, but *his* father. My grandfather. Trying to make amends for his son, I guess. There would be no acknowledgement that I was related to them. But they would do this one thing. So generous. Downright mag-fucking-nanimous, don't you think?"

Dmitri was silent for a few beats. "Please explain the circumstances for which you were put in the Miramar Brig, Mr. Mehran."

"Don't you have this information already? It was all over the news, and I'm sure you can do a Freedom of Information Act request for it," he protested.

"We would like to hear your version of events."

"You people are a real barrel of laughs, aren't you? Fine. Officially, my conviction was for *mishandling of classified information* and *murder*."

"In your view, was that the reason?"

Roz exhaled. "My boss at the time—Colonel Milena Janek—was into some shady shit. I found out some of it, but she was way more devious than I realized. I didn't get along with her chief of staff—we'd gotten into a fight that day, witnessed by several people. I embarrassed him. It was an easy sell that his death resulted from round two of our disagreement, and that I took things too far."

Dmitri pressed. "And what did you learn that caused her to frame you for his death?"

He laughed bleakly. "I never could quite figure it out. Not totally. I could see the parts here and there, but she got to me before I could put it together. She thought I knew more than I did."

"Is it not true that you were engaged in an extramarital affair with Colonel Janek at the time? Something she denied vehemently—and claimed that you sexually assaulted her?"

Roz breathed out. In. Out. In. *How did they find out?* The

media reports only covered the assault angle. His version was shunted aside. Buried.

"Mr. Mehran?"

"Yeah," he husked. "We were having a consensual affair."

Another longer pause. "Thank you, Mr. Mehran. That's enough for now."

"Are you sure? 'Cause I was really enjoying this trip down memory lane." But there was no response, and the unit powered down. The pod hatch unlocked and ascended silently upward. He clawed roughly at the monitoring equipment. Hurled it off. Roz found himself all alone—the lids of the other pods all sat raised in the air. Except the ninth one, the one that didn't get used. Silence. He looked down. The dog sat there, looking at him with those accusing, judgmental eyes. Not alone, after all.

"What are you looking at? You're not perfect, you know."

"CAMERA TWO, CAMERA TWO, SOMEONE GET ME THAT ANGLE BACK," Hazel ordered, voice taut with urgency. She stress-ate from a giant, party-size container of peanut M&M's. They weren't supposed to have any peanut products in the operations center, because at least one other staff member was allergic. Justine didn't care at the moment. It was game time. IT minions scampered back and forth, troubleshooting cable connections and improper software settings. At a certain point, all this tech was like magic, Justine mused. She doubted if even the experts had a complete grasp on all the problems.

Any sufficiently advanced technology is indistinguishable from magic.

The old Arthur C. Clarke line. And that was the entire problem, the very thing the foundation was trying to redress. Our ability to create world-destroying technology has outstripped our ability to responsibly steward it.

Justine sat next to Hazel in a swivel chair. Watched the group of selectees on the monitors. The flutters in her stomach came in waves—she got them whenever she engaged in something so stressful and high-stakes. Particularly something that was of such importance to Nicky.

So far, so good.

She wished he were here to see it all happen. Justine took a deep breath to tamp down on the nerves. Nicky's dream for the succession plan was no longer an abstract thought experiment, but real. And it was working. The selectees had already navigated a series of challenging obstacles—places of legitimate danger. They had only a few minor injuries to show for it. Tabitha had been an unfortunate loss, so early. She was in stable condition—taken to San Francisco General. Plek had an Artificial Generalized Intelligence running simulations based on all the inputs for each of the potential candidates, trying to divine the probabilities that each would survive. So far, the results had been inconclusive, with Matamua and Gabrielle leading the pack, alternating with Harkness. She had her doubts about the model's ability to predict the outcome. Humans were too messy.

Justine took off her glasses and rubbed her forehead. Sleep had been a distant, irregular acquaintance for a long while now. Pills helped from time to time, but she hadn't wanted to get addicted. That left her with long hours spent thinking about Nicky and how to best honor his memory. His legacy. That there was no body to bury made processing his death and finding closure all the more difficult. Her eyes fixated on one poster, part of a set that seemed to cover every square foot of the walls in the operations center. It was a wildlife action picture showing a spawning salmon leaping up a set of river rapids, right into the waiting mouth of a grizzly bear. The caption read *"Ambition—The journey of a thousand miles sometimes ends badly. Very badly."* She smiled, despite having seen it over and over for months as the tower project had come together. Someone had alternated the posters. For every serious one—concepts like *Leadership, Courage,* and *Teamwork,* there was a humorous one mounted on the walls between them. You could walk around the room like an art gallery if you were bored, oscillating between bubbly earnestness and bleak irony at each stop. She leaned back and listened to the soft hum of activity in the operations center.

From her position in the circle, Justine watched her people move about with practiced, purposeful precision. Dmitri was a tornado of activity—he rocked and darted his wheelchair to either side of his workstation as he directed cameras and other specialists to choreograph and curate the selection process. Kathy was on the phone with someone, dark-blond hair tightly bound. Always planning the next step. Playing chess, not checkers. The recent Georgetown public policy grad was a great addition to the team, recommended by an old friend from the intel community. Speaking of buns, Manbuns himself was here as well, speaking to Hazel in low tones. That was the name that she and Kathy had cooked up one night after a few bottles of Pinot. The former Ranger was head of her security detail and kept her safe with a quiet professionalism. Hazel nodded and made a note of something, and Manbuns ambled off.

Sighing, Justine pulled up a video of Nicky on her phone, ensuring that the sound was off. Old footage of a rare vacation. They had been in Port au Spain, Trinidad and Tobago, staying in an off-the-books hostel. The proprietor, a rail-thin fifty-something woman who went by Zuzu, had a dozen rooms spread between three old Antebellum houses. They were old but clean, maintained by Zuzu and her staff of half a dozen friends and family. Nicky didn't like to stay at expensive, high-profile hotels when they traveled—he preferred to remain *sub rosa,* as he called it. Under cover of anonymity among the locals, rather than the tourists.

"What do you want to do today?" he asked on the screen as he looked up at her. She knew all the words by heart by now. They lay entwined on the bed, trying to avoid moving in the heat. The heat. She remembered the sticky waves of heat lancing up from the asphalt in the midday sun.

"Stay in bed with you," she replied from off camera. Justine watched the smile grow on his features, from his lips to his eyes, until he laughed.

"Get over here. And turn that damn thing off." He pulled her close. The camera wobbled. The phone fell onto the bed and caught them in a kiss before Nicholas grabbed it and tossed it across the room. Justine exited the video, wiping her eyes. It hurt to watch, but she felt compelled to do it. Like a mouth with a ripped-out tooth, she kept sticking her tongue in the hole, triggering the nerve over and over.

As if the pain would distract from the loss.

A *whump* rattled the room, and the air pressure changed. Alarms blared in the distance, muted by the separation of several walls.

"There! Front entrance." Hazel pointed at one screen, the bottom right of which showed a rotating feed of their external building cameras.

"What happened?" Justine asked. The team was a flurry of

action, talking on phones and radios. Fingers flew over keyboards.

Hazel stood and updated her on the situation in tight tones. “Ma’am, someone detonated what looks like a large Molotov cocktail at the front entrance of the building. We have them on camera, but they were masked. I have safely accounted for all our personnel. Emergency services from the city are en route.”

“How many? Where did they go?”

“Three of them. Headed toward the waterfront.”

“Do we have a patrol outside the building?”

“Not yet, but we’ve deployed a response unit, and a drone is going up now.” She could see the flatscreen on the wall, where the grainy, black-and-white image of a camera winked into view as the device went airborne from a nearby balcony.

“Okay. Let’s talk to Detective Reinholm and get ahead of the law enforcement response.”

“I just notified him. He’s on his way over as we speak,” Hazel affirmed.

Justine nodded. “Well done, H. Bring him in through the back way to my office when he gets here. We don’t need him to see all this.” She gestured around the operations center.

“Understood.” Hazel nodded.

Justine took a last look at the selectees on the screen before turning to stride out of the room. She had calls to make.

CHAPTER 14

Roz—Saturday, 3 AM

I came to a place, stripped bare of every light and roaring on the naked dark,
like seas wracked by a war of winds.
Their hellish flight of storm and counterstorm through time foregone,
sweeps the souls of the damned before its charge.
Whirling and battering it drives them on,
and when they pass the ruined gap of Hell, through which we had come,
their shrieks begin anew.
Inferno, Canto V

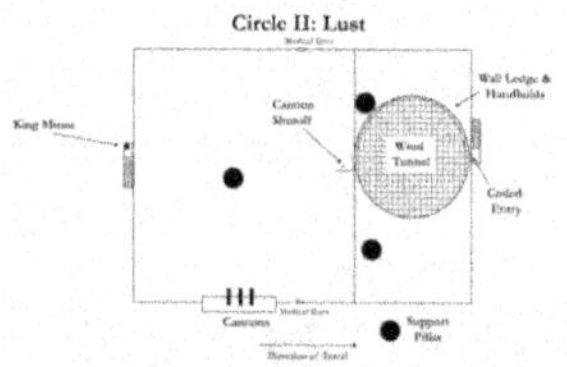

HARK STOOD NEAR THE EDGE OF THE TURF, looking up the stairs. The dog bounded over and Hark gave him some love, scratching his snout affectionately. "Everyone's up at the next landing."

Roz grunted. "How was your pod time?"

Hark bit a piece of beef jerky, chewing as they started walking up the steps. "Bunch of shrink questions. Asked about my dad dying, a few other things. You?"

"Same. Digging into personal stuff." A sound grew in their ears as they ascended, a slow-building rhythmic pulse he felt in his teeth. It soon became clear what it was.

Human voices.

Dozens.

Hundreds.

During the odd moments Roz could pick out an individual voice from the larger group, powerful emotion stood out. Arousal and excitement. Rage and anger. No discernible rhyme or rhythm, save an uneven up and down of the pitch. Like a churchgoer speaking in tongues, conveying the ecstasy of the divine that normal words could not. As he crested the last step onto the landing, Roz found most of the group crowded at the top of the stairs, watching someone inside the massive main room of the level. Tucked at the edge of the landing stood a statue, covered in robes, its face hidden by a dark hood. The statue had a motorized tail that whipped back and forth. Roz walked over, out of range of the tail. A small placard hung at the front, which read:

"Avoid the strike of the hailstones of Hades at all costs. If they touch your body, you must return to me and begin your journey anew. On the other side is a switch you may trip to provide a break in the stone fall. But beware the winds of Hades. They are most irregular." —King Minos

ROZ TURNED to face the group. The sonic susurration made talking almost impossible. In the middle of the vast open area of the circle, past the building support pillar, a short pylon stuck out of the ground, a strobing light on top. To the right of the pylon, as viewed from their position at the entrance, a barricade sheltered the pylon from the right side. Past the pylon, a long wall of plexiglass bisected the larger open area from right to left, but he couldn't see what was behind it at this distance. The ceiling arced three stories above them, banks of cameras spaced regularly across its width.

Abeni jogged back to the landing, massaging her shoulder. "Your turn, old man," she yelled over the din to Danault as she passed. She wore a helmet and goggles, and Roz saw that there was a small bin of the gear next to the door.

No one outranks safety.

He stared at the far-right side of the vast room, where a row of cannons perched midway up the wall. Lacrosse balls littered the floor. One of them rolled into the entry, and Roz picked it up. On closer inspection, it seemed the size of a golf ball, but the heft was such that it must pack quite a punch.

"I'll go," he said, shouldering his way to the front of the group. No one much minded him budging in this line.

"Want protection?" Abeni offered, holding out a helmet.

He shook his head. "I'm good. I have a hard head."

"If you get hit, you have to come back—"

He cut her off and sprinted into the open area. Immediately, a projectile whizzed past his head. The cannons appeared to be powered by compressed air, judging by the sound. Roz took the next one on the Aegis, wincing at the impact. He sidestepped at a comfortable jog, trying to anticipate the firing pattern. Three total cannons firing at odd intervals, a few seconds between each one. The pattern seemed to be left, right, center, in a repeating cycle. They changed tactics when he was about halfway across to the pylon, pausing to use the support pillar as shelter. The launchers fired at the ground and tried to skip the projectiles into him when he moved again. Then they began to fire one shot as a decoy and then another in quick succession to get past the Aegis. Thankfully, they didn't try the latter tactic until he was nearly all the way across. The pylon with the flashing light held the cutoff switch in a plexiglass alcove, sheltered from the barrage.

He looked back at the group. They were all in various stages of celebrating his success. Hark gestured, miming pressing the button. Beyond the alcove, ringed by a long wall of plexiglass bisecting the level, lay a shadowy, cavernous hole, perhaps thirty feet wide. It extended downward into blackness. High-velocity air screamed up, separated from the alcove by an open entryway door. There was no way to get to the far side of the circle and the exit. Roz leaned down and noticed a narrow ledge below the lip, with handholds moving around the arc of the pit. On the other side of the abyss stood a closed door, leading to the exit for the circle. Roz paused, staring up at the vents in the ceiling, where the high-pressure air funneled.

Could it be?

Only one way to find out. He got to his knees, strapped the Aegis to his pack. Snugged it tight. Roz glanced over at the group again. Tau ran out from the entrance and took a rubber ball to the shoulder. Hark slung his bow and prepared to use his pack as a shield. The Texan shook his head at him. Even at this distance, Roz could see the disappointment.

Whatever.

He'd made it across just fine—the rest of them could do it too. Wasn't this thing supposed to be an assessment? He held his hands out and leaned most of his body forward, into the surging air. Sure enough, it held him in place horizontally. It felt right. Helluva thing to risk your life on.

Fuck it.

Roz came back to his feet in time to see Hark make his way across, sheltered behind his pack. He wished he had earplugs. Between the slithering madness of the voices and the keening of the gusts, it was loud.

He took a step back, paused for a beat, and launched himself into the maelstrom.

CHAPTER 15

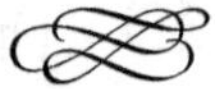

Roz—Saturday, 4 AM

THE WIND HELD HIM.

Cradled him in a choppy embrace. Roz buffeted back and forth until he relaxed into a stable "box man" position—hands out in front of his head, his legs kicked upward at the knee. Eyes squinted nearly closed to deal with the gale. Thirty feet below, enormous fans spun too fast to track, below a safety net of thick twines of steel wire. Miscalculating here would be dangerous, but likely not fatal. He banked his body in the stormy currents of air and "flew" across the circular opening by extending his legs. The circular-shaped portal on the other side—the exit of the wind tunnel—was closed and featured a piece of artwork on its face. A bearded, god-like figure appeared in the foreground, with several other human and angelic figures flanking him on either side. Roz tried to open it and found it wouldn't budge. There was a small alphanumeric keypad next to the portal.

Roz turned, saw Hark make it to the sheltered area. The Texan slammed his hand down on the switch, which triggered compressed air to erupt from the base of the pole and the launchers mounted on the walls. Roz grabbed a pair of handholds on the wall and hung there. He tried a few entries on the keypad—"Dante," "Hell," "Inferno"—but none of them did anything. He glided back across at the same time most of the group made it to the pit entrance. As he clambered back onto the floor, the alcove plexiglass sheltering them from the launchers began to retract. At its current rate, the little shelter would be exposed to the balls in a minute, two on the outside.

Hark prepared his pack and bow to make the transit. "Would it have killed you to hit the button?" Hark asked. Danault glared at him. Tau examined the handholds on the pit edge.

Roz shrugged. "I knew you'd figure it out."

"What's with the exit over there?" Audrey yelled, gesturing with her spear.

"Not sure." Roz described it a little, talking into her ear, then recounted the keyboard next to the portal.

Tau climbed down into the opening. Grady and Gabrielle tethered to each other with rope and followed onto the handholds.

"I can figure out how to get that door opened if you get me over there," Audrey said.

Roz considered. He certainly hadn't made any progress on his own. "Fine. This is what I need you to do." He described the body position for her to assume while they transited over. "Ready? The key is to relax," he said, staring into her green eyes, one normal, one unseeing. No fear there, just the resigned weariness he'd glimpsed earlier on the balcony.

Audrey clasped her hands on his forearms, her back to the abyss. "Ready." She'd secured the spear through a belt loop and her pack straps. Being so narrow, it shouldn't catch enough wind to make a big difference in their flight. But they'd find out soon enough.

Roz stepped off into the wind. She bucked and flung her arms around, while he tried to keep her stable with grips on her arm and thigh. They lurched up and down in the air. A choppy gust caught her scarf, unraveled it from her neck and face. She reached to keep it from getting sucked away, distorting her body position. She grabbed the scarf, but the motion destabilized their movement. The two slammed into the side of the pit and fell downward.

Toward the blades.

They hit the steel netting, fans screaming just below. Though it was impossible to talk, Roz gave her a wave of a hand, the thumb and pinkie extended in a surfer's *shaka* gesture. The universal symbol to relax. He gave her a three count with his hand, and then they were floating again. Roz guided her the rest of the way across the chamber, past the stares of the trio traversing the pit on the handholds.

Once to the portal, Roz swiveled her so she faced the painting. She nodded once she saw it and yelled something at him that was lost to the wind.

Roz watched her type in "Blake," then "Lust," and finally "Minos." At the last one, a green light flashed on the keypad and a deadbolt retracted into the circular door. He slid it open and levered her up onto firm flooring, following close behind.

"It's William Blake. His *Dante* art!" she yelled. "King Minos, judging the inhabitants of this circle of Hell! The guy in the hall with the whippy tail!"

"I don't care!" Roz yelled back, staring across the space. Tau and the Corsteads were almost to the portal. Hark looked like he was in a heated discussion with Richard, who pointed at the wind tunnel and shook his head violently. At last, Hark shrugged his shoulders and walked over to Abeni. Richard climbed down below the lip, started across on the handholds. Roz leaped into the wind and flew back. Had to get the mutt.

"Afraid of heights!" Hark yelled in his ear when he got there, gesturing at Danault.

"Maybe he'll fall," Roz yelled back.

Hark shook his head. He guided Abeni out the door and floated across with her. Hark pushed her in right after the Corsteads and Tau went through.

The dog stared up at Roz and barked.

"Yeah, yeah. I know you don't like to jump."

The dog stared back with a panting, mildly interested expression.

Roz picked up the dog and got a firm grip. "No squirming."

Thankfully, the hound kept it together for the several seconds it took to glide across without incident. Shortly after, Richard made his way to the portal and Hark helped him climb out.

They followed the others into the stairway. As the noise receded, Hark pulled on his elbow. They stopped and let the rest of the group continue. "What's going on with you?"

"What do you mean?"

"First, you didn't want to help Winkel, and now you had a chance to help the group, and you went off by yourself."

Roz shook his head. "I carried Zhou across, didn't I?"

"Yeah, because she could do something for you."

"Hark, I'm in this for one reason, and one reason only.

Get a lawyer, keep my daughter. She's the only family I have left. She's all I have left."

"That so?" Hark said, pulling his bow out. "No friends?"

Roz frowned. "You know what I mean."

"You don't have to do this alone. That's all I'm saying."

Roz looked down the stairs and lowered his voice. "I don't know these people. They mean nothing to me. They're between me and my kid. You're my brother from another mother, but the rest of them can go to hell as far as I'm concerned." He walked off, leaving Hark standing there.

"We're already *in* Hell!" Hark called to his back.

Roz ignored him.

CHAPTER 16

Roz—Saturday, 5 AM

His eyes are red,
his beard is greased with phlegm,
his belly is swollen,
and his hands are claws to rip the wretches and flay and mangle them.
And they, too, howl old like dogs in the freezing storm,
turning and turning from it,
as if they thought one naked side could keep the other warm.
When Cerberus discovered us in that swill, his dragon-jaws yawed wide,
his lips drew back, in a grin of fangs.
No limb of him was still.
Inferno, Canto VI

Circle III: Gluttony

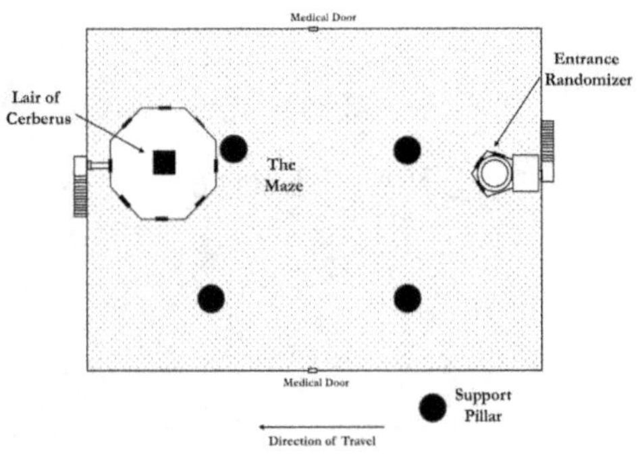

ROZ STOMPED UP THE STAIRS, the dog's claws clicking on the rough concrete behind. He hated when the Texan got preachy. Normally he left Roz alone, let him blunder his own way. The dog was the only thing Hark had been adamant about him taking, back when Roz was in a bad way. At the top of the stairs, he found a hotel lobby-style revolving door painted in dull gold. He caught sight of Tau disappearing through the door, leaving only Gabrielle remaining to enter.

She whirled a baseball bat idly, looking at him. "Bold move, not hitting that switch," she said. "But I get it. I understand."

Roz squinted at her. "You never mentioned what card you drew for yourself. Back in the conference room."

She laughed. "The Priestess. Naturally. All in divine order."

"THE DOG GOES IN SEPARATE, MR. MEHRAN," said a voice from a wall-mounted speaker.

"Why?" he replied. There was no response.

"See you later, Feroz," Gabrielle said, closing herself through the door.

"You catch all that?" Roz asked Hark, who came to a halt at his side.

Hark nodded. "You remember what was in the Gluttony Circle?"

"Cerberus."

"Yep. Should be a real hoot."

Roz made a face. "I don't think that's how you use that word."

He gestured for the dog to go in, and it turned to stare up with curious eyes. Roz bent over. "Look, I don't know what's behind there. Maybe I'll see you again, maybe I won't."

The dog snorted and padded into the opening. Roz swiveled the door shut, and it continued turning in a circle of its own accord.

After a minute, it ground back around to face them in the open position.

"Age before beauty," Roz said, and gestured for Hark to go next.

He gave the faintest dusting of a smile and walked past him. "Catch you on the flip side, amigo."

"I'm getting real tired of hearing that," Roz replied. But he couldn't help but smile back. It was hard to stay mad at that mustached son of a gun. When it was his turn to go, he stepped in with the faintest tendril of unease coiling in his guts. Roz breathed out as the door rotated counterclockwise, passing one, then a second opening, before grinding to a halt at the third. It moved too quickly for him to step out on the earlier openings, and he wasn't about to test it by putting a limb in the way.

It's a maze. He stepped out and immediately noticed the temperature had dropped twenty degrees. Roz recalled going to the U.S. Marine Corps museum in Quantico, Virginia. They had an indoor exhibit for the Chosin Reservoir cooled to a frigid temperature to simulate the conditions of the

Korean War battle. *The Frozen Chosin*. But there was no rain inside the Marine Corps museum.

Here, cold water sluiced down from massive shower heads several stories above, draining into grates on the floor. A chill breeze gusted across the passage. Not the turbulence of the previous level, but enough to make the wetness completely miserable. It trickled down his back, and he shivered, his body's natural response to keep its core temperature up. The sensation took him back to his early days of SEAL training. The class had been preparing for hell week, conducting small boat drills and physical training with the logs. Several of the cadre members pulled the students aside for some personalized, one-on-one "mentorship." They laid on the pavement outside their classroom on a cloudy January day, resigned to the wretched hour to come. For some reason that none but King Neptune himself could fathom, the normally sunny city of San Diego grew gloomy and rainy during SEAL hell weeks. It was as if the gods themselves wanted to add an extra measure of challenge to the trainees. Roz remembered lying there, soaked from countless trips to the ocean, covered in sand, aching back pressed onto the asphalt, body jack-hammering uncontrollably. His class lay prostrate before the Lords of Pain and Misery, embodied in human form as Basic Underwater Demolition/SEAL instructors. They worshipped at the altar of woe on pyres of sand and saltwater.

"God, how I love the water," began Instructor Murkowski, standing above them. "It is cold, but it is good." He was a compact but powerfully built man and spoke so softly you had to lift your head off the soaked pavement to hear. "It makes me strong; it makes me pure. God, how I love the water."

The class lay there, shaking and shivering, as hoses held

by other instructors gave them a good measure of freezing spray.

"Say it with me."

The students repeated it, first in halting and low tones. "God, how I love the water. It is cold, but it is good. It makes me strong; it makes me whole. God, how I love the water."

"Again."

They repeated it, over and over, until finally, they were screaming, belting out the lines with every fiber of their being, every puff of breath they had.

"GOD, HOW I LOVE THE WATER. IT IS COLD, BUT IT IS GOOD. IT MAKES ME STRONG; IT MAKES ME PURE. GOD, HOW I LOVE THE WATER."

"God, how I love the water," Roz murmured to himself as the water dripped down his nose. Sometimes, you just have to be cold, and that's the way it was. Your body had ways of dealing with it. One of them was shivering. And if you were shivering, things were okay. It was when you stopped shivering that you had problems. It meant the body was giving up on efforts to maintain a stable core temperature. He pulled a black beanie from his pack and put it on. It was another piece of kit Hark had recovered. In his first platoon, all the new guys had sewn handcuff keys and razor blades into their beanies after attending SERE school.

The walls appeared to be composed of modular material, like a classroom divider. He'd seen this setup in plenty of kill houses—training venues where military and law enforcement could train with live ammunition. Roz adjusted his grip on the shield and slowly advanced down the corridor, listening. Yells reached his ears from other parts of the maze. They didn't seem far, but difficult to tell with the sound bouncing around. The walls topped out at fifteen feet, while the actual ceiling of the level loomed at least twenty feet above them.

He tried the same tactic they'd used in the woods—find

his way around the outside edge. Roz watched his breath plume in front of him as he came around a corner. The place couldn't be *that* big. It was inside a building. He could see one of the massive support struts, but he couldn't tell which one it was of the four. Roz activated the camera on the dog's harness. The watch showed a grainy shot of the hound moving somewhere in the maze. He couldn't hear anything except the dog's breath over the feed. Roz checked his compass. Heading north. At present, he needed to go northwest to move toward the exit to the level. When the passage he walked came to an end, he had an idea. The walls were tight enough to "chimney," a rock-climbing technique that involved putting your hands on one wall and feet on the other. Using it, he ascended until he could grab a handhold at the top. The width of the wall top was only about six inches, but he found he could perch there, legs balanced on either side.

The spot gave him a bird's-eye view of the maze. There was a large open space near the exit, with several paths converging there. Roz walked carefully—heel, toe, heel, toe, toward the exit. He jumped between the walls in two spaces, and each time he landed with a sharp grunt of exhalation, head and chest leaning over the next section. When he made it to the edge of the clearing, he discovered a shed-sized structure at the center. Light wisps of fog drifted across the area, which made the already dim lighting even more shadowy. Seven total paths led into the clearing.

Something smacked hard into his side, hard.

He lost his balance, fell.

Experience born of years of parachute landings gone sideways led Roz to instinctively put his legs together, bend his knees, and relax. His feet hit, then his ass, and then the pack kept his head from bouncing against the rough floor. As it was, he lay stunned on the ground, struggling to draw a breath.

Roz stared out at the center of the room, at the entrance to the shed, cloaked in shadow.

He saw the eyes first.

Quick scrabble of claws on stone as three dogs exploded from the hut. Rottweilers. Big animals, easily over a hundred fifty pounds each. A harness tethered them together. They made no sound as they bounded toward him. Too late, too slow, he brought the shield up.

A dark shape blotted out the light above, and there stood Tau, fending one dog off with his club and beefy mass. From his right came a whirling axe that impacted another hound. A flash of dirty blond fur from his left.

The Meat Missile.

The dog and one of the Rottweilers battled, jaws snapping at one another's exposed flanks. Tau roared as he swung the club at the first dog. Roz staggered to his feet and found Gabrielle close by, bat at the ready.

"It's good to have friends," she said with a twinkle in her eye, and she swung at one dog. Roz heard a yelp, and over the rim of the shield he saw one of Grady's axes embedded in the rightmost dog's side. The mad animal snapped at the axe handle, trying to rip it out with its teeth. It fell out as the hound dodged and tried to get around to bite Roz.

He was just starting to feel things were turning their way when a soft beeping chimed, and the leashes holding the Rottweilers together separated. The animals broke apart and circled the humans. Only the one with the axe wound lagged a step behind the others. They renewed their attack. One battered into Roz, who met the charge with his shield, and slid back. The dog lunged at his legs, probed for an opening in his defenses, panting fetid breath. From the side, a spear lanced into the animal, and Roz turned to see Audrey, mouth set grimly as she worked the weapon with both hands. Together, the two of them drove the hound back.

An arrow flicked across the clearing, then another. Hark and Abeni came out of the same entrance. One dog went to the ground, blood pooling and filling the air with a coppery scent. The other two ran off down a corridor. Richard came out behind Abeni, crossbow at the ready.

Roz looked at Tau, who stood in the center. "Thanks. You saved my ass back there."

The big Māori gazed at him for a moment before nodding.

"Nice spear work," he said to Audrey. "You look like you know how to handle that thing."

The scarred woman smiled faintly. "My mom made me train when I was a child. Clichéd Tiger Mother. I never expected it would pay off until now. Please don't tell her I said that. She'll become more insufferable than normal."

Roz smiled. "Your secret is safe… For now."

"People, can everyone identify which entrance they came from? Let's try to figure out the way out of here," Hark said. He kept an arrow nocked on the bow.

The group all pointed to their respective doors and found only two were not accounted for. The dog was sitting in front of one, tongue dancing in the air.

"Well, there's our answer. Lassie wants us to go that way," the Texan replied.

"Who is Lassie?" said Grady, brow furrowed. "Is that someone's nickname?"

Hark winced. "Never mind. It's not important. Diogenes wants us to go that way. Anybody hurt?"

Roz's ribs ached from the fall. He wondered what had knocked him off the wall. Nothing on the ground in the clearing.

"Let's get out of here before those—" Grady began.

"Cerberus," Gabrielle interrupted.

"Yeah, that. Let's get going before they come back."

CHAPTER 17

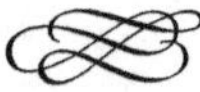

Justine—Saturday, 7 AM

SHE CRAVED A CIGARETTE.

Craved the *idea* of a cigarette—the tang of secondhand smoke in the air, the sharpness of the inhale, the fiery flare of the tip in a shadowed room, the satisfying *tap* when you flicked the ash. She'd quit years ago—decades—but it didn't stop her from thinking about it. Justine stared around the circle of the workstations in the ops center. Her staff was only now settling down after the attack, as they adjusted and made sense of the event. Reinholm and her security chief confirmed the culprits vanished, and the probability of finding them was low. What concerned Justine was what she was missing. What aspect of the problem wasn't she seeing?

Inattentional blindness.

The kind that allows a gorilla-suit-wearing undergrad to walk through a crowded group of peers passing a basketball and remain unnoticed by observers. The magician's sleight of hand that obfuscated the obvious with a fog of the mundane and a flamboyant misdirection.

What was she missing?

"How does this level work, exactly?" Justine looked up to see Hazel, her operations chief, talking to Dmitri. The woman pointed to an overhead video feed of the Greed Level as the selectees prepared to enter.

"Oh, it's quite diabolical," he answered, then winced. "Apologies, that was in poor taste."

"Nice to see you're upping your game," Hazel responded.

Dmitri wheeled his chair to face his screen. Justine never understood the appeal of those huge trucker hats. They looked *ridiculous*. "Here, let me show you." He opened up a screen on his MacBook, revealing an overhead diagram of the circle.

"They start in the VR pods—round two is a follow-up on any outstanding threads of inquiry from the first session, and then they segue into prisoner dilemma scenarios. At the conclusion of that, since there's an even number of selectees, the ones with the two highest scores will advance without having to do the wheel." Justine's eyes flicked to the only casualties so far, denoted on a wall screen showing face shots of all nine selectees. Tabitha's face greyed out. Justine listened to Dmitri continue. "So, the big 'weiners' get to come out of their pod, go through the door here. Plus the dog. We won't make the dog do what comes next. The others will be randomly assigned to either of these two chambers."

Hazel twirled a lock of red hair as she leaned over Dmitri's workstation. "And what comes next…this thing is like a big tug-of-war?"

Dmitri adjusted his hat, leaned back in the wheelchair. "More like a reverse tug-of-war. Pushing instead of pulling. If we look at the mechanism like a clock face, each of the chambers is at three and nine o'clock, respectively. In *The Inferno,* the hoarders and the spenders constantly fight with each other here, so you can think of each of these chambers as one of those groups. The exit to the circle is at twelve o'clock, while the pit opening is at six. The chambers connect to one another through a track system, so as one moves clockwise, the other—"

"Moves counterclockwise," Hazel finished. "Wow, you weren't kidding about the diabolical part." On the screen, they watched the selectees leaving Gluttony on the way to Greed.

"Would you trade places with one of them if you could?"

Dmitri looked up. "I'll stick with my day job. Besides, that pit on Lust might have given me some trouble."

Hazel grabbed one of his biceps and gave it a playful squeeze. "You would have done just fine."

"Ma'am, you're going to want to see this." Kathy stood at Justine's side, an iPad in manicured hands. It pulled her from spectating some sort of budding workplace romance, which was undoubtedly in violation of one policy or another. "We've been monitoring social media traffic, and anything related to the selectees. Gabrielle hasn't posted to any of her platforms in over nine hours. Her followers are getting worried."

"Followers?"

"Several million on Instagram, decent numbers on the other platforms. Sub-Kardashian, but still significant."

"Let them worry. Maybe she's down with a flu or something."

"No, Ma'am. You don't understand." Justine caught the faintest whiff of Gen Z condescension, although Kathy did an admirable job keeping it under wraps.

"Okay," Justine replied, favoring her young aide with an indulgent smile. "Please, enlighten me."

"We have her phone here, in the Plek building. Her close friends have access to her location data in several apps. They can see that she's here. If they don't hear from her soon, some of her friends are going to come and try to figure out where she is, what she's doing. They could draw a great deal of attention with a video or two that hits the algorithm at the right time."

"Oh, dear." Justine closed and rubbed her eyes, pondering. "What do you suggest, as a mitigation strategy?"

"With your permission, I'd like to send a team with her phone to a local Airbnb. Send in someone that roughly matches her description. While we do that, we can spoof her account and send out a post on…damn, so close to Mercury going into retrograde—that would have been perfect. We'll say she's taking some personal time to reflect on something. Self-care, toxic friends. Oh, and she wants to see the Tenderloin District, see the real San Francisco. We'll handle it, Ma'am."

Justine looked around the room, marveling at the talent the foundation attracted. A commentary on Nicky's vision, his ability to bring in a big tent of all varieties of humans. "I do not know what the planet Mercury has to do with all that, but approved. Make it happen. I'm sure we'll have to explain the violation of her privacy later, but it sounds like the best way to keep attention off the process until it concludes."

Kathy nodded and moved off. On the screens, Justine watched the selectees slow to a stop and pause at the landing before Greed. Good pace so far. The model predicted the loss of at least one selectee by now, but not which precise one. It surprised her that the group had navigated the first part of the tower so quickly. She couldn't decide whether that was a good or bad omen. Too early to say. *We'll see,* like the old Zen master said when confronted with a succession of fortune and calamities. *This would make one hell of a reality show,* she thought as she surveyed the monitors set to other levels of the tower. *What was that Stephen King story that they butchered as a movie with Arnold? Ah. Running Man.* Frankly, she was surprised that someone hadn't done something like this already for a reality TV show.

Only a matter of time.

"Ms. Lipton?" A woman's voice came from behind her.

"Ah. Teela. Thanks for stopping by. I trust the space in the chamber above Treachery is adequate for your purposes?" Justine beamed at her chief scientist. It was a coup that the foundation had gotten Dr. Phillips poached away from Johns Hopkins after a groundbreaking neurobiology study on psychedelics and transcranial stimulation.

The woman gave her an uncomfortable smile. "That's what I wanted to speak to you about. Are you sure you don't want to wait until we're back on the island, to begin the nootropic and neuro-pollination modalities? It would be much safer than doing it here."

Justine held up a hand. "I get it. I do. It makes sense to me." She exhaled as she nodded. "However, Dr. Berenger was clear about this part. Very specific. He wants the Berenger Blend administered to those who make it past the Treachery circle. I know it makes your job more difficult, not to mention the security risks—"

"—And those are significant, given the advanced nature—"

"Yes, which is why we have everything in the tower above the Treachery level completely separated from the rest of the building. All the access codes, cameras, servers—it's routed straight to our offsite location in an independently encrypted system." Justine smiled at the woman. "Your research is safe."

Teela shook her head, tightly coiled braids shaking. "I still don't like it, Ms. Lipton. It's an unnecessary risk. I wanted to give you my honest opinion."

"Thank you for your candor—it is a risk," Justine allowed. "But it is one we're going to take."

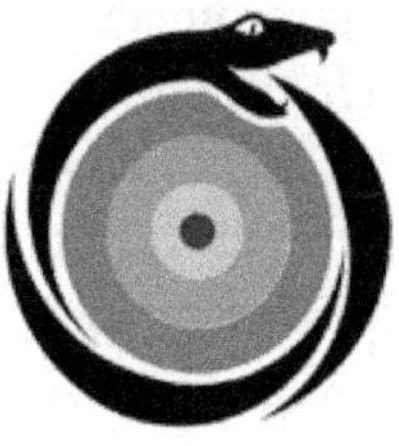

Roz—Saturday, 8 AM

AT THE LANDING HALFWAY BETWEEN THE LEVELS, the group halted and took a break. They didn't talk about it—but it was a collective decision. Roz sat on his haunches, pulled a collapsible bowl from his pack. He poured water in, watched the dog slurp. "Good boy." He stroked the dirty blond fur. Roz exhaled with a shudder and tried to clear the excess adrenaline from his body.

"Seems like a good match for you." He looked up to find Audrey staring at him. She was always watching, observing with a quiet intensity that most overlooked.

Roz glanced over as he finished refilling the water bowl. He wasn't about to share details with someone he'd just met. "He's a match for something, that's for sure." His eyes flicked to Hark, and he knew the Texan would not let him get away with stonewalling.

"Don't let him fool you," Hark interjected. "He won't talk about it, because he's a horse's ass, but I will. When I got out, I started a non-profit with a few old teammates of mine. It's focused on helping vets transition out of the service, particularly if they're having any challenges. Reintegration. Mental health. I figured old Roz here needed a little canine companionship."

Hark was leaving out the unpleasant details. Roz remembered all of them, even if he didn't want to. He had been in a bad way. Getting high all the time. Didn't really see the point of living. People tried to talk to him, but he couldn't hear them. Roz hated the dog when Hark dropped him off. He tried to ditch him several times, but the hound proved resourceful. Having the animal around at least gave him something else to think about, rather than the broken ruins of his life.

"Where did he get the name Diogenes?" asked Abeni, pulling a black North Face fleece from her pack.

"I never knew the trainer who gave it to him, but it comes from an old Greek philosopher. Maybe philosopher isn't the right name. More of a performance artist of sorts, trying to shock citizens of the city of Corinth out of their slumber. Diogenes of Sinope, who himself was sometimes called a dog because he lived on the street. He did things like masturbate in public, drink water without a cup," Hark explained.

"Hopefully not in that order," Roz clarified.

Abeni frowned. "Sounds lovely."

Hark continued with a mischievous grin. "So, the story he's most famous for, the one that people love, is when Alexander the Great visited Corinth. The great conqueror stood in the city square, surrounded by his retinue of guards, and stared down at this wild-eyed, bearded, half-naked man. Alexander asked Diogenes what he could do for him. 'You're blocking my sun,' Diogenes answered. To which Alexander replied, 'If I were not Alexander, I would be Diogenes.'"

"Stand out of my light," Audrey said. "Supposed to be the exact quote."

Hark nodded. "That sounds better anyway. More dramatic."

Abeni smiled and patted the hound on the head. "Well, I'm glad you're here with us, Diogenes."

The dog returned the grin as he panted and reveled in her attention.

Roz walked up to where Tau was sitting. He stuck out a hand. "Thanks for saving my ass back there."

Tau grunted. Took the offered hand in a meaty, callused grip. "Right thing to do."

"Did anyone get the answer to the nine-dot thing?" Grady asked the group.

Roz said nothing, and the rest of the group shook their heads and replied in the negative. Except Tau. "Arrow shape. Start outside the dots." He traced the outline of the arrow in the air.

"Damn. Functional fixedness," Audrey replied. "When you can't see past some preconceived assumptions you have about a situation. Should have seen it. Like the candle, box of thumbtacks, and matches experiment. You're supposed to figure out a way to attach the candle to the wall, so it doesn't drip wax on the table."

"What's the solution?" Asked Grady.

"I know this one," Hark replied. "Take the thumbtacks out of the box, use it as a base and attach it to the wall with the tacks. Instant candle holder."

Audrey nodded. "Hard for people to see old things with fresh eyes."

CHAPTER 18

Roz—Saturday, 10 AM

"Master," I said, "tell me—now that you touch on this Dame Fortune

—what is she, that she holds the good things of the world within her clutch?"

And he to me:

"O credulous mankind, is there one error that has wooed and lost you?

Now, listen, and strike error from your mind:

That king whose perfect wisdom transcends all,

made the heavens and posted angels on them to guide the eternal light

that it might fall from every sphere to every sphere the same.

He made earth's splendors by a like decree and posted as their minister this high Dame,

the Lady of Permutations.

All earth's gear she changes from nation to nation,

from house to house, in changeless change through every turning year.

No mortal power may stay here spinning wheel.
The nations rise and fall by her decree.
None may forsee where she will set her heel:
she passes, and things pass.
Man's mortal reason cannot encompass her.
She rules her sphere as the other gods rule theirs.
Season by season her changes change her changes endlessly,
and those whose turn has come press on her so,
she must be swift by hard necessity.
Inferno, Canto VII

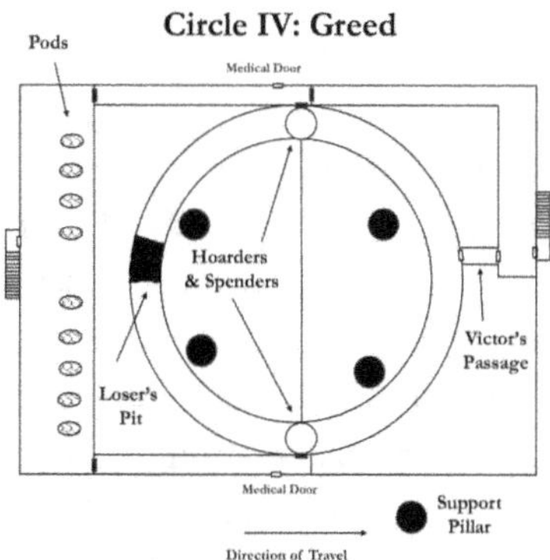

THE VIRTUAL REALITY PODS—NINE OF THEM, lined the wall immediately outside the stairwell. A long barrier kept most of the level from their sight. Two locked doors on the wall—one on either end. They looked too sturdy to force their way through. The rest of the group was getting settled in the pods. When he found he could delay no longer, Roz walked up to the one marked with his name and slid in. "*Blijf*," he told the dog as he shut the pod hatch.

With the earphones, the VR mask, and the silence of the

pod interior, it was like entering another world. Which, he supposed, it was. After a brief pause, the questions about his past began again, picking up where they left off from the last time. An image flashed on the headset screen: *Vanders.*

"All right, Mr. Mehran. Let's pick up from where we ended before. With Iraq." Same voice from before. He tried to imagine what the guy looked like. Short, running to fat, sipping an enormous 7-Eleven soda. Wiping Cheetos on his shirt. Something like that.

"Why don't we talk about you instead? How's your day going?"

The man laughed. "It's been...eventful so far. But we're not here for me, are we?"

"We could, though, couldn't we?"

"Someday, maybe. Could you please expand on the events leading to the death of Major Jeffrey Vanders?"

"All this is open source now—it was all over the news. I'm sure the resources of the foundation would have no trouble finding out the specifics."

"We're not interested in the media narrative, Mr. Mehran. Nor the internal military explanation of the event. We want to know what happened, *in your own words.*"

Roz thought about just bailing. Getting out of there. Pop the top off the pod, walk over to the medical stairs. Walk out. Keep walking. The dog could stay with Hark. He'd probably rather stay with the Texan, anyway. But if he walked, he might as well kiss seeing his daughter again goodbye. He breathed out, as if he could banish the frustration from his body with the exhale. "First of all, Vanders was a huge asshole. That should be established, right off the bat. He had a reputation for ducking danger and hard decisions, and nothing I saw in five months changed that reputation. Vanders was the XO—Milena's second-in-command, for

Milena—on Task Force Valkyrie. You probably never read *Once An Eagle*, have you?"

"Nope—but I have this beautiful Google machine here—and here it is." A pause. "This looks super boring."

"Okay, so Vanders was Massengale to the core—typical staff officer, political, from an old-money family."

"Does that mean that you're Sam Damon in this metaphor? Integrity, honor, and a…'deep sense of duty?'"

Roz shrugged, even though he knew the man couldn't see him. *Or could he?* He didn't know if there was a camera on him in the pod. "No, I served with some Damons, but that wasn't me. Anyway, my point is Vanders was a self-centered prick. That doesn't mean that he deserved to die, but it should be noted for the cosmic records. My SEAL platoon deployed to Iraq, and I was pulled to work for the task force once we got in country. Because I knew Farsi. Grew up in Iran. Janek put the word out she wanted men and women who could pass as locals. I did ops for them for a couple months—brought Hark in for a few for backup. Over time, I started to get suspicious about Janek. At first, it wasn't anything I could put a finger on. Glances here and there, a sentence she said in passing or during a briefing. But I had a feeling."

"About what?"

"The Berenger rescue was what really focused things. She acted weird during that whole op. I think she wanted to order us not to go, but everyone in our operations center could hear what she was saying on the phone. I think she didn't want to be seen ordering us *not* to rescue an American. Bad for business. Bad for her promotion prospects. Something changed after that op. She was colder, distant. I started checking into some things. For one, I had collected a cell phone from one of the guys who captured Berenger. It had a call log and texts with a few phone numbers from the day they stormed Berenger's NGO compound. One day I happened to be standing outside our operations center and called it. It started ringing right behind me, in the phone locker."

Prior to entering an area where classified information was discussed and worked on, you checked your electronics at the door, to avoid potential exploitation as listening devices for any adversaries.

"So, I hear this phone going off, and I take a closer look. It was one of Vanders' phones—he had three of them total, which by itself wasn't that unusual, but having his number in a shithead's phone definitely was."

"What did you do?"

"What I should have done was take a pause, go find Hark and talk it out. But he was back home on emergency leave, saying goodbye to his father. Instead, I confronted Vanders about it directly."

"And then?"

"That…didn't go so well. He became evasive, and I had to rely on some…non-standard methods of questioning."

"Non-standard?"

Roz gestured with his hands. "It got a little physical. Nothing that would leave a mark. After a while, he let on that Milena had engineered the kidnapping, at the behest of some of her defense contractor friends. They wanted to sweat Berenger for some project he was working on, and they had no other way to get the information."

"Did he say what project?"

Roz swallowed heavily. "No. I didn't understand what was happening. I misjudged it. What screwed me was that a few people might have overheard our rather *spirited* discussion in Vanders' living quarters. I went to find Milena, but she was out of the camp. Over in the Green Zone talking to some folks at the U.S. Embassy. She conveniently stayed there, not answering my phone calls, until well after they arrested me later that night."

"Was that after Vanders turned up dead?"

Roz nodded. "Eight hours. She put the entire thing together in eight hours. Murdered him and framed me for it. Milena swept her two biggest liabilities right off the board, in one move. An illicit lover and the only person connecting her to the kidnapping attempt. And then she plays the victim and becomes a media darling in the process. Elegant, really."

"Elegant?" Notes of disbelief in his ear.

"If I hadn't rotted in a cell for a few years, I might appreciate it more. Like Clausewitz said, I didn't understand the nature of the war I was in."

"Couldn't you prove what happened?"

"By the time I figured out what was happening, four military police were tackling me in my CHU—my room. Vanders' phone was long gone. Someone made it disappear. All that was left was a bunch of people who said they heard me beating on him that morning, and those who could testify we had a long-standing adversarial relationship. Which we did, of course. Because he was an assclown, of epic proportions. Like Gilgamesh-level clownery. And then the colonel, the poor, poor colonel who, it must be said, that woman could *talk*. She persuaded the jury her loyal aide was murdered while valiantly protecting her from an out-of-control operator. The tragic strain of combat, I guess. She could give a master class in acting." Roz's shoulders slumped. He'd betrayed Colleen, repaid her love and loyalty with infidelity. Betrayed their vows. He was going to lose Bella, too, if she wasn't already lost. "But you know all this, don't you?"

"Yes," the man answered after a beat. "What would you have done differently, knowing what you know now?"

Roz laughed. "Kept my powder dry, for when it counted. Not confronted Vanders until I figured out what was going on." After the questions, the darkness in the VR goggles resolved into a virtual interrogation room, a grimy cliché of every police procedural he'd ever seen. Camera in the corner of the ceiling, one-way mirror. He could hear a low ambient noise, some kind of background sound they piped in his earphones to make it immersive. He was able to stand by moving his fingers in the haptic gloves, regarded himself in the mirror. A reasonable image of himself, in virtual form. His avatar wore an orange prison jumpsuit. A pneumatic hiss within the pod, and a sour smell washed over. Stale sweat, old cigarettes, and something he couldn't identify. Piping in scents, as well. A new level of devious. He knew this room, recognized it instantly. Not this room exactly, but the idea of it. Most of the time, he'd been on one side of the room—asking questions rather than answering them. But he'd been arrested by local law enforcement in more than a few unsavory locales over the years. As he watched, an image flashed onto his viewing screen. Another prisoner like himself, judging by the jumpsuit. It looked like Tau.

"Prisoner's dilemma. Defect or stay silent, those are your choices. If you both defect, you each lose twenty points. Both stay silent, you each win five points. If you stay silent and he defects, he wins ten points. If you defect and he stays silent, you win ten points. Choose." A pair of red buttons floated in the air above him, with both choices labeled.

Roz selected "defect."

Hovering cursive words swam across his field of view. "Winner, ten points."

Over the next minutes, an image of each of the remaining selectees flashed before his eyes, followed by the choice. He defected in every choice but when paired with Hark. After the first round, only Gabrielle had defected in his pairing, giving him a net-positive score. This showed up in a floating chart that revealed everyone's point totals. In the second round, everyone defected but Hark, and now his score was in the negative. In all, they played seven more rounds.

Roz's score kept tumbling.

After the final round, it was near the bottom. Hark was somehow the winner, followed by Tau, and then Audrey. The screen faded to black, and he waited for the pod door to unlock.

One of the maxims driven into his head in SEAL training was that "it pays to be a winner."

Roz didn't know what last place would get you, but he was certain it wasn't good.

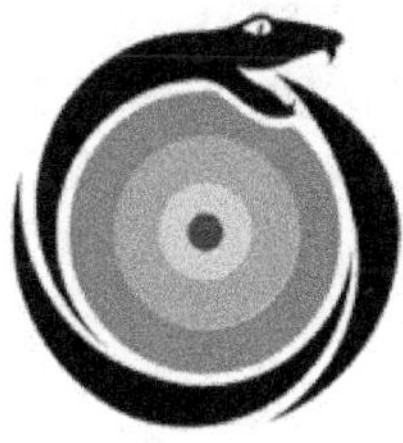

THEY WERE WAITING for this moment, wondering if it would ever come. When it did, they had a rush of adrenaline unlike any they'd ever felt. A deep, lancing spike into their side, a hammering of heart they hoped no one in the ops center noticed. There was a Pinterest board they checked every hour. On the board, a new graphic on how to deep clean your bathroom.

At last, the signal.

It was like the old Sinatra song their great-grandfather used to play, "In the wee small hours of the morning." *That's* when you make moves.

Stealing the access card was easy—Dmitri was a total slob, and it lay lodged under a succession of wrappers on the side of his workstation. Child's play to distract him with a question and slide it out. Getting to the server room was a little more challenging, but not impossible. They'd scoped out a route weeks ago, out of sight of cameras and inquisitive coworkers. They hid the device inside an oversized picture frame on their desk, a photo capturing the Plek succession team on a camping offsite a few months ago. The trip had been fun, but not fun enough to turn down the offer, when it came. The money was just too good. They had things they wanted to do in this life, and slaving away at a job wasn't in the plan. They inserted the device, the male end penetrating the female port on the server rack. Spreading a seed of control and dominance. Their work done, they slipped back to the ops center.

CHAPTER 19

Roz—Saturday, 12 PM

"I DON'T SEE AN ALTERNATIVE," Audrey said. She stood at the opening to the circular structure, next to Abeni and Roz. When the pod door finally unlocked, he found Hark and the dog gone, as well as the Corsteads, Richard, and Tau. Only the three of them remained. The other opening to the circle stood closed. "Look at this." She gestured with her foot to the area where the wall met the floor on the inside. The floor itself was rough concrete, and the wall was a type of hard plastic, painted a dull sheen of brown. There was a skirt on the bottom of the wall, between it and the floor.

"Well, nowhere to go but forward," Roz responded, gesturing at the door in the corner of the level past the pods. He stepped inside. After a moment, the women followed. As they entered, the door slid shut.

Once within the interior of the chamber, they found they

could see the inside of the circle. Roz looked across and saw an identical chamber the other doorway fed into, with the Corsteads and Richard inside. No sign of Hark, Tau, or the dog.

"Is that—" Roz began but stopped when a light flashed in front of them on the track.

A voice boomed from unseen speakers. "We have divided you into hoarders and wasters. This chamber is your rock. Push it to the flashing white light in front of you and you will find freedom. Behind you—" they saw crimson tones pulse "—is a flashing red light. You don't want to end up there with your rock. If you fall from the circle, your time in selection will end. Push hard." They heard an ominous *chunk,* and the walls moved a touch. Their chamber moved backward, away from the flashing white. As they slid, the other chamber moved forward around the arc. As Roz stared out the clear plastic window, the contours of the situation became clear. Their chamber and the other one were on opposite ends of a circular track that moved independently from the floor. When one chamber advanced toward the exit, the other retreated. All it took was one glance in the opposite direction from the exit to see what awaited there. The shadowy maw of a pit. No telling how deep it was, or what lay below.

Roz pushed forward, trying to arrest their backward progress. He cursed under his breath as his heels found no purchase on the stone floor. "Little help here."

"Stop! We can figure this out!" Audrey shouted over at the other group. It was no use. Gabrielle watched them, face set in a mask of studied indifference. Grady and Richard pushed, without looking over at them.

Roz put his back against the wall and leaned. With the addition of Abeni's power, they slowed their movement backward. With Audrey, they made up some of the ground lost before the other group fought the track to a halt. A back-

and-forth battle ensued over the next few minutes. Relentlessly, the superior mass of the other group began to win the day. Roz, Audrey, and Abeni inched inexorably, inevitably backward.

They screamed obscenities.

They begged.

They bargained.

Nothing worked.

"Okay, we're going to have to give it another minute, and then look for handholds," Roz gasped, as they were pushed toward the pit. They were exhausted, lathered in sweat. It seeped and ground into their cuts and scrapes, under the mud of the Gluttony circle.

"There's nothing. There's nothing to hold on to," Abeni husked out.

"Can you wedge your spear?" Roz gritted. The other chamber grew close to the exit. Which meant that their chamber was nearing the drop into the pit.

"Maybe." Audrey searched for nooks. "I don't think it will take much weight, though."

"Will it take your weight?"

"We'll see, won't we?"

Roz laughed darkly as the dropoff crept under the back wall like a dreadful sunrise he never wished to see. "*Okay*, wedge it."

She stopped pushing, pulled the spear out from her pack straps. Losing her weight caused the pace of their backward movement to increase.

"Abeni...can you see anything to grab?"

"Maybe the lip here, where the clear plastic meets the other material."

"Okay, go for it," Roz ordered. There was no time. No time. As Abeni turned, the other group seemed to give one last vicious lunge for the finish line. The chamber began to traverse over the pit, cutting off their standing room. Roz could see the steep side wall on the other side of the pit come into view. Too far to jump. The next bit happened fast. Without two of the group members pushing, the chamber sped up. Roz popped up, extending his hands and feet to connect with the walls on either side.

Chimneying again. Useful life skill.

He gritted his teeth and held the pose, every muscle taut and quivering as he looked down into the pit. It went down about fifteen feet, and then the bottom was full of padded material. The fall wouldn't be bad, but elimination from selection was. The speed of the rotation helped cut down their time in the danger zone. As the chamber crossed the pit opening, the far side floor came into view.

They were now approaching the starting position of the other group's chamber. Abeni gave a yell and peeled off the wall, falling. She landed on the cushions and immediately slammed her hands into them in frustration. The bottom of the pit passed from their sight as the flooring on the other side came under them. Roz hopped down and pushed into the opposite wall to slow their speed. Audrey dropped down and helped push. The other group was out of their chamber, so there was no resistance.

"We were so close. One more second or two and she would have made it," Audrey whispered. The chamber slid rapidly, and they soon came to the opening. The rest of the group stood next to the chamber exit. Hark, Tau, and the dog were there to meet them.

"You know, we could have figured out a way to solve that, without losing Abeni," Audrey said, staring down the twins. Her ruined eye blazed with anger.

"Maybe. Maybe not," Gabrielle replied. "But hey, you made it right? No harm, no foul." She gestured toward the exit doorway. "Hark even scouted the next part for us."

"Why weren't you in there?" Roz asked. "Could have used your ample glutes."

"When my pod opened, they told me to go through the bypass door that went around the circle, and to take Dio. Guess it pays to be a winner. Isn't that what they say at BUD/S?" Hark replied as they walked away from the circle.

"Hold up a minute," Audrey pulled on Roz's arm. He stopped. She waited until the rest of the group moved out of earshot. "Thank you," she said.

"For what?"

"For getting us through. Keeping it cool in there."

Roz shrugged. "No choice. No sense panicking, doesn't help anything."

"There's always a choice. The options might not be the best, but it's still a choice."

"You weren't so bad yourself."

She smiled, a gentle sunrise dawning on her face. "Lady Fortune shined on us. I'll take that any day."

Roz PUT his back against the wall and slumped to the concrete floor. A deep ache filled his lower body from all the pushing, like the aftermath of a heavy leg day in the gym. Right now, the cold on the floor felt relaxing. Soon, it would be unpleasant. He recalled sleeping in the jungle, years ago. He went to bed in sweat-drenched fatigues he'd spent the day patrolling in, sprawled out in a hammock or on a ground pad, depending on the scorpion situation. Sometime around midnight, he'd wake up shivering and change into a dry top for the rest of the night. If he put it on too early, he'd sweat right through it.

A few steps above him, Audrey was lying down as well, facing the opposite direction. The rest of the group had hunkered down toward the entrance to the next circle, past the next landing. He stared at the ceiling, trying to tamp down his frustration at losing in the wheel. Roz replayed the events in his mind over and over, searching for a way they could have prevailed. If it was there, he couldn't see it.

"Not much for team sports, are you?" Audrey put down the dog-eared copy of *The Inferno* next to her on the rough cement.

He shrugged. "I know I can count on myself. Mostly. Hark, yes. The dog, sometimes."

"I get it. I know what it's like. To feel violated and betrayed." She didn't gesture to her face, but she didn't need to.

"Sucks, doesn't it?"

"I saw you on the news," Audrey replied. He was wondering if and when that comment would materialize.

He was practiced now, watching for the moment that people recognized him. The pariah, the sociopath, the monster.

"Is it true what they say?" No trace of the edge in her voice he assumed would be there. Just a neutral, frank curiosity.

"Did I get in a physical altercation with one of my coworkers? Yes, that part is most definitely true. That I murdered him in a fit of drunken rage later that night, and then left his body to be found in my room? No, that part isn't true," Roz replied.

She was silent for a moment. "Can you prove it?"

He shook his head lightly. "I *had* evidence. I was going to the inspector general when the military police came for me. While in custody, someone broke into my room and took my laptop and the backups."

"Didn't you want to clear your name when you got out?"

Roz paused for a long while. "Part of the condition of my pardon was giving Janek a wide berth. I thought about what I could do. Dreamed about things I could do to get revenge on her. I...went off the rails for a while when I got released. Wasn't in a place to do much of anything. I tried to drown it all. I almost succeeded too, if it wasn't for that pesky Texan over there."

Audrey smiled. "And your wife?"

Roz laughed darkly, staring up at the whorls in the concrete. "We were having problems *before* the deployment. Before...the affair. Went back to her maiden name, changed Bella's last name too. Started the divorce proceedings."

Audrey nodded. "I can see how you wouldn't want to rely on anyone."

"It's easier this way. No one can let you down." He looked over at her. "How did you deal with the...attack?"

She laughed. "When I find out, I'll let you know. It's a work in progress. I'm still pretty suspicious, but I'm getting there."

Roz grunted. "Just hang it out there and be ready for it to be crushed again? No thanks."

"What else are you going to do with your life? Sit in a gutter and wait to die?" She looked at him. "You have to try, at some point."

He was silent for a long while. "What about you?" he asked, in what he hoped was a smooth change of subject.

"Married? Kids? I heard you talking to Justine back on the balcony."

The others were talking about something or other on the steps above. Dimly, he heard Grady's staccato tone, the gentle boom of Tau's voice, interspersed with the higher pitches of Gabrielle's.

"No husband. No kids." She smiled, lighting up her face. "My mother has cancer. It doesn't look good. But she's survived much worse getting out of China in the '90s. She'll die with grace and poise. Just like she lived."

"Just like her daughter."

Audrey laughed. "I wish I had half her poise. What about your parents?"

He gazed into her eyes. "My father was an American oil guy in Iran. Fled the country when the Ayatollah came back. I never knew him. He's in Texas. My mom and I moved to LA when I was ten. She passed away when I was in college."

"Do all SEALs go to college?"

Roz smiled. "We are a highly educated lot, generally. But no, not all. When my mom died, I derailed a little, flunked out of the Naval Academy. I enlisted to pay back the schooling." He pulled a protein bar from the backpack, offered her half. "What was it like for you? Growing up in China and being in the State Department."

She took the offered food gratefully. "You mean, was I trusted? Was I always trying to overcome a nagging suspicion from coworkers that I wasn't *really loyal*?"

"Something like that."

"A mixed bag. Were you trusted in the teams?"

Roz paused. "Yeah. There were a few assholes, to be sure. But I think they wouldn't have liked me no matter what. You make it through training, prove yourself—the trust of your teammates is yours to lose." He took a sip of his water. "How did you know him, anyway? Berenger."

"About five years ago, he came to Somalia. I was posted at the embassy—Mogadishu, not Nairobi. We'd moved back by that point. State had to give him a minder, and my incredibly lazy department chief volunteered my name. I spent a week driving around in protective motorcades as he looked for something. I never found out what it was, only that it was left over from the period when the Italians governed the country, back in the 1920s and '30s." She sipped water from a bottle.

"Did he find it?"

"I couldn't tell for sure. I think he got more information, at least." She shrugged. "What about you? Where did you cross paths with the mysterious wandering billionaire?"

Roz smiled. "Old Hark and I were be-bopping around Baghdad—as one does—and when we found out he was about to get kidnapped, we...intervened."

"Berenger must have been grateful."

He shrugged. "I guess. Seemed like a good dude."

Hark peeked his head around the corner of the stairs. Gave a chopping motion with his hand. "Break time's over."

BOOK III

SURVIVAL

CHAPTER 20

Roz—Saturday, 3 PM

Returning to my theme,
I say we came to the foot of a great tower;
but long before we reached it through the marsh,
two horns of flame flared from the summit,
one from other side, and then, far off,
so far we scarce could see it across the mist, another flame replied.
I turned to the sea of all intelligence, saying:
"What is this signal and counter-signal?
Who is it speaks with fire across this distance?"
Inferno, Canto VIII

Circle V: Wrath

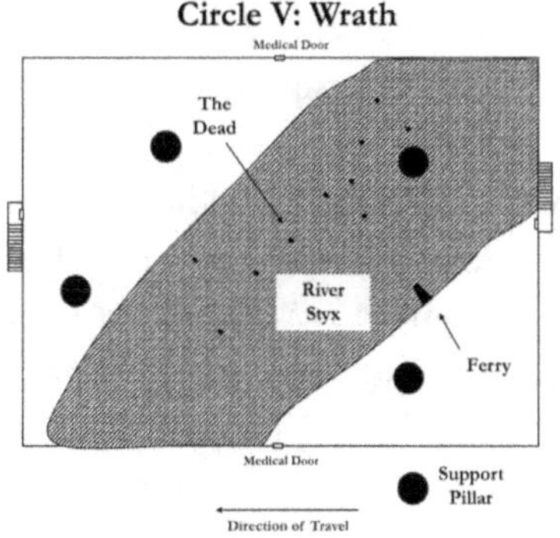

THE SMELL HIT THEM FIRST, like a physical wave.

Roz watched Gabrielle visibly recoil from the odor. The scent rippled down the line, as though they'd crossed some invisible barrier, until at last it engulfed Audrey and Roz in a sulfuric embrace. The dog sneezed in consternation. The smell brought back memories of slogging through the swamp down in Stennis, Mississippi. Fighting ticks, leeches, snakes, and constant wetness. Jungle warfare.

"What do you remember about this level?" Roz asked as they reached the last landing before entering.

"It holds the second of Hell's four rivers—the Styx." Audrey pointed at it.

Roz surveyed the place. Flat, like most of the earlier levels, but the floor looked like a wet, swampy mess. Plants and small trees dotted the area, blocking a complete view of the far side of the open area. A boat with an unmoving, cloaked figure perched on the edge of the swamp, nearby.

"Are those…" breathed Audrey. "No. Fakes. Have to be."

The rest of them looked at where she was pointing. At various parts of the swamp, a dozen humanoid shapes bobbed and moved in unseen currents.

"Guess this is the only ride in town, eh?" Hark said,

gesturing at the vessel. He walked over to check it out. The rest of the group followed behind in a loose line.

"Who is the boatman supposed to be?" Grady asked, gesturing at the figure.

Audrey answered. "Phlegyas. He holds the crossing of the River Styx, which divides upper and lower Hell. This represents a delineation point in *The Inferno,* between sins that—"

"I'm falling asleep listening to this," Grady interrupted. "Phlegyas, can you talk?" But the boatman did not respond.

Roz gave him an experimental touch. "Robot, like the others," he said.

Like Chuck E. Cheese robots.

Roz thought of the last time he'd been at the establishment with his daughter, and he winced inside. You don't know it's the last time you get to do something until much later. The last time you'll see your daughter squeal with delight, uncensored by the self-consciousness of later years. Unburdened by the accumulated weight of growing up.

The group clambered aboard the craft. With seven of them and the boatman, it was full. The dog sat, sandwiched in the middle. No sooner had they settled when the boat slid into motion, drawn across the water by an unseen force. A submerged cable, likely. They slid past the bobbing figures, who turned and watched with a gaze reminiscent of something reptilian. They looked like rejects from a wax museum —a mix of men and women, young and old, hair and clothing swaying with the movement of the water.

"So Phlegyas, you got any good tourist spots down here?" Richard asked, giving the boatman a playful elbow.

"CITY. OF. DIS." Came a response from inside the figure, a wheezing of sound from an unseen speaker.

Richard flinched, sliding as far forward as he could in the craft. His movement disturbed the equilibrium of the boat, causing it to oscillate back and forth.

"Hey! Watch it!" Audrey said as he pushed into her.

A high-pitched whine approached. Another drone. A quadcopter, ferrying a mannequin made up like the Grim Reaper, complete with a scythe. The drone floated in the limp air, and from it, an angry voice barked in Italian.

"Argenti," said Audrey under her breath. "Politician in Florence during Dante's time. Supposedly, he slapped Dante during a disagreement, and rumor has it Argenti's brother took the Alighieri family holdings when they were exiled. Kept them from returning to the city. Nicknamed Argenti because he put silver shoes on his horses."

"Huh. I didn't catch that part," Hark replied, swiveling to keep the figure in sight as it circled them above, arrow nocked.

"No one reads anymore," Audrey replied, shrugging. She had the spear cradled in her lap. "Not much, anyway. Besides, the whole silver horseshoes thing seemed over the top. Made it stick in my memory."

Tau stood up, club in hand.

"Maybe wait until we get on land, broham?" Grady suggested as the big man's movements rocked the boat.

The drone swooped down; the scythe whooshed through the air rhythmically as it approached. It trailed wisps of cloth and the whirling rotor blades sent ripe air blowing over the group. The figure had a misshapen skull for a head, wore a frozen grin as it berated them in Italian. Tau swung at it, missed, and nearly fell out of the boat.

They were most of the way across the swamp when one of the corpses attacked. It lunged onto the boat from the port side, arms scrabbling for purchase. Gabrielle and Audrey were the closest and fled to the other side of the boat. The thing grabbed at the edge as two others surged up on the same side, fingers scraping the aluminum frame like nails on a chalkboard. Audrey stabbed at the first one, and her spear went straight through the grinning mouth. It slid back into the water, knocking into the other two, pulling them off the boat. Up close, it was clear they were not actual corpses, but more robots.

Since all seven of them huddled on one side of the craft, the drastic change in balance caused it to overturn.

They plunged into the dark liquid.

Shock from the cold stole Roz's breath.

He fought to the surface to find a scene of chaos. The group was in various stages of moving toward the shore, swimming as best as they could in clothing and gear. The dog paddled efficiently. He was the only member of the group who seemed unperturbed by the turn of events. Argenti buzzed around, swooping down at them. Roz dove under and it kept going, hunting the other humans in the water.

"Go!" Roz bellowed as he saw bobbing heads converging from all directions. The group made for the shore, pawing at the water with waterlogged arms. He heard a cry, saw Audrey go under. He swam over and grabbed her pack, pulling her upward. She surfaced and sucked in a great mouthful of air, grabbing onto him fiercely. He had to work to disengage her and turn her around in the water so that he could tow her. "I got you," he repeated, scissor kicking out with his legs.

"Get it away," she sobbed in panic. Hark and Grady reached the shore, boosted themselves up, with Tau and Gabrielle close behind.

Audrey climbed up with Hark's assistance. Richard struggled. Roz felt a great welling up of water underneath his legs, and two of the robotic corpses surfaced, latching onto Richard. The man yelled as they took him downward. Roz felt one do the same to his leg, and he barely had time to suck in a breath. He ripped at the hands on his legs, tore them free and spun the robot and gave a vicious shove with a foot. Roz surfaced and caught his breath. No Danault. He tossed his pack onto the dry ground and turned to push off the wall.

Hark grabbed his arm. "No—he's gone. You can't do anything but get yourself hurt or killed." The Texan nodded gently. "If there was a chance we could save him, you know I would try."

Roz slammed the water in frustration. He climbed out with a rapid motion and knelt, looking at the river, foul moisture dripping off his body. The cuts and abrasions all over his body stung. Richard's pack floated listlessly in the water, doing a slow counterclockwise spin near the far shore. A corpse grabbed it, took it under with barely a ripple. "How's everyone else doing? Everyone okay?" Roz finally said, looking over.

Everyone that hasn't been drowned by a robotic zombie?

He heard a slamming sound, and Tau bellowed in triumph. The voice box grew garbled, and he watched the drone spin out of control and plummet into the water. "Now I'm okay," the man answered. Tau took off his shirt and wrung it out. Tattoos covered his back—swirling, dark whorls of ink, and other patterns that seemed to writhe as he moved.

Roz stood up unsteadily as the rest of the group walked off toward the exit. Hark stood to Roz's left, and Audrey his right. The dog behind, investigating one scent or another.

"He was an asshole, but that was a shitty way to go," Hark commented.

Roz nodded. "And then there were six."

"And then there were six," Audrey repeated. She squeezed his shoulder lightly. "I'm glad you're still here."

Roz froze for a beat. Then, loosened his muscles.

"Tell me again, how does this prepare us for stewardship of a multi-billion-dollar foundation? I still can't figure that one out. Couldn't they...I don't know, interview us?" she asked.

"Hell of a job interview." Roz shook his head. "I don't care anymore. The only way out is through."

"I need to get through. I have to get back to my mother." She stared off into the middle distance, shivering.

"You will. Probably. Maybe." Roz pulled a water bottle out of his pack and offered it to her.

Dasani, official sponsor of the Plek Foundation Succession Challenge.

She took a long pull. "Thanks for getting me back there. If you're not careful, someone might think that you're getting soft."

Hark clasped a hand on Roz's shoulder. "He's a knucklehead, but like Churchill said about America, we can depend on him to do the right thing once he's exhausted every other option."

"Thanks, old man. I think."

"It can't get any worse, can it? Can it?" Audrey asked them.

Roz laughed darkly, taking the water back and drinking. "Oh, it can get much, much worse."

THE ROOM WAS SILENT, save for the soft clicking of keyboards and the hum of the electronics. Church-service silent.

According to the script for the Wrath level, the General Dynamics robot "corpses" were there to serve as window dressing, nothing more. Not to engage with the selectees. Not to drag them to watery deaths. Legal was going to have a mess on their hands.

"Will somebody mind telling me what the *high holy fuck* is going on?" Justine asked, as they watched Tau club the drone apart on the screen in high definition. She saw some of the looks exchanged by her people. In a past life, Justine had used expletives like a proverbial sailor, but at her age she preferred not to stoop to such a coarse rhetorical level. Certain moments cried out for their use, however. This seemed to be one of them.

"Working it, working it," Dmitri replied from his workstation in a flurry of keystrokes.

Chewing on a pen cap with a landline phone in her hand, Hazel said, "Ma'am, I'm spooling up legal and PR to deal with this. The medical team in the stairwell is ready to respond. But I don't want to send them in until I know if we have, err, control of the situation with the underwater robotics." She listened for a few seconds, and set the phone to her chest. "Medical outside the Wrath Level is reporting the door to the circle is jammed shut. It's not responding to their key cards."

"Shit, shit, shit," Dmitri cursed. "J-Bone, what are you seeing?"

From across the room, Jarvis responded. "Someone is inside our firewall—they have got partial control of our subsystems, looks like a zero-day exploit, can't find a point of origin—"

"—Can you reroute server configurations to bypass?"

"—infrastructure and internal security functions offline—"

Justine walked over to Dmitri. "English, please," she said, with a hand on his shoulder.

"We just lost control of the tower," he reported tersely, staring at one of his monitors. "Someone else directed those floating robots to get homicidal. There should have been a cooperative puzzle to get the boat to move across the swamp. That part of the level never initiated. I also lost link with the Argenti drone midway through the selectees transiting across the River Styx."

Justine kept her features hooded. She felt violated, but nodded thoughtfully, as though she had received a weather report. "Do you assess it more likely to be the Hopf Collective, or Laughlin Carmichael?"

Hazel shook her head. "No telling. Could be either of them at this point."

Laughlin Carmichael. Had to be. "Okay, let's get a list together of the affected systems, and we'll put together a mitigation strategy."

Her red-haired ops chief nodded and moved off.

"Kathy—let's get a conference call with legal and PR in my office in ten minutes." She looked around the room. "We still have a job to do, people. The next steward, or stewards, are up there. If anyone has any ideas, I'm all ears."

CHAPTER 21

Roz—Saturday, 5 PM

The Master freed my eyes.

"Now turn," he said, "and fix your nerve of vision on the foam there,

where the smoke is the thickest and most acrid."

As frogs before the snake that hunts them down churn up their pond in flight,

until the last squats on the bottom as if turned to stone—

So I saw more than a thousand souls scatter away

from one who crossed dry-shod the Stygian marsh into Hell's burning bowels.

With his left hand he fanned away the dreary vapors of that sink as he approached;

and only of that annoyance did he seem weary.

Clearly he was a Messenger from God's Throne, and I turned to my Guide;

but he made me a sign that I should keep my silence and bow down.

Ah, what scorn breathed from that Angel-presence!

He reached the gate of Dis and with a wand he waved it open, for there was no resistance.

"Outcasts of Heaven, you twice-loathsome crew," he cried upon that terrible sill of Hell,

"how does this insolence still live in you?

Why do you set yourself against that Throne whose Will none can deny,

and which, times past, has added to your pain for each rebellion?

Why do you butt against Fate's ordinance?

Your Cerberus, if you recall, still wears his throat and chin peeled for such arrogance."

Inferno, Canto IX

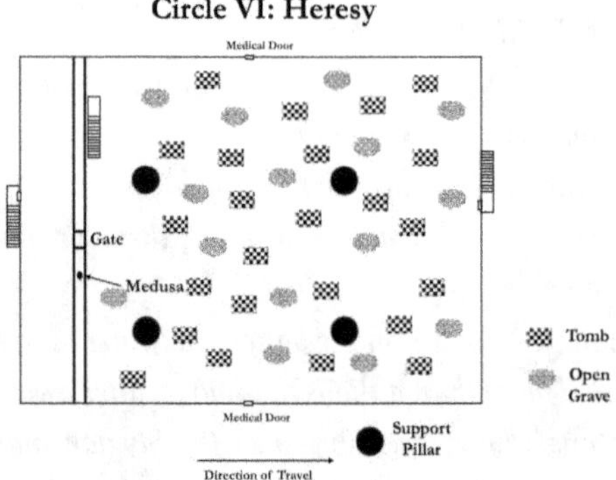

THE SIX OF THEM STOOD AT THE BASE OF THE WALL, taking in the three-story slab of stone and mortar. This was easily the tallest of the levels they'd been in so far—the ceiling soared another twenty feet above the top of the barrier. Directly in front of them stood an enormous, closed set of doors—large enough to drive a semi-truck through.

"The City of Dis," Audrey said, adjusting her scarf, tucking the stray hairs away. Seemed to be a habit of hers. Some sort of physical tic. The rampart at the top of the wall was ringed with flaming sconces, putting out fiery, flickering blooms of light toward the ceiling. After the cacophony and sonic assault of the other circles, this one was strangely silent.

"Well, 'Dis' sucks," Grady said, drawing more groans than chuckles from the exhausted group. "Someone had to say it."

Audrey continued as if he hadn't spoken. "The Sixth Circle of Hell is for Heretics."

The floor below them was made of a sandy material. The air full of a sharp astringent odor that Roz couldn't quite place.

"What do you say, amigo?" Hark asked him, eyeing the face of the wall. "Want to give it a go, or cover me with the bow?"

"You're the search and rescue climber-type. High angle is your thing."

"Fine with me," Hark said, and handed him the bow. "Just don't shoot me. You Frogmen are a tad trigger happy sometimes."

"Yeah, yeah. Throw the damn line, old man."

Hark pulled climbing rope from his pack, along with a grappling hook and a set of gloves. A quick toss, a tug to set the hook, and the Texan started to ascend the knotted line. Hark was halfway up when Roz heard the drones. They came over the wall, held aloft by several rotor blades each. Feminine figures that, like Argenti, were clad in cloaks. They held torches and knives in gnarled hands, with faces that radiated hostility.

"The Furies," Audrey said in a low voice, barely audible over the vibration in the air.

"GO AWAY," boomed a voice.

"YOU ARE NOT WELCOME," said another.

"WE WILL SUMMON MEDUSA," claimed a third.

One of them swooped toward the group. Roz got off an arrow, missed, and cursed as he nocked another. The drone hurtled toward Gabrielle and froze no closer than six feet from her. Gabrielle flinched back. Then it pivoted and swooped toward Roz and Audrey. Audrey stabbed at it. Roz abandoned the bow and unslung his shield, moved in to cover her. The spear struck a rotor blade, and the spinning metal flew apart. His Aegis kept most of the hot fragments from their midsections and heads, but Roz felt the angry impact of at least one piece on his thigh. The Fury gyrated away from them and pancaked into the stone with a boom.

Roz looked up, saw Hark reach the top.

A wail echoed from the far side of the parapet, and something stirred there—the figure of a woman with wavy hair that shimmered sinuously, even from a distance. Her eyes glowed with an ominous light. The dog began barking madly, back hair raised in a canine mohawk.

"Turn away!" Roz yelled, but he was too late. The woman's eyes supernovaed, and although Roz closed his own, he felt their power. Hark yelled out in surprise, then confusion, and finally pain.

Roz crouched behind the shield and moved up, squinting at the parapet. When he saw the beam of the light slide down the wall toward them, he moved his shield and reflected it directly back at the figure. Roz heard a slight pop, and the light faded. The figure remained motionless.

The only sound Roz could hear in the silence was Hark's low keening, up on top of the wall.

"I can't see!"

Then a glow of a different sort came, from behind.

MILENA STOOD, steaming coffee mug clutched in pragmatically manicured hands. She stared down the length of the plane at the row of technicians. The half dozen IT contractors Grace had retained through a shell company were digitally running through the Plek Foundation's electronic village, virtually pillaging as they went. The official story was that this was a training exercise with a company under a larger corporate umbrella. All the same, they'd plastered the contractors with NDAs. Laughlin Carmichael had leased a cargo plane for the flight to San Francisco, filled the interior with a mobile telecommunications package.

Barrett approached. "I contacted my folks through Signal and our usual message boards. They'll be ready for tonight, should you decide to go that route. They think Plek is a linchpin in a globalist cabal."

"Close enough," Grace replied, sliding up to stand between Milena and Barrett. "Our selectees found the cache the asset left for them. Gabrielle is ready for her viral moment."

"Did I miss anything this morning?" Milena asked.

"The exploit went live around noon, thanks to our asset inside Plek. We have control of cameras, doors, and the moving parts for levels five through nine. Danault drowned crossing the Styx, after the aquatic robots got a little frisky."

"He should have taken our offer."

"Too greedy," Grace replied. "Our pair, plus their big Kiwi helper, are in the lead, heading into the seventh level now." Grace pinched her fingernails on each hand as she looked down at the contractors. "One little wrinkle."

Milena sipped her coffee. "Yes?"

"Even with the exploit, we haven't been able to access the top level of the tower, the suite above the Ninth Circle. We think there's something there, but it's not managed by the subsystems we have admin rights to."

"Alright. Keep working to get access. Worst case, our agent can give us the details on what's in there."

Grace nodded.

Barrett pointed at a dark-gray module in the corner. "What's this?" Cables snaked out of the back, bundled and taped to the floor as they made their way to a server rack on the wall.

"Virtual-reality setup. Mimics what Plek has inside the tower. We can control the centaurs, harpies, and demons from it," Grace explained.

"Centaurs, harpies, and demons, oh my," Milena replied.

Barrett gave a polite chuckle and gestured at the contractors. "What about them? What if they find what you're looking for?"

Milena shrugged. "They won't. Lipton is no dummy. Ever heard of the Department of Nonlinear Affairs? She was one of their agents, when even my aged ass was in elementary school."

"Do you trust the Corsteads?" Barrett asked.

Grace looked at him sharply. "That is not—"

Milena held up a hand. "It's okay. Grady, I trust completely. He wants what we can provide him. His sister, though—she's a wildcard. And this Matamua character is along for the ride. Gabrielle is leading him around by his... appetite for her."

Barrett brushed some lint off his jacket. "I guess we'll see, then."

"Speaking of," Grace injected, "I can pull up a live feed right now." She opened a tab on an iPad Pro, showing the Heresy Level, the place dotted with open pits, filled with flames.

"What happened to Harkness?" Barrett pointed to the screen.

"I blinded him with a laser a few minutes ago," Grace shrugged nonchalantly.

Barrett squinted his eyes at her. "You did what?"

"Just call me Medusa, baby," Grace replied.

"It had to be done," Milena replied, a chastened expression stealing over her features. "Josh Harkness is a good man. And I didn't want things to come to this."

Barrett nodded. "What's next?"

Grace looked up from the iPad with a twinkle in her eye. "Ever wanted to be a minotaur?"

Milena's phone rang, and she excused herself when she saw who it was. Carlton Bero. Vice chairman of the Laughlin Carmichael board of directors. "Mr. Bero, I thought you were in Turks and Caicos this weekend?"

"I am, General Janek. We have cell reception down here."

"Please, Mr. Bero, call me Milena."

"All right, Milena," he began, with a voice that sounded in need of a good clearing of phlegm. "I don't believe in beating about the bush. Never have. The board has reached a critical progression in our thinking about your leadership. We've been able to keep the skeptics at bay for the last six months, but no longer. There's an emergency meeting called for Tuesday morning, and we expect you to present an update with regards to the status of *Project Wayfarer*. We need that program online and securing Defense contracts yesterday, to shore up losses in other markets."

Her stomach did a backflip, and she fought to steady herself.

Deep breath. In. Out. Belly breathe.

"Mr. Bero, as we speak, I am putting the final touches on an initiative that will put us into position to draw from the Gibbons Act—"

"That isn't going anywhere, and you know it."

"Once I can show them progress—"

"Tuesday, General Janek. See you there."

"Yes, Mr. Bero." But he had hung up before she could answer.

Milena swallowed. She felt betrayed—a panicked bewilderment slowly transmuted into something approximating vengeful rage. Milena had a good idea who defected into the skeptic camp. There was still a rump contingent on the board, angry about Admiral Stents' dismissal to make room for her.

No matter.

By this time tomorrow, she'd have the keys to the kingdom and then a long night to prep a triumphant presentation to the board next week.

She'd make them pay for violating her trust.

CHAPTER 22

Roz—Saturday, 6 PM

THE GLOW EXPANDED, and shadows fled before the baleful light. As Roz tracked this new floating object through half-closed eyes, it slowly passed over them, coming to a halt in front of the door. He couldn't get a clear view in the brightness. Screeching tones issued from the orb, and after a pause, the two remaining Furies departed, winging back into the city. With a sharp click, the doors unlatched and groaned open. Then the orb slid back and returned to a recess in the wall behind them. Silence again reigned over the level.

"Hark! You good?" Roz shouted, ran over to the base of the wall. The Corsteads moved forward with Tau through the door, heading to the right with a curious sense of purpose.

A dry chuckle came from the parapet above. "Besides the fact that I can't see shit, I'm good."

"All right, stand fast. We'll be there soon." He gathered their packs, looked at Audrey. "Could you— Um, do you think that—I mean—" Roz stopped to take a breath. "I'm not very good at this. Do you think you could help?"

Her eye twinkled. "Thought you'd never ask." Audrey took the bow, and with the dog at their side, they moved through. The door opened into a wide expanse. Glowing openings in the ground interspersed with small structures around the landscape. Once inside, Roz moved to the left, locating a metal stairway leading upward. They hurried.

"It's us. No stabbing," Roz called as they approached. Hark relaxed a tad, sitting with his back to the wall, a Winkler knife in his hand. "Let me look," he said, and shined a flashlight into Hark's eyes. "Can you see that at all?" No sign of overt damage to his eyes.

Hark wiped away tears. "A little. I can see some light. It's blurry and far away. Flash blindness, brother."

Roz swore under his breath. "Okay. Let's get you out of here."

Audrey was at the top, staring out at the others as they moved. "Why does it look like that Fury is guiding them through the tombs?"

Roz stood and looked for himself. Sure enough, one of the remaining Furies floated in front of Grady as they followed a twisting path across. "Huh." Audrey stood and watched the trio's progression as Roz pulled the rope up and wrapped it, stowing it back in Hark's pack. He walked down the parapet, empty save the frozen figure at the end. The Medusa spoke in a soft voice as he approached, his shield up, even now, until he pointed her head in a safe direction. He pried a plate off the back of the head with his multi-tool. The snake-hair was eerily lifelike up close. Underneath a wide woolen cloak, the Medusa had a robot chassis with a tank track rather than legs. He walked back to Hark and Audrey.

The dog sat with his head in Hark's lap, and the Texan stroked his head, staring out into the city.

"The device said five watts," Roz reported.

Hark nodded. "Powerful. The damage might be temporary." He looked up at Roz. "Might not. Time will tell."

"You feel up to moving?"

Hark laughed. "You're not going to carry me? Be a pleasant change of pace."

"Negative. Lose a leg or two, then we'll talk about you getting carried."

"Fair enough. Point me in the right direction, then."

"Let me see if I can paint the picture for you a little," Roz began, as they watched the others file through the portal on the other side. "We're going to walk down the stairs in front of you, turn left. We'll be facing a wide plateau. It's filled with grave-sized openings, and small structures. We're going to have to weave our way through. No telling what we'll find, but we know what we've encountered so far."

"These are the flaming tombs of Heretics," Audrey replied. "Not surprisingly, there are a lot of politicians and religious leaders in this part of *Inferno*." She gestured with her spear off to the left side as they looked at the scene. "There's a solid path on this side. Do you want me to get him to the medical stairs?"

"Yeah, let's go that way."

"Hell no. I'm not quitting. If my sight doesn't come back after a while, we can try that option."

"And I'm the hard-headed one," Roz responded. "You're the pararescueman, but I thought 'life, limb, or eyesight' was the criteria for getting medical care. I guess that doesn't apply when we're talking about ourselves?"

"I will not quit just because I can't see right this second," Hark grumbled.

"Audrey, will you take the lead with the mutt? I can follow

and guide this pain in the ass as we move," Roz asked as he helped Hark get his pack on. He stowed the bow and quiver, wondering if the Texan would ever use them again. *Too early to tell.*

Audrey nodded, but then realized that Hark couldn't see, so she gave a verbal confirmation. The group headed down. The sound of the Furies returning broke the silence of the massive room. They floated into view, circling around the building struts.

"Okay, here we go, old man. Try to keep up."

Hark chuckled darkly. "If I knew that going blind would get you to finally carry your share of the load, I would have done it years ago."

They walked for a minute or two, and they seemed to avoid being seen by the Furies. Then, in front of them, the dog sniffed and turned in a semi-circle before he sat.

"Audrey, freeze," Roz said.

The dog whined.

"Aww, shit," Hark said. "What do you see? Victim-operated or command-detonated?"

Roz gazed around the immediate area. The floor was rough concrete, with broken, irregular patterns, but there was a distinct two-foot-by-two-foot square shape in front of Audrey. As he continued searching, Roz realized there were more than a few of them on the floor, some better disguised than others. "Probably victim. Okay, we're going to retrace our steps. Carefully."

Audrey, come to the sound of my voice." They retreated to the first open grave they'd passed. A skeleton lay inside, lit by orange, recessed lights. Roz pried a piece of heavy brick from the side of it and lugged it forward.

"What are you doing, amigo? I hope it's not what I think it is."

"Get down," Roz said. He waited a beat, then lobbed the

brick at the two-by-two floor squares. It skidded and tumbled across the ground before sliding onto the space. He had time to register the faintest of *thunks*, and a massive whoosh of air and material erupted from the spot. It wouldn't have killed someone but likely knocked them into one of the adjoining pits. Wouldn't be pleasant.

"Probably explosively actuated. That's what Dio was smelling."

With that in mind, they continued to make their way across the tombs. The other three selectees had left minutes ago, without sparing so much as a glance in their direction. As Roz watched the two remaining Furies, they both fell to the floor, pinwheeling and crashing to a stop on the other side of the level. Hark flinched, and Roz described what had happened.

"Strange for them both to run out of power or have a mechanical issue at once," the Texan commented.

They reached the medical door without further incident, and Roz tried it. Locked. He slapped it with his fist, making a boom that echoed in the enormous open level.

From behind the bottom of the door, he heard a man's voice. On the younger side, anxiety in his voice. "Hey! I can't open the door—it's locked. We're working on the problem now."

"What do you mean, 'it's locked?' I got a guy that can't see in here—he needs someone to look at him."

Long pause. Finally: "There was a, some kind of breach. Someone hacked the tower operating system. They have control of the locking mechanism for these doors. The IT guys are trying to find a solution."

Roz looked over at Audrey and Hark. "That must be what happened with the corpses in the Wrath Level."

Hark nodded. "I felt a change when we were crossing the

swamp. Something felt…off. Different. Can't really describe it better than that."

"Like a *feeling* feeling? Spidey-sense feeling?" Roz asked.

"Yep."

Roz turned back to the group. "Let's get out of here before something else tries to kill us."

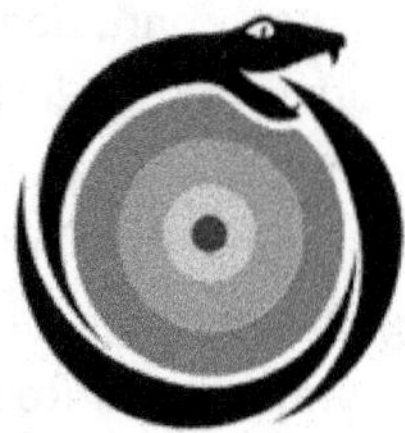

ON THE STAIRWELL LANDING, they found nine cots arranged in two lines along the walls of the place. Each had a name placard on the pillow, complete with the Plek Foundation symbol—an ouroboros encircling a multi-colored bullseye, and a neat pile of fresh clothing. A long folding table pressed up against the concrete wall, filled to the brim with still-warm buffet bins. Coolers squatted on the floor, filled with ice and cold drinks.

Roz guided Hark into a resting position on a cot. The Texan grimaced. "Gonna be sore tomorrow, eh?"

"Beats the alternative," Roz replied.

"I need to rest my eyes a little, and then we'll go on," Hark said, flushing them with saline from his med pack.

"Let's give it some time, see if your vision comes back," Roz said. "We could all use some rest."

Audrey looked over at them. "Did you notice something when that drone attacked us back there?"

"Nothing in particular," Roz answered, fixing a plate of food for Hark from the table.

She sighed. "You didn't notice how it came up to Gabrielle, paused, and then turned to attack us?"

"Now that you mention it, that seems strange. I chalked it up to a glitch."

"Then why was a Fury leading the others through the tombs?"

Hark shrugged. "Maybe it was doing a pre-programmed patrol pattern, and it seemed like they were following it. Who knows?"

Roz looked over at her. "So, whoever was controlling the drone didn't want to attack Gabrielle?"

"I don't know. It could be coincidence, like them following the drone across."

He nodded. "So, Professor, what do we need to know about the last three levels?"

"Violence, Fraud, and Treachery remain," Audrey replied, wolfing down a plate of steaming stir-fry. "They are, in Dante's view, the worst of the seven sins. They get progressively worse as you descend. Or ascend, in our case."

"Treachery, huh? That's what he thinks is the worst?" Roz made a face. "I'd think Violence would be the worst."

"Violence is bad—it's near the bottom," Audrey countered. "But to betray others, to betray God, Dante viewed that as the worst thing a human can do. It destroys the trust in a society. Without trust, there is no glue to hold things together."

Roz stared at the wall and said nothing.

Audrey continued. "So. The Seventh Level. Violence. The Eighth Circle is for the sin of Fraud, and comprises ten pouches or ravines, called *Malebolges*. The Ninth Circle is Treachery, a place of cold and darkness.

"What things did Dante have to deal with?" Roz pulled a

few icy Gatorades out of the cooler and got each of them a bottle.

"Minotaurs, centaurs, snakes, demons, rivers of blood. The worst sins of humanity are on display."

"This sounds like the plot of *Big Trouble in Little China*."

"We *are* in San Francisco," Hark mumbled, eyes closed, turning over on the cot. "Wake me up to stand watch. My ears still work—I can still hear if someone's sneaking up on us."

No one spoke for a long while. Then came the sound of Hark softly snoring. The man could fall asleep at the drop of a hat—whether on a C-130 flying to a remote outpost or kitted up on a helo waiting to assault a high-value target.

Audrey looked at Roz. "Tell me about when you met Berenger."

"I'd rather not."

"Why?"

"I...I don't know. It hurts to think about. The last good thing that I ever did. It all went to shit after that."

Audrey took a drink of the Gatorade. "I'll make you a deal. I'll tell you about the attack. You tell me about when you met Berenger."

He looked at Hark, slumbering peacefully. "Fine," he said at length. "Besides, if I don't, the Texan will give you his version, which won't be as good."

She grinned. "Well, I want the good version." Taking a deep breath, she began.

"Becoming a diplomat was everything. It's what my father wanted. What I thought I wanted. It was a good fit for my personality. I was pretty idealistic about the whole thing, growing up watching my father work overseas. I got the chance to go out into communities, see what was actually happening on the ground. I wasn't one to stay cooped up in the embassy and collect a paycheck." She paused, adjusted her scarf self-consciously. "Between overseas postings, I worked the Near East Desk at Foggy Bottom. I could push out all over the place, even locations where the Diplomatic Security Service would rather we didn't. Hot. Long hours, sleeping on hard cots at military forward operating bases. Like these. What am I saying? I'm sure you've had it way worse than that."

Roz shrugged. "Sometimes it's five-star hotels, sometimes you're shitting in a bucket. Your mileage will vary. These things are actually pretty comfy." He patted the cot appreciatively.

Audrey smiled, then the expression fled from her face, vanquished by a thought. "One of my trips was to Pakistan. We were a few hours outside of Lahore. Near the end of our visit, a man burst into our tent. Somehow, he made it through all the DSS protection we had." Audrey stared at the wall. "I was talking to a young girl, and I heard a noise. The man was in the middle of throwing the acid when I looked up. It arced toward my face, and I barely had time to turn my head. Thankfully, none of it got on the little girl. It could have been so much worse. Then he started beating me with his fists. It took three men to pull him off."

"That's horrific."

"Four surgeries later and this is as good as it's gonna get," she smiled sadly, waving a hand at the side of her face. "A real-life two-face."

Roz looked at her. It had been an intense eighteen hours. Nothing to lose from being honest. "I think you look beautiful."

Audrey laughed. "Intellectually, I understand that you probably mean that. And it's taken fifty hours of therapy to get that far."

"I'm sure you've heard all the clichés."

"I'm beautiful on the inside, right?"

"I think you're beautiful on the outside, too."

"That's generous of you."

He laughed. "Generosity was the last thing on my mind. I was thinking of asking you out on a date. Just a lunch or something, nothing serious."

"Isn't this experience like one long date?"

"The worst first date in recorded history."

The two laughed, then settled down into a companionable silence. They each stared at the ceiling as they lay on the floor.

"You think we're going to get out of this?"

Roz looked at the stairs moving relentlessly upward. "I don't know. I don't know what our probability of making it to sunrise is. When you jump out of an airplane, you're streaking toward the earth at around a hundred and fifty miles per hour, depending on your body type and position."

He paused. Looked over at her.

"Until you pull that ripcord—until you have a good silk above your head—for all intents and purposes, you are dead. You're dead until the chute opens."

"Huh." She looked back, the slightest of twinkles in her good eye. "I never realized that SEALs had such a flair for the dramatic."

Roz chuckled. "Oh, honey, we do dramatic better than anyone. Almost anyone—aviators are really competitive in this arena."

"Okay, your turn."

"Do I have to?"

"A deal's a deal."

He sighed. "Fine." Roz cast his thoughts back through the years, back to the heat and the dust.

CHAPTER 23

Roz—The Past

"YOU DRIVE LIKE AN OLD MAN. Did I ever tell you that?" Roz asked as he glanced through the back window of the sedan to check for their follow vehicle. There it was. The old Renault van lurked four cars back, a wolf in sheep's clothing. The mid-afternoon traffic on Al Jami'ah Street oozed in both directions. Opportunistic drivers made lane changes wherever a car width would allow. Walking would be faster. The sun lanced down on the Baghdad streets, a vengeful deity seeking to incinerate all foolish enough to expose themselves to its gaze. The air-conditioning of their dusty white Opel sedan fought a fruitless battle to cool the air inside the vehicle. "You're not out on a wagon trail outside of San Antonio."

He swerved to avoid a pair of kids selling gum and put his eyes on Roz in the rearview mirror. "You tell me that every time we do a close-target reconnaissance. This ain't LA either, amigo." Hark and Roz both wore white *dishdashas,* the outfit Coalition soldiers referred to as "man dresses." Hark's beard was patchy and blond, but he'd dyed it dark brown. Roz needed no such help. He trimmed it like it was his own personal bonsai tree to keep it looking properly Iraqi. Both of their faces were deeply tanned from hours spent in the Mesopotamian heat.

"Misty 26, Blazer One. This mess clearing up soon?" Roz asked through his earpiece. The "bone phone" style conduction device allowed him to speak without a headset and avoid drawing attention to himself. Three miles above the city, an Air Force Liberty MC-12 airplane floated in a racetrack orbit, like a hawk scanning a meadow for prey.

Misty's sensor operator responded after a moment. "Primary route clogged with traffic for another kilometer, then it opens." A woman's voice.

Hark listened on his own headset. "Think she's hot? She sounds hot."

Roz shrugged. "No idea. Haven't met her yet." He liked to meet up with the flight crews after missions to debrief and learn their operating procedures. Putting a face to the voice was helpful, but building the relationships even more so.

Roz's phone rang, the default Nokia ringtone filling the air in the car with strident tones. He recognized the number. Phil, a SEAL junior officer. The young Frogman served as a liaison at the Baghdad Operations Center, the nexus of command and control for all Iraqi forces in the capital city.

"*Shaku Maku,* broham," he answered. "What's up?"

"Roz—" The strain in Phil's voice came over the line. "The Iraqis just gave me something—kidnapping threat on an American, down in the Karada District." Roz could hear raised voices, yammering in Iraqi Arabic in the background.

He could picture the scene. An enormous room full of hairy, mustached men at rows of desks, smoking cigarettes and yelling into cellphones. A Dubai soap opera or soccer game playing on one of the wall-mounted televisions. "It's going up the chain now, but it's taking forever. I needed to tell someone because it's imminent. Place called Plek Relief. Some NGO."

"How imminent?" Roz asked, making eye contact with Hark in the mirror. A non-governmental organization was a civilian entity—in this part of the world they were usually doing humanitarian work. Compared to a military or diplomatic location, they had limited security.

"Like the next hour imminent. I sent it to headquarters, but I don't think the Quick Reaction Force from FOB Trenty can get there in time. Not in the traffic right now. You're the only unit I know in the area."

"Yeah, we're in Karada now. What's the location?"

Phil relayed the grid, and Roz plugged it into the imagery software on his navigation device. He whistled. "Three clicks away. Take a left and head south," he said to Hark. "Okay, we'll go check it out."

He ended the call with Phil and hailed the plane overhead. "Misty 26, Blazer One, new sensor tasking." He relayed the coordinates.

"Standby, One," came the response. Miles above, the plane swiveled its high-definition lenses to the new location. The pair came up with a hasty navigation route and briefed the follow vehicle over the radio. Roz asked the aircraft to relay his intentions on their change of mission to headquarters. The ISIS safe house reconnaissance was going to have to wait.

"Be advised—we are seeing lots of activity at that compound. I count two vehicles static at the main entry point, with multiple armed military-age males milling about. Relay from Blazer Actual—the colonel requests you contact her," the sensor operator in the air reported. Hark took a left through thick oncoming traffic, earning a chorus of honks from irate drivers. The unmistakable tang of burning trash filled Roz's nostrils as they blew past flaming pyres on the side of the road. He cursed under his breath.

"Mom's mad," Hark said, weaving through traffic. He found an open lane and went with it, zooming up the shoulder of the road. The follow vehicle struggled to keep up through the syrupy flow of cars.

Roz dialed the number by heart as he slid the *dishdasha* off, revealing body armor and a trio of rifle magazine pouches underneath.

"What are you doing?" Milena asked without preamble. He sensed notes of impatience and annoyance, with a dabbling of weary resignation in her voice.

"Err, Colonel Janek, we received credible reporting from a liaison officer of a hostage threat to an AMCIT. My intentions are to check it out, see if it's legit." Silence. Roz took the phone off his ear to see that he hadn't lost the call when she finally responded.

"I don't think that's a good idea. You don't know what you're walking into. I will not tell you no, but I advise against it. Better to let the QRF handle it."

In his earpiece, he heard Wally, the team leader in the van behind them, come up on the radio. The SEAL informed them he was stuck behind a garbage truck. "We're just going to get eyes on. If it's too hinky, we'll pull back and wait for the boys from Trenty to show up."

She was silent again for a long moment. "Fine. Don't say I didn't warn you." Another pause. Then—"Remember, we're supposed to play cards tonight."

"We're still on—we'll be back for that. Wouldn't miss it for the world."

"See to it." He thought he could detect the faint trace of a smile in those last few words.

"Roger that...Ma'am." Roz ended the call and looked up to find Hark's eyes on him in the rearview mirror.

"What's that look mean?"

"You're playing cards with the colonel now?" Hark's features were inscrutable.

Roz looked out the window at the concrete houses and their courtyards. He massaged the burned skin running up his neck toward his chin. "Just a friendly game of poker."

"That's all?"

"Emphasis on the friendly."

Hark shook his head. "You have a toddler at home, brother. What are you thinking?"

"It just kind of happened. There wasn't a lot of thinking involved."

Hark said nothing.

Roz pulled down a residential street and braked to a stop. Silence filled the vehicle. Without the meager air-conditioning, the heat invaded the interior immediately. Hark pulled the Iraqi garment off, revealing an enormous Texas state flag centered on his body armor, faded and salty from sweaty hours in the arid elements. He grabbed his med bag and slung it onto his back, press-checking his Heckler and Koch 416 to ensure a 5.56-millimeter round was chambered.

Roz pulled the Aegis from where he had it stowed, an irregularly shaped one-by-two-foot plate of Kevlar. He loped up to the pedestrian entrance, MP-7 aimed at the faded red door. Locked when he tried it. "Gimme a sec." He knelt and took out a set of lock picks, got to work.

Hark eyed Roz's primary weapon with a flicker of disdain

before glancing up and down the street. "You know that is a bitch-ass gun, right, amigo?"

"Your face is a bitch-ass gun."

"That doesn't make any sense."

"Whatever." The compound had the usual eight-foot concrete wall, topped with broken glass and other unsavory items to deter climbing. Shots rang out from inside the compound, the deep booms of an AK-47. A woman screamed. Hark turned and mule-kicked the door. The lock splintered in the frame and the door swung open.

Roz sighed and put his picks away.

Hark scanned the inside of the compound from behind the sights of his long gun.

Roz took point, sweeping past him into the compound with his MP-7 locked into the nook of the shield. Hark flowed in behind, covering his six. They crept toward the voices. At a building corner, Roz glimpsed a group of men and women sitting in the shade of a building in an open courtyard. Three armed men milled about, gesturing and yelling. A fourth held a pistol to an older man in the middle of the space and, as Roz watched, forced him roughly to his knees. Two crumpled bodies lay in small pools of blood on the far side of the courtyard.

"One, this is Two—we are dismounting, moving to the south entrance." Wally's voice came over the earpiece, and Roz heard Hark click his push-to-talk button twice in acknowledgment.

He pulled back and looked at Hark. "No time to wait. Four tangos. They're about to execute a hostage. Ready?"

Hark gave him a sly smile. "Always ready to meet God, amigo. On you."

Roz nodded and turned back. With a swift move, he swept into the courtyard and put his sights on the pistol-wielding man in the center, the foregrip of the MP-7 nestled securely in a notch of the shield.

He exhaled.

Stroked the trigger.

Roz sent a flurry of 4.6-millimeter rounds hurtling into the scorching Baghdad afternoon at over twenty-four hundred feet per second. The first several hit the man in the neck, and the rest slammed into the middle of his face. He crumpled to the courtyard stones, discharging his pistol into the concrete as he did.

One down.

As Roz swiveled to another hostage-taker, he heard Hark open up with the larger 416 carbine.

Two down.

People yelled out in fear at the sharp cracks of bullets, and the escalating violence. Through the chaos, Roz acquired his next target, watching the masked man bring his rifle up in what seemed like slow motion.

Sight, slack, squeeze.

He hit the man center mass with a quartet of rounds. Roz flinched as a round hit the shield squarely and ricocheted off. The impact thrummed through the Kevlar, into the bones of his arm, but the bullet did not penetrate.

Three down.

He scanned the rest of the courtyard for threats as Hark engaged the last man.

Four down.

Roz bounded over to the old man as Hark covered the open areas between the buildings. Roz quickly frisked the dead man at their feet, extracting a phone and a wad of cash from his pockets. American cash. Had to be close to several grand in hundred-dollar bills. "You okay?" he asked the man.

"I think so, yes," the man replied, running hands over his body to ensure he had no wounds. Mid-sixties, with gray hair and a white beard. A cut on his forehead leaked blood where it looked like someone had struck him. "My name is Nicholas Berenger."

"Feroz Mehran."

In front of them, Hark engaged someone with his rifle out toward the main compound entrance, a *tut-tut-tut* of suppressed fire. AK-47 rounds snapped past their heads, whining into the sky.

"Blazer One, multiple personnel maneuvering toward your position," the sensor operator reported through their earpieces.

"Copy—we are troops in contact," Roz answered. To the group of civilians, he yelled, "People, we need to move. *Yamshee! Yamshee!*" He pointed back toward the pedestrian gate. They made no move to leave. "Will they listen to you?" Roz asked Berenger.

"Let's go!" Berenger bellowed, waving his hands. Most of the people needed no further encouragement, streaming past Roz toward the entrance.

"Two, this is One—bunch of civilians heading your way. Request you set a corridor and deal with the main entrance."

"Blazer Two," came Wally's acknowledgement.

Roz helped Berenger out of the compound, with Hark covering their movement. At the gate, he found Wally and another SEAL. Gunfire near the compound entrance. Roz got Berenger to the Opel, eased him into the back.

"Can you take me to the airport? My plane is there," Berenger asked him. "Those men were after me. As long as I'm here, my people will be in danger."

Roz nodded. Called out on the radio. "Misty, find us a decent route to the airport." Baghdad International Airport—BIAP—for short, lay to the northwest.

"I can get us to BIAP from here, amigo," said Hark, moving past and heading into the driver's seat.

"Wally, break down and follow—we're heading out," Roz called over the radio. Hark did a U-turn and roared away from the compound.

"Ditty Mau," Berenger said from the backseat. He trembled.

Hark looked back at the man in the mirror. "Where did you serve?"

"2/6 Marines. Beirut. Lots of old Vietnam vets trained us for that operation."

"Tough duty. Were you there for the barracks bombing?"

"I was out on patrol when it happened. Worked the recovery and the redeployment."

Roz handed him a water bottle from the small cooler in the front seat. "Any idea why someone would want to kidnap you, Mr. Berenger? You realize this is not the safest neck of the woods for Americans, right? We're not the most popular folk here."

Berenger took a deep pull of the water, gulping half of the bottle down. "Many reasons. Someone could fetch a large ransom for me if they wanted. When you get to my age, the things I've done, places I've been, friends come and go. But enemies accumulate."

Roz grunted. "I don't mean to insult you, you being familiar with a combat zone and all, but this isn't a place that suffers the naïve or the foolish. Usually, their bodies get strung up somewhere as a lesson."

Berenger closed his eyes and nodded. "I had to meet with someone. She had something that I need for my…work. She refused to meet anywhere else. I thought the threat was manageable. I brought guards—those were the men lying in the courtyard. That reminds me—I need to send someone to retrieve their bodies. I didn't expect the lengths that my adversaries would go. But like a miracle from beyond, you two appeared to save me. Like avenging angels."

Roz shook his head. "Two guys trying to do the right thing. Trying to get through deployment."

"Not all of us have little babies waiting for us." Hark drove with his knee and packed Copenhagen chewing tobacco into his cheek.

"You have a child?" Berenger asked. He seemed calmer.

"Yep. Three-year-old daughter. Scary-smart already."

Berenger smiled. "A wonderful age. Reality hasn't shown its darker colors yet."

Roz nodded. "With any luck, she can enjoy being a kid awhile."

Private contractors guarded the back entrance to the airport. Nigerians wielding AKs with a casual but deadly air. "*Habari Yako,*" Hark said, flashing a special-access badge for the airport. The guards let them pass with a cursory inspection of the undercarriage for explosives. They drove in silence for a few minutes, down a dusty and potholed access road.

"May I ask you gentlemen something?"

Roz looked over at Hark. "Sure."

"What is the biggest problem facing mankind, at our present juncture?"

Hark answered first. "Huh. I don't spend a lot of time cogitating on that particular subject, but if you forced me to answer, I would paraphrase Pascal and say that people can't sit alone in a quiet room. They'd rather shock themselves than be bored."

Berenger nodded. "And what about you, Mr. Mehran?"

Roz considered. "We can't seem to accept we're all connected. That what we do to one, we do to all."

"My foot is connected to your ass," Hark retorted.

The three of them laughed, and it felt good.

"Thank you both, excellent answers. Ah, there it is,"

Berenger said. He pointed to a nearby strip of weathered tarmac.

Hark let out a low whistle. "G6. Nice."

A perimeter of Army soldiers surrounded the plane. On the side, it bore a unique image. A circular snake, eating its own tail. And in the middle, a multi-colored bullseye—blue on the outside, then red, green, and finally purple in the center. The sentries waved them through after a radio call. The follow van with Wally and assorted pipe-hitting Frogmen hung back, outside the perimeter.

As they pulled up at the stairs to the plane, Roz was surprised to see Milena and her aide, Major Vanders. They stood and spoke with a tall, blonde woman.

"Huh," was all Roz said as they slid to a stop. A pair of men in civilian attire with long guns slung hustled Berenger out of the back of the Opel. He turned to face Hark and Roz.

"I owe you two a great debt for what you did today. Come to San Francisco to see me when you get back to the States."

Roz nodded and Hark tipped his faded Dallas Cowboys ball cap. Berenger shook Roz's hand, a firm and callused grip.

The blonde woman handed him two business cards. Below the same symbol adorning the side of the plane, the cards bore the words PLEK FOUNDATION in clean black print, along with a ten-digit phone number. "If you need anything, please reach out," she said with a smile.

Milena approached. "Tech Sergeant Harkness, thank you for letting us borrow you for the operation. I'll let Lieutenant Colonel Rickover know what an asset you were today. Senior Chief Mehran, let's debrief back at the FOB."

"Aye, Ma'am."

Her eyes lingered on him for a long moment before she turned to converse with Berenger. A peppy smile migrated onto her features while she pivoted to the billionaire and put her arm on his shoulder.

"Time to go?" Hark asked, staring over Roz's shoulder at Major Vanders, who stood next to the aircraft stairs and favored them with his best stink-eye."

"Seems appropriate," Roz answered. He blew Vanders a kiss as they drove off. The officer watched them depart with an expression reserved for cleaning dog shit off a shoe. They pulled back into the forward operating base, parked near the armory. Silence filled the car, save the tick of the engine as it cooled.

"Clean weapons?" Roz asked finally.

Hark shook his head. "I need to get back. Call my dad."

"Any changes?"

"He's got maybe a month left."

"Sorry to hear that, brother. You going home?"

Hark nodded. "Yeah. Try to settle all the old arguments. As best we can, anyway."

"When my mom died, I derailed pretty hard for a while. Dropped out of the Naval Academy. She was the only family I had in the States."

"Yeah, but on the bright side, it kept you from being an officer. What do you call it in the Navy?"

"*Cake Eater*?"

Hark wagged his finger in the air. "That's the one."

Roz cocked his head. "Technically, I would have been both a *Cake Eater*—a Naval officer—and a *Ring Knocker*—a Naval Academy graduate."

"This keeps getting better and better," Hark laughed. "You Navy folks have the best names."

"Seriously, if you need someone to talk to, let me know."

"Thanks, amigo." Hark got out of the Opel, rifle in hand, and grabbed his med bag with the other. Then he leaned back into the car. "Watch out for Vanders. He's a snake. Toxic reputation in Air Force spec ops. Keep your wits about you."

Roz smiled at him in the fading light of the afternoon. "Luckily, his boss likes me."

Hark grunted, spat on the gravel. "Like I said, keep your wits about you. We need to have a conversation about your life choices. Careful who you trust in here. I'll be back in a few weeks, after I say goodbye to the old man." He extended his hand.

Roz grabbed it. "Safe travels—catch you on the flip side."

He watched Hark amble out the gate of their FOB, heading back to his own unit, down the dusty road.

CHAPTER 24

Roz—Saturday, 8:30 PM

The scene that opened from the edge of the pit was mountainous,

and such a desolation that every eye would shun the sight of it:

a ruin like the Slides of Mark near Trent on the bank of the Adige,

the result of an earthquake or of some massive fault in the escarpment

—for, from the point on the peak where the mountain split to the plain below,

the rock is so badly shattered a man at the top might make a rough stair of it.

Such was the passage down the steep,

and there at the very top, at the edge of the broken cleft,

lay spread the Infamy of Crete,

the heir of bestiality and the lecherous queen who hid in a wooden cow.

And when he saw us, he gnawed his own flesh in a fit of spleen.

And my Master mocked: "How you do pump your breath!

Do you think, perhaps, it is the Duke of Athens,

who in the world above served up your death?

Off with you, monster; this one does not come instructed by your sister, but of himself to observe your punishment in the lost kingdom."

As a bull that breaks its chains just when the knife has struck its death-blow, cannot stand nor run but leaps from side to side with its last life—so danced the Minotaur, and my shrewd Guide cried out:

"Run now! While he is blind with rage! Into the pass, quick, and get over the side!"

Inferno, Canto XII

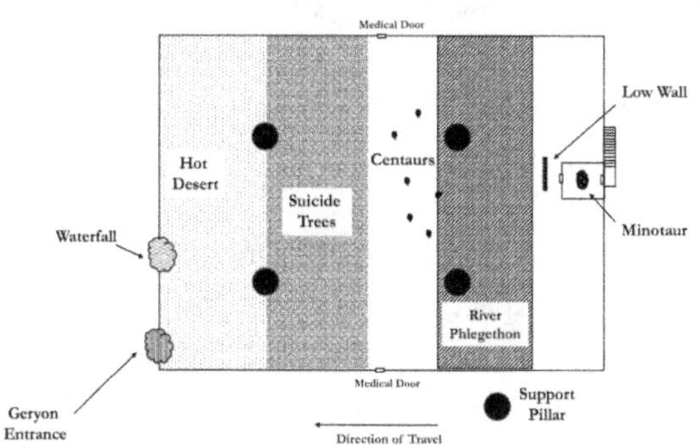

ROZ SQUINTED AROUND THE CORNER. Looked back at the group. "What's the name of the bull thing? The half-man, half-bull creature?"

Audrey stood next to him. "Minotaur. From the labyrinth of Minos. King Minos sacrificed beautiful men and women to it. Finally slain by Theseus, who escaped with the help of

Ariadne, Minos' daughter. One of my favorite stories from Greek mythology."

Roz grunted and stepped off to the side so she could see what he was looking at. The entrance to the Seventh Level was a square, twenty-by-twenty-foot room. A colossal figure blocked the exit leading out of the room, enticingly visible between its large, tree trunk-sized legs. The minotaur stood fourteen feet tall, covered in fur and a giant loincloth. Ceiling three stories above. It stirred, and a booming *broooh* sound boomed from unseen speakers. Bull noises in surround-sound high-definition. Roz stared at the Minotaur's face, startled to see it blur and morph. A manic grin, a wistful frown, a cheerful snarl. He shook his head and looked again. The face was just a face.

Must be the psychedelics.

"You guys feeling weird?"

Hark laughed. "Brother, weird does not begin to encapsulate how I feel right now. I'm mostly blind, going through Hell, and we're microdosing."

Audrey scrunched up her nose. "In Olde English, *wyrd* means fate or destiny."

"So, that's not the question I asked."

"Yes, I feel funny. I've never tried anything like this, so I don't know what to expect."

"Expect it to get weird." Roz stepped forward, and as he did, the nostrils of the minotaur exhaled a yellowish gas. The legs swept outward; arms swooped down. Roz looked behind it and saw a long cable connected to its body, extending to the wall behind it.

Audrey sneezed once, then again. "Something in my eyes."

Roz looked back, then at the minotaur. "CS gas. Coming out from the bull's nostrils. Gotta be." The acrid scent and tightness in his chest brought him back to SEAL training.

The obstacle course on San Clemente Island had a section where the sand was full of the chemical. When you crawled through a tunnel, you stirred it into the air.

Audrey rubbed her eyes. "What's CS gas?"

"Tear gas. Don't rub—it'll make it worse. Just when I'm starting to see again," Hark grumbled.

The minotaur snorted, sending another jet of gas into the room.

"Okay, time to go." Roz watched the movement of the massive limbs. He tried to time the sweeps of arms and legs, and almost succeeded.

Almost.

One of its legs swung out. Roz barely got the Aegis up before the massive kick sent him airborne. He hit the floor and slid to the wall; the impact stole the breath from his lungs. Audrey ran over, coughing.

"You're supposed to avoid the legs." She palpated his chest. "Nothing seems broken. How does it feel?"

Roz gave her a squinty-eyed, grimacing smile, and a thumbs-up as he struggled to his feet. Another snort from the minotaur. Without another word, Audrey launched herself forward. She moved gracefully, and as the minotaur swung a fist, she dodged to the side and slid past. She got to her feet and let out a whoop, giving an excited wave back at them. Then she peeked out the door and darted out into the main part of the level.

"Brooh!" came the bull sound, and another snort. The dog had an easy time of it, skirting the limbs of the minotaur with nimble ease.

"I'm going to try," Hark laughed manically. "Can't do worse than what you just did." Somehow, the Texan found a break in the pattern of the swings and made it through untouched.

Lucky bastard.

"He's blind, and he's doing better than me," Roz muttered. "And he's trolling me." He tried again. As a hairy, tree-trunk-sized arm came down, he lay prone on the shield like a sled and skidded across the floor, under the swooping paw, and past the doorway.

Way past.

As his momentum carried him out into the open, Audrey yelled something. Roz was dimly aware of Hark and Audrey crouched behind a low wall as he flew past, down into an open area in front of another body of water. Arrows flitted by as he ground to a halt, and he brought up his Aegis just in time to block one. It shivered angrily off the Kevlar shield, knocking it into his face.

Roz scooted back to the low wall. "A little warning would have been nice."

Hark peeked over the edge and ducked as an arrow whisked past.

"Can you actually see?" Roz asked.

"Close enough, amigo. Blurry movement. Halos on everything. Seeing auras, man! Yours is red. You're angry, Feroz."

Roz nodded. "That checks out. What is that ungodly smell?" More sulphur; more decay. Rotten eggs, like month-old water at the bottom of a garbage bin.

"Get it—ungodly? Because we're in Hell," Audrey answered, elbowing Hark.

"Please, leave the punning to me, 'Rey." The psychedelics seemed to have infected the three of them with a devil-may-care attitude to the dangers posed by the level.

More devil-may-care than usual.

Roz looked at his shield, using the metal edge banding as a mirror to see what was out past the barricade. On the other side of the wall, there was a body of water, and what appeared to be a horse, half-submerged on the banks of the far side. Beyond, on a slightly inclined ridge, a pair of centaurs trotted back and forth, holding giant bows with some sort of reloadable cartridge and mechanism for the arrows.

Audrey stared at him. "Did you just give me a nickname?"

"No. 'Course not." Another arrow smacked into his shield, ripping it from his hands. He snatched it back with a sigh. "Any bright ideas, you two?" he asked.

"We're supposed to ride a centaur across the water. Nessus." Audrey blew snot from her nose, a reaction to the tear gas. "But it's on the other side of the water."

A deep booming echoed around the open space. It pulsed up and down in volume, seeming to come from all directions.

Hark adjusted an arrow on his bow. "*That* can't be good." As discordantly as it began, the noise faded.

Roz sighed. He unslung his pack, handing it to her. "Give this back to me if I'm alive on the other side."

"What are you gonna do?"

"Take those things out. Or die. That's a strong possibility."

She looked at him, the faintest promise of a smile on her lips. "So don't die."

He stared back and nodded. Roz looked at Dio, who watched with quiet intensity. "*Blijf*," he told the hound.

Stay.

Then he sprinted for the edge of the water and dove.

There was a salty, oily viscosity to the liquid that stung the various cuts on his skin. Like sliding into a warm bath. The water was only four feet deep, which he discovered after smacking into the bottom. He hugged it until he reached the other side. Whatever targeting system the centaurs had could not traverse low enough to fire at the water's edge. As the four-legged automatons swiveled to engage him, he moved. The centaurs looked uncanny up close—robotic chassis under Hollywood special effects. He bowled into the first one with the Aegis, sending it tumbling down the ridge into the water, where it promptly sank. Roz blocked a projectile from the other one. As a new arrow moved through the reloading mechanism, he darted forward, grabbed a leg and lifted until it fell over. He located a control panel underneath the chassis and pounded it with the Aegis until the centaur ceased moving. Roz moved down to the submerged horse. Near its neck, he found a manual switch and flipped it. The robot whirred into action, moving across the water toward Audrey and Hark. While he waited for them to load up, Roz turned his attention to the rest of the circle.

A grove of strange and misshapen trees lay ahead, filled with a macabre sound.

CHAPTER 25

Roz—Saturday, 9:15 PM

AUDREY AND HARK CLUNG TO THE SIDES OF THE CENTAUR as it crossed the water. Dio doggy paddled daintily nearby.

Roz pointed at the trees when they came within earshot. "What are we looking at here?"

Audrey handed him his pack. "The Seventh Circle of Hell is for the Violent. It contains three subcomponents. The outer ring houses murderers who committed violence against others and property. The middle is for those who chose suicide—violence toward themselves. The final and inner ring houses blasphemers and sodomites, those who were violent toward God, art, and nature."

"So, if that was the outer ring," Hark said, gesturing back the way they came, "this part is…suicides?"

Audrey nodded, giving a flip with her spear that looked practiced.

"Were you a baton twirler or something?" Roz asked.

"Something," she answered, gesturing with an arm for him to enter the woods.

"That's it. That's how you paid for college, wasn't it? But you don't want to talk about it because you're humble."

Audrey rolled her eyes, shaking her head slowly. "'Rey will not dignify that with a response."

They walked into the grove. It was thicker than Roz expected. He couldn't see the end. Easy to get disoriented. Dio trotted along, snout to the earthen floor. A keening pierced the air, then another, and another, until the sound grew and braided itself into a mournful susurration. Talking was difficult. He looked closer at the trees, found humanoid faces bulging from the bark, locked in expressions of pure horror. Dante's idea of what happened if you committed suicide. Roz wondered if he would have ended up in a place like this if he'd taken the jump from the bridge all those months ago. Back then, he'd just wanted the pain to stop. These folks probably felt the same.

Dio oriented to one side, ears on high alert. Above the wailing, Roz detected a familiar buzzing in the air. More drones.

Getting really tired of these things.

Barely had time to form the thought when the first of them burst through the trees. Like the Furies from Heresy, but smaller.

More like faeries.

He bashed the first with his shield, sending it skittering away. Dio growled, and Audrey slashed her spear into another. Hark swung his bow, keeping a third at bay.

Roz led them in a race through the woods. After a tense few moments where he was certain they were lost, the trees ended and transitioned into a sandy flat. Searing hot air smacked them in the face in pulsing waves. On the far wall of the level, twenty yards away, a ten-foot plume of water cascaded down in front of a darkened pool. As they sprinted across the sand, Audrey yelped as glowing flakes landed on her from a pair of blazing, ceiling-mounted bellows. The faeries remained in the woods. Roz staggered to a halt in front of a small, rusty sign, driven into the sand. He read the slender cursive script aloud.

"Sacrifice something of real value to the waters, in order to proceed."

Roz peered into the pool. At the bottom, he could see a bracelet, watch, and a small dagger. He looked at the others. "Any ideas?"

Audrey pulled her scarf off her face, slowly unwinding it. "No more hiding." She dropped it unceremoniously into the depths.

Hark fished a skeleton key from his pocket. Tossed it into the waters. "Something best left in the past," was all he said.

The two of them looked at Roz. After deliberating, he pulled a seashell-encrusted string off his neck. "Last thing my daughter made for me. First grade." He flipped it into the water. It plummeted into the liquid to join the other pieces of their past.

The group stood in silence, with no sound save the murmur of the waters and the faint wails from the suicide trees. The moment felt holy almost, like a benediction.

Then, from the dark opening next to the waterfall came a churning groan of metal, and a long, cylindrical shape slithered into view. A set of rails led upward, into a shadowy tunnel.

"Geryon, the snake," Audrey murmured in fascination.

"I HAVE BEEN SUMMONED TO FERRY YOU TO THE EIGHTH CIRCLE," boomed a voice from speakers mounted on the walls high above. "CLIMB ABOARD AND STRAP IN."

Audrey found a ladder on the side and clambered up to discover a roller coaster-like sitting area. Dio scrabbled up with Roz's help and sat at Audrey's feet.

"You first, broham," Hark said, looking back across the circle. "You know, this thing is supposed to be nine levels. But they don't count the woods and purgatory. So, it's really eleven. False advertising, if you ask me."

"Nobody asked you," Roz replied as he climbed up. "Shut up and get on the snake train, old man." He snapped his seat belt into place.

Just then, a flock of the faery drones burst from the wood, making a beeline for the opening.

Hark turned to face the new onslaught, setting his feet to meet them, swinging the bow like a sword. He sent several of the drones crashing into the sand. Geryon began to move. Roz tried to unbuckle, but there was a lock on the seat belt. As the train gathered speed, he pulled out a knife and hacked through the nylon. Hark bellowed, and Roz leaped to the top of the moving serpent.

Audrey screamed out a warning.

Something hit Roz's shoulder, knocking him off balance. He fell from the train.

The last thing he heard was Hark call his name, echoing off the concrete walls of the tunnel.

JUSTINE STOOD, CORPSE STILL. She stared at the video feed on the flatscreens at the front of the room. Harkness swarmed by drones in high-definition. Drones *she* should be in control of. For every one he struck down, two more seemed to take their place, like the Hydra of old. They were supposed to be a window dressing for the levels, an aesthetic trifle that was never intended to be perverted for such a purpose. To hurt and kill. An unlit cigarette dangled from her bony fingers. Justine had gotten it from one of her drivers. She badly wanted to light it. She could, if she wanted. No one would say a word. But it wasn't about flicking the gorgeously dried tobacco flakes into combustion. As the primary caretaker of the foundation, it was her job to set the example and chastise departures from that policy. Right at the moment, she desperately wanted to grant herself an exception to policy.

The damage from the building attack turned out to be minimal. The thought of what might come next, the uncertainty, filled her with greater worry. She looked over at the men and women in the operations center. So young. So talented. A flashing notice in the corner of her monitor drew her attention.

"Rena. What is it?" Justine looked over at the French woman, who seemed to be distressed by something. She always looked so fashionable, a simple yet distinct sense of style different from most of the other women in the operations center.

Rena brushed a wisp of hair from her face and cycled through the screens on her monitor. "*Mierde.* Hazel, could you please rewind the beginning of Violence footage and playback on screen two?" After a few moments, the video appeared on one of the big screens. "It's Gabrielle, Ma'am." She pointed up. "She just sent out a social media post."

"I thought we were spoofing her from another location?"

"We are. Or rather, we were. But this is coming from within the Plek building."

Justine imagined taking a drag from her cigarette, exhaling a white cloud toward the ceiling. Watching the smoke spiral and drift in the air currents. "*Mierde* indeed."

"Here's the post itself," Jarvis called, gesturing with a finger to another screen.

A shaky video began—the phone held by Gabrielle's hand. The robot centaurs paced in the background. Next to her, Grady waved a pistol. "Hey beautiful people, it's me. As you can see, I'm trapped in some kind of nightmarish *Squid Game* scenario. I call upon all of you to join me downtown. Right now. There is a great alignment underway, a nexus point of cosmic energies. It's all going down at 140 Montgomery Street. Come down. It will be wild. Promise."

Justine put her hands on the table and gazed at the team. "Can someone explain to me how these people got electronics and firearms? And now that they've disqualified themselves—"

"Actually—" One of her lawyers interrupted from the other side of the circle. Vanessa something. "The rules as written and agreed to forbid selectees from *bringing* firearms and electronics into the tower. They don't actually say anything about possession of them *once inside*."

Justine pushed down the rage and frustration and worked to keep it out of her words.

"What are our options?"

Her staff digressed into a flurry of heated, micro discussions.

Dmitri raised a hand. "We can shut down the Wi-Fi if we need to."

Justine squinted at him. "Explain yourself. What do you mean?"

He swallowed and maneuvered his wheelchair out into the center to address the group.

"We built the tower infrastructure to respond to this sort of scenario. It will degrade our monitoring capability—we'll be relying on the hard wires running from the building to the ops center here, instead of the mesh repeaters throughout the tower. But we can do it. And if we put the EM, the ah, electro-magnetic sheath up, her device will lose connectivity to the outside cellular towers and wireless networks in adjacent buildings."

Justine considered. Choices and tradeoffs. Another of Nicky's aphorisms: *Pick your poison and drink it, mon cherie,* he used to say in an exaggerated French voice. That was the rub, though. Which poison was the least lethal? It was always so hard to tell. "Do it," she ordered finally, with a conviction she didn't feel.

"And Ma'am, this last story she posted is getting a good deal of engagement." Rena pulled up the social media feed on a big screen.

Justine set the unlit cigarette on the table in front of her. "Can you do anything to alter the video now? Can we take it down with her phone—the one we have in our possession?"

Jarvis raised his hand again. "Ma'am, I have a few friends at Instagram, and I know my way around their systems decently enough. We *could* do it, but at this point that is going to make it worse. Red meat for all the conspiracy theorists. Gasoline on the fire."

"Okay, I don't care about all the details. Throw enough chaff out to get us through until sunrise. If she makes it through, we'll cook up a story to explain it—a reality-show audition or something. If she doesn't…"

"We'll come up with a different story," Rena finished.

Justine nodded. "Chaff, people. Another few hours of

chaff. People will move on to the next shiny object after a media cycle or two."

"Isn't chaff flammable?" Rena asked.

"We're about to find out," Justine answered.

"Can we talk in your office?" Kathy stood before her; a set of folders cradled in her arms. Justine nodded and they walked out the back of the ops center. She felt the eyes of other staffers as they departed.

"What is so important we need to speak in private?" Justine leaned against her desk once inside. She felt exhausted—sore back, tight neck, and a light yet growing headache. She needed a nap.

"I'm just going to say it. I believe that we have someone—someone *inside* the ops center—reporting to Laughlin Carmichael. Someone definitely slipped the phone and guns to the Corsteads. Likely at the food and drink station between the Sixth and Seventh Circles. The same someone that engineered a back door into our system."

"How long were you planning on sitting on this information? Do you have a suspect list?"

Kathy paused. "I needed to be sure before I came to you." She handed Justine a folder. "I've narrowed down five possibilities. Those who had the access and placement."

Justine considered. Since coming onboard a year previously, Kathy had established herself as a savvy judge of both character and context. Despite her youth, she read the room like no one Justine had ever seen. Finally, she nodded. "Okay. Let's monitor them for now."

Kathy pursed her lips. "Agreed."

"Is that it?"

"For now, Ma'am."

"Very well. We can't let the process derail at this point."

Kathy fiddled with a ring she wore on her right hand.

"Are we sure they have to finish selection? Can't we call it good as it is and get them out of there?"

Justine nodded and moved a stray lock of silvery hair out of her eyes. "I know. It's a lot of time, money, and blood to find the heirs to Nicky's fortune. But I owe it to him to carry out the process as he intended. It sounds hyperbolic, but the fate of the world may rest on the results."

"I don't think it's hyperbolic at all. We need leaders to rise. The moment demands it."

"Besides," Justine said with a wry smile, "we're so close."

Kathy nodded and followed her from the office.

CHAPTER 26

Audrey—Saturday, 10 PM

There is in Hell a vast and sloping ground called Malebolge,

a lost place of stone as black as the great cliff that seals it round.

Precisely in the center of that space there yawns a well extremely wide and deep.

I shall discuss it in its proper place.

The border that remains between the well-pit and the great cliffs forms an enormous circle,

and ten descending troughs are cut in it,

offering a general prospect like the ground that lies around one of those ancient castles

whose walls are girded many times around by concentric moats.

And just as, from the portal, the castle's bridges run from moat to moat to the last bank;

so from the great rock wall across the embankments and the ditches,
high and narrow cliffs run to the central well,
which cuts and gathers them like radii.
Here, shaken from the backs of Geryon, we found ourselves.
My Guide kept to the left and I walked after him.
Inferno, Canto XVIII

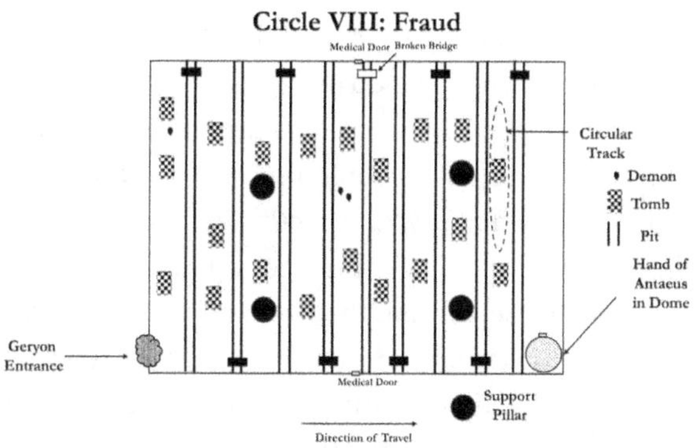

GERYON WAS TERRIFYING.

The journey, lashed on its back in the darkness, seemed much longer than the minutes it took in actuality. The tracks led on a twisting helix of a pathway around the outer periphery of the building. Audrey realized this must have been the sound they all heard, inside the Violence level.

Geryon passed flaming vistas of demons, fire blowing strongly enough to scorch hair. Prompted dark memories, best left forgotten. They had to be getting close to the top of the building. She tried to do the math in her head about how far they had ascended. As she was working, the upward grade of the tunnel flattened. At last, Geryon slowed—groaned to a stop with a shriek of sparking metal on metal. The seat restraints came loose at some unseen trigger.

Diogenes jumped down. He took off back down the tunnel like a rocket, through a gap between Geryon and the wall. Though Audrey's frame was petite, the space was too small for her to fit.

She stared at the bizarre vista in front of her. The Eighth Level was a long line of ascending tiers. It must take up at least six floors of the skyscraper. Maybe more. As with the other levels, four support columns broke the perfect openness of the space. The tiers reminded her of rice paddies built into the slopes of a steep hill. In *The Inferno*, these were supposed to be ten concentric rings, descending toward the bottom of Hell. Barricades and small structures littered the tiers, and she caught movement on several terraces. She couldn't make out who, or what exactly, was moving.

"Well, well, well, look who it is," came a voice from across the ten-foot ravine separating the first and second tiers. The Corstead twins looked at her smugly. Tau was nowhere in sight. Gabrielle filmed her with a phone, and Grady held a gun. As the weapon came up, Audrey broke into a run. A round spanged into Geryon, showering her with dark flecks of paint and metal. She flinched and ran down the terrace, seeking cover.

"Watch out for the demons!" Grady's words echoed mockingly against the walls as she fled.

ROZ LAY ON A BED. He recognized the place. It was the bedroom of the house they used to rent in Coronado. A cozy little mission-style bungalow, built for a different time. Bella jumped on the bed. She was three, maybe four years old. That put this moment before Iraq. Before it all went to shit. She grew up so fast. He was busy deploying overseas. Bella was busy growing up. Roz knew he wasn't here. Not really. But he didn't want to leave the moment. He wanted to linger in the memory for as long as he could.

A shame you couldn't recognize the good old days until they were well in the rear-view mirror.

"Daddy, Daddy! Jump, Daddy, jump!" Bella yelled, pulling on his hand.

He seemed frozen, glued in place, watching her hair fly up and down as she bounced into the air.

"Daddy, get up! GET UP!"

Like a battleship pulling away from a pier berth, Roz willed himself into movement. When he did, the bedroom vision faded from his sight. It was as if motion in the dream banished it. Cloaked in the murk of the tunnel, he saw light in the distance. Struggled to his feet. Staggered forward, relying on blind, bone-deep instinct. He had the Aegis from Iraq in his hand—the one that took a round for him in Sadr City.

Now it streamed back to him—like an ancient computer booting up.

Berenger. Selection. Hark. Hark!

He broke into a shambling run.

Christ, his head hurt.

Like there was a little pixie in there swinging a hammer and chisel. Roz found Hark at the opening. A scattering of destroyed drones lay on the floor around his collapsed and broken form. Two still lurked nearby, and he savaged them with his shield, heedless of fragmentation damage to himself.

Then he shook his friend softly, assessed his wounds. Blood everywhere. Hark had applied one tourniquet to his arm and tried to apply another to his leg before passing out. Roz cranked that one tight, which prompted a groan and a grimace from the Texan.

"Hey," Hark croaked, staring up through squinted eyes.

"Let's get you over to the medical doors—maybe they're unlocked by now," Roz said, pulling off Hark's pack. "I know you packed a Matbock litter in here somewhere. Probably under this useless HEEDs bottle."

"You never know," Hark husked out, "when it could come in handy."

"Here it is." Roz pulled the litter out. He was still woozy from the hit that he took on Geryon and put a hand on the floor to steady himself. It took long minutes—too long—to set the litter up and drag Hark to the doors—the sand made things easier once he got past the waterfall. Thankfully there was a path through the trees at the edge of the building. Roz pounded on the doors. No response. From his pack, Roz pulled out a small hooligan tool—a tactical crowbar. He jammed it into the seam between the door and the frame near the locking mechanism and pounded it in with the Aegis. With a great shriek of metal, he levered the door open.

Two men were coming up the stairs, no doubt drawn to his pounding. He recognized them as the same two who took Tabitha away.

Seemed like two lifetimes since then.

"I need help!" Roz called.

To their credit, the men rushed across the doorway and grabbed the stretcher.

"No use, amigo… Lost too much… Going hypo… volemic." Hark reached and grabbed his shoulder. "Take my pack… More goodies. Tell Sophie…sorry."

"Negative, old man."

"Get your…shit together…" Hark's arm slid to the ground as consciousness left him.

The men did a rapid evaluation on Hark, grim-faced. Finally, one of the men looked at Roz as they hefted him on the stretcher. "We have an ER doc a few flights down. We'll do our best."

Roz nodded, looking down at his hands, bloody with his brother's blood. He faced back toward the Geryon tunnel as another drone floated up. It didn't have the same aggressive posture as the other ones and stayed out of reach. A tinny voice came out. "Mr. Mehran. Hey, it's Dmitri. Remember me? From the VR pod?"

"Yeah."

"Oh, I can't hear you. This thing doesn't have a microphone. But if you give a thumbs-up, I can see it on the cameras."

Roz held up a middle finger.

"Yeah, cool, cool, cool, that works too. We're in a major cyber battle right now, which sounds like a first-world problem, I get it. I snuck into this little guy, but I don't know how long I can keep control. Anyway, I'm sorry about your friend."

Roz waved a *get to the point* gesture.

"Yeah, okay, okay, I wanted to let you know, the Corsteads and Matamua? They got a cache of stuff from someone—we don't know who yet, but I think we can guess who. I saw pistols and a phone, at least. Not sure what else. I'm sorry that—" The drone lurched, almost falling to the floor before it regained its balance. It froze, regarded him for a moment, then swooped toward him aggressively. He swung his shield like a baseball bat and sent it splintering into pieces.

Roz watched the drone parts rain down to the floor, amidst the fiery flakes from the ceiling bellows.

He'd never thanked Hark for everything he'd done for him.

For introducing him to Dio when he was at his lowest.

All the hours they had spent together—hell, years.

Training trips all over the country, long days in the heat, running and gunning and blowing things up.

And that was *before* they got downrange on deployment.

Closing down bars and keeping each other out of the local jail.

Weddings, birthdays and funerals.

Too many funerals.

They never seemed to end.

He stood up wearily, grabbed a few things from his pack, transferred them to Hark's.

"I'll make them pay, brother. Promise."

Roz shouldered the pack, walked into the tunnel.

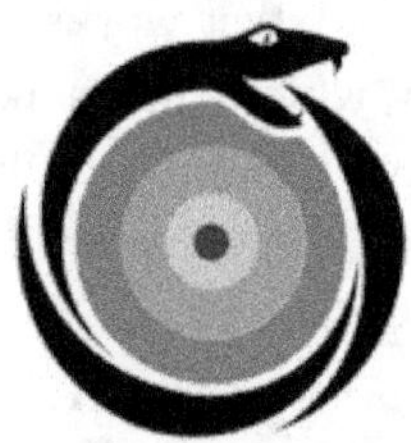

MILENA STABBED HER FORK INTO THE PAD THAI. "Tell me something good," she murmured between mouthfuls. The flight had been smooth, besides that jarring phone call from Bero. Now they were setting up in a 1980's-era airplane hangar. Contra Costa, she thought the airfield was called. Almost entirely deserted, thankfully.

Grace gave her a stressed look. "So, I can give you good news, and some mixed news."

"What's the mixed news?"

Grace took a sip of a drink. Some sort of acai mungberry something or other. "We still can't get into the software code for the level above Treachery. It's a subsystem completely walled off from the rest of the infrastructure. A black hole. They must be running that completely remotely. Our exploit won't give us access."

Milena exhaled, chomped the noodles. Damn, it was good. "Fine. Above Satan is a void. We'll figure it out through the Corsteads. Speaking of, how is that going?"

"Much better. They recovered the cache that the asset so thoughtfully left them. They are now armed and dangerous." Grace's features brightened. "You know what the best part is?"

Milena finished her plate with a satisfied sigh. Pushed it aside. "I'm all ears."

"The documents we've recovered pertaining to the rules of selection say nothing about possessing an electronic device or firearm *after* you enter the tower. It clearly says that you cannot bring one *into* it. But once *inside* the tower, if you happen to find a firearm, it's fair game."

Milena smiled. "So Plek can't disqualify them from selection?"

Grace nodded her head. "Legally speaking, we are in the clear. Or rather, the selectees are."

"Now we just need these two and their hulking companion to pull through. What's this?" Milena pointed to a camera feed.

"That...is Zhou. Barrett is in the VR tank, chasing Zhou with a demon avatar." Grace gestured over at the pod. "Old One-Eyed Willy is faster than she looks."

Milena nodded. "So, either we'll get her with the demons, or the twins will."

"Most likely," Grace hedged. "It's her against the three of them. We took Harkness down on the previous level."

"A shame." Milena looked at the ceiling. "And Mehran?"

"He's a pain in the ass. Still moving—on foot on the tracks between seven and eight. The dog is around there somewhere, too. I'm going to reset the train and see if I can nail him. Worth a try."

Milena's phone vibrated with a message from her husband. "Okay. Go for it. Good luck—he's one tough cockroach to smash." She walked out of the hangar to check it. A video. Maybe it was an old one of the kids—Henry was a junior at James Madison, and Jenny was a freshman at Penn State. Time went by so fast.

It started with a dark screen and a wobbly camera. Elrond was away on a guys' getaway in western Virginia. Last she'd heard, he was day-drinking somewhere on a golf course. "Hey Goon." Close-up shot of his face, part of his shirtless chest. Behind him, the bland monoculture decorations of an upscale hotel room. "Listen, I've wanted to talk to you about this for months. But I could never—could never find the time." He was completely sloshed. Slurring his words. He was having trouble even sitting upright. Blackout drunk. "I'm done, Goon. I can't do it anymore. Look, I stood by you, for every promotion, smile on my face, the loyal hubby. I stayed when you fooled around, again and again. Now the kids are out of the house. We did it, Goon. We raised 'em. You had a brilliant career. But...I don't wanna, I don't wanna live like this anymore. I'll be by next week sometime. Grab some things. But for now, I'm gonna stay away, turn my phone off for a while. See ya." As it cut off, the phone wobbled, and she saw another shirtless man in the background.

Son of a bitch.

With effort, she resisted the urge to hurl her phone into the chilly twilight.

After all this time.

So many miles together, to be betrayed like this.

But she had a job to do.

Milena set her jaw, turned, and walked into the building.

ROZ ZOMBIE-WALKED UP THE SLOPE. The commanding officer of SEAL training when he went through was an old Vietnam vet, a short, thin, unassuming old guy, late 60s. Captain Pete Winfrey. Every time he talked, he sounded so kind. The class called him Mr. Rogers behind the scenes, where the instructors couldn't hear them. It shocked Roz when he found out that the man had three confirmed knife kills in Vietnam. Captain Winfrey used to tell the training classes that the one thing that he looked for, above all else, was the simple ability to put one foot in front of the other. To keep moving forward. Even as the damage and fatigue grew. It was what separated those who finished training from those who did not.

Through the pulsing headache and his bruised body, and whatever strange chemical cocktail he'd ingested, the tendrils of loss snaked skyward from his stomach.

Like some fiendish squid, bent on consuming him.

He stopped and leaned against the wall. Turned away and closed his eyes as hard as he could. It wasn't supposed to be like this.

It should have been him.

The Texan was one of the finest humans Roz had ever

known. The thought of a world without him in it filled Roz with an emotion he didn't have a word to describe. It was both an aching loss and a berserker level of rage that threatened to explode from his battered ribcage.

All the Texan wanted was to help others.

From his time as a pararescueman to the nonprofit he built himself, to keeping Roz from ending his life by giving him that fucking dog.

Diogenes.

He hoped Dio was okay. Probably bouncing along next to Audrey.

Another soul broken by service to the nation. They were alike in that way. He had to find her. He couldn't let the Corsteads have their way with her.

He wouldn't.

He heard it only a few seconds before it arrived, in a storm of wind and sound. Geryon screamed by inches away from him in complete, inky darkness. If he hadn't stopped to rest, he may not have had time to get to safety. He pulled out a water bottle and took a long drink. If the foundation *was* microdosing them in the water and the food, he was long past caring. As the mechanical moan of the serpentine train slowly faded, Roz heard another sound—a quiet, regular clicking. Dio bounded from the darkness. The dog ran up and nearly bowled him over with enthusiasm.

"Hey there." Roz gave him some love. "Don't let this go to your head, but I missed you a little. And I have to tell you something."

The hound stared up at him expectedly.

"Hark is, Hark... He... I think he's gone," Roz finally husked out the words, wiping his face and exhaling raggedly. The dog put his head in his hands, and Roz stroked it gently.

"We have to live for him now, okay? I'm gonna need your help to do that, okay? We need to find Audrey."

Dio's ears perked up at the mention of her name.

Roz tried to recall what he read about the Eighth Level. All the circles blurred together in a mush in his mind, but he remembered something about demons. He thought about his mother—how weak she'd been in those last days. Child-like, confused. His only tether back to Iran, and his life back in L.A. "Run your race, Feroz," she whispered in his ear on one of the final days, while she clutched his face with withered fingers. The smell of wildfires lingered in the air, a touch of brimstone he'd forgotten about until now. Everything he'd done in his life; he'd given it his all. There was a lot that he fell short on—he flunked out of the Naval Academy, Milena outplayed him in Iraq. He failed to see the effect his actions would have on the others in his life. He couldn't fix any of that.

All he could do was take the next step.

With Dio beside him in the tunnel's darkness, Roz took it.

Then another.

And another.

BOOK IV

SUBLIMATION

CHAPTER 27

Roz—Saturday, 11 PM

ROZ GAZED AT THE ROWS AND ROWS OF TERRACES, marveling at their construction. Each looked to be slightly higher than the one before, with a ten-foot pit between them. A gunshot rang out, then mocking laughter echoed from above. He turned to the left, crept toward the end of the terrace, where a footbridge spanned over the gap. Handrails and a long, graceful, U-shaped piece of metal swept into the air above the pit, supporting the bridge. Roz stayed low and skirted around the statues and grave markers. The edge of the floor dropped straight down, fifteen feet, to an open area. From the sheerness of the walls, it didn't look like it would be an easy climb if you fell into one.

From behind a statue, a figure popped out from around a structure. Clad in a long black cloak that covered a hunched back, with a face painted in an ugly leer. Yet another robot, made to look like a demon. Not a terrible job, all things considered. As Roz stared, the face appeared to morph, shifting colors and expressions. Whip in hand, the demon advanced in a steady, purposeful gait. Dio growled.

"Feroz," it said in a flat monotone voice. "I was hoping Geryon got you. Sorry about your friend. He definitely took one for the team there."

Roz sidestepped to put a four-foot-high tombstone between them. "You got a name? You know mine, after all. So I can look you up after I get out of here."

The rictus-like expression on its face did not change, but the demonic robot wagged a finger at him. "Come now, Mr. Mehran. Surely you don't expect me to answer that. Besides, you're not getting out of here. This is the end of the line for you."

He stared stonily into the demon's eyes. "Is Milena there, wherever you are?"

Silence.

"Who is Milena?" it finally replied, after ten long seconds. It flexed an arm, and the whip flashed out. Roz ducked and held the Aegis out to parry the strike. Roz closed the distance, slipped behind it. Gave a vicious shove. The demon plummeted to the abyss below.

It clambered to its feet and looked up. "Don't worry, there's more of me to play with. See you around." The demon gave him a jaunty wave.

Roz crossed the first bridge on faded wooden planks and walked into an invisible wall of filth. Manure crossed with other rancid odors that he'd rather not identify. The funky smell motivated him to keep moving. Still no sign of human life, but he couldn't see far. Each of the twenty-foot-wide levels seemed to have different objects that blocked a full sight line. The fourth terrace featured mannequins buried face up, their heads on backwards. Moans of pain pumped from hidden speakers. The abyss between terraces four and five held black water, steam rising from the surface. Dio growled. Humanoid shapes writhed in the dark liquid, and Roz didn't feel like lingering. They kept going.

On the fifth terrace, a pair of demons barred their path. They moved in a haughty creep and separated to flank him.

"Milena!" he yelled, smashing into the first one before it could lash the whip, knocking it down.

The second landed a blow, and fire spread across his back, like the thrashing flail of a jellyfish tentacle. Cursing creatively, Roz knocked the demon down. He pulled the whip from its hands. Tested it. Not bad. Pushed it into the nearest pit.

The bridge between the fifth and sixth terraces was gone. Not completely—the planks and the handrails littered the floor of the pit, but the U-shaped strut still arced over the abyss. He looked at the strut.

"Hmm." Roz flicked the whip out. It hit the span and glanced off. Over the next few minutes, he played with the whip, trying to get it attached. He was pretty sure someone had debunked this on the show *Mythbusters*, but he still wanted to try. Once he got it really locked in, he found he could add a last wave of the whip to get the end piece to cross over itself. Roz leaned back with all his weight, and it seemed to hold. "Mind over matter," he mumbled to himself. *If you don't mind, it doesn't matter*—an old saying from SEAL training. He didn't know how he'd fare with the added weight of the pack, but he didn't want to leave any of the items.

Both the whip knot and his grip held on the downswing.

The upswing was another story.

Both the knot and his grip loosened.

Instead of landing on his feet, he slammed into the concrete lip of the terrace.

The "Dirty Name" was an infamous component of the SEAL training obstacle course. A pair of horizontal logs raised high in the air. In order to traverse the obstacle, you hurled your midsection into them in a bold leap. Back when he was a young, pipe-hitting Frogman, he used to run the obstacle course wearing body armor. Once, as he negotiated the Dirty Name, his impact smacked the bottom ridge of the Kevlar plate into his chest so hard that it bruised his ribs for weeks. This impact felt much the same. His vision strobed with white flashes as he gasped for air and tried to keep from falling into the pit. Through the agony, he levered a leg up, then rolled to his back on the concrete. The knot unfurled and fell down from the strut, and he gingerly reeled it out of the abyss.

"That's gonna leave a mark," he gritted.

He looked up just in time to see Diogenes sprint at full speed at the gap, launching himself into the air. The hound landed and squatted low on his haunches, claws scrabbling to slow his drifting slide.

"Huh. Wish I could do that." Roz made sure his immediate area was clear of any threats before putting his back to a low wall and resting for a few minutes. He probed gently with his fingers, wincing.

"Feroz!" he heard a voice call out. Close by. Grady. He didn't respond. Although Roz yelled out earlier, he realized it was a dangerous proposition now. The Corsteads were armed, and Tau did not look like he would be easy to deal with, even unarmed.

Grady yelled again. "Feroz! Remember that fall you took off the wall? When Cerberus almost ate you for breakfast? That was me, baby." Coming from the next terrace over.

As Roz crept down the sixth terrace, he found a line of mannequins robed in thick material. The attire looked like the lead shawl radiology techs stuck over patients before their X-rays. A low wall and other mausoleums shielded most of the terrace from view. Staying low, he moved from cover to cover. Now he could hear voices but couldn't make out the words.

He and Dio crossed to the seventh terrace.

"Whoa." Roz peered down into the pit between the seventh and eighth terraces, feeling a building dread at the spaghetti-bowl mass of churning reptiles in the pit.

Snakes.

Lots.

They slithered sinuously over one another, coiled, hissed, fought. Roz caught sight of several Komodo dragons as well. The big lizards received a wide berth from the serpents, lying lazily below the footbridge to the next terrace. Only the occasional flick from a tongue revealed they were, in fact, alive. Roz crawled where he needed to stay out of sight.

He sent Dio forward with a command to search and checked the camera feed on his watch. It showed the hound advancing in a bouncing fashion. Then, the camera microphone caught Grady speaking to someone out of sight, on the next terrace.

"Let's go. He's taking forever to get here. Probably fell in a pit. Maybe he can't get over that broken bridge behind us."

"That's fine," Gabrielle answered. "We can still bring her as an insurance policy. Tau found a path up, and our friends have opened the medical stairs for us. Straight shot to the top."

He slid between the small buildings, narrowing the distance to the voices. Got close enough to make out the words.

"Alright, let's get going, two-face. You get to stay alive a little longer." Grady stood up and glanced down the alley that Roz was creeping, saw him. "He's here!" Grady yelled.

But Roz was already in motion, sprinting with the Aegis

up. Grady fired the pistol and Audrey dropped to the ground. Roz felt two rounds snap past him, and a third spanged off the shield. Then Roz was on him, bowling into Grady, knocking him to the ground. He had no interest in staying on his feet with a Muay Thai guy. His midsection made its displeasure known.

It felt like a vindictive donkey had settled in to tap Morse code on his chest.

Roz struggled to breathe, but adrenaline gave him a shot of biochemical help, providing both strength and pain relief. Nature's hormonal boost, just when he needed it.

Roz fought for control of the pistol and dodged a vicious knee to the groin. He could hear Gabrielle yelling, but it was all he could do to fend off Grady's attack. Roz couldn't draw a decent breath.

Have to end this quick.

Back to the abyss, Roz clambered to his feet. Took grips on Grady's shirt and spun him into a judo *Seo Nage*. He flew through the air, landed in a sprawl on the ground behind Roz.

Then Grady slipped and toppled backwards, into the pit.

From the other terrace, Gabrielle screamed.

He seemed dazed by the impact. The snakes scattered at his sudden appearance, but one of them lunged, striking Grady as he called out for his sister. Roz leaned over to watch. It was hypnotic—the snakes converged on Grady, bit him, and moved away. At certain points, it was difficult to tell where Grady ended, and the snakes began. They appeared to be morphing together, into one another. A Komodo roused itself from its torpor and ambled toward him, its flicking tongue questing the air for his scent. Roz watched as the reptile closed in on Grady. Gabrielle fired, but not at Roz. She hit Grady at least once in the head. Roz slumped down to his knees behind the cover of a tombstone, working to get air into his lungs.

Audrey crawled over. "Let me see." She lifted his top garment to examine his chest.

"There. Are. Easier. Ways. To. Get. Under. My. Shirt," Roz gritted. Audrey shushed him and felt all around the injury. Together, they watched Gabrielle move off.

"Bad news—looks like one, maybe two cracked ribs, from the bruising. Have you had those before?"

Roz nodded. "Who. Hasn't?" he husked out.

"You will not be running any marathons soon."

"Who. Wants. To. Run. Marathons?"

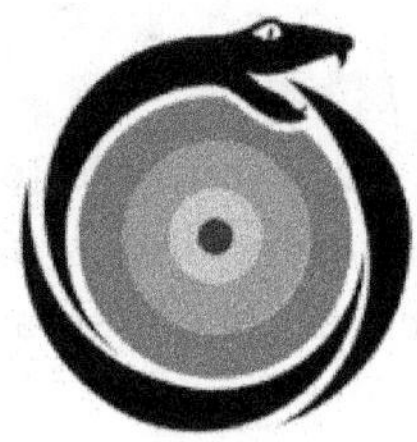

THEY WALKED THROUGH FIRE.

Columns of flames sprang from the ground on the eighth terrace. Audrey told him that these metaphorically represented the "false counselors," which Roz interpreted as either Jerry Falwell evangelist types, or maybe Bernie Madoff-style investment advisors. Either way, it was hard to see ahead with all the flames. After crossing the footbridge, they encountered a circular track, running in a long oblong oval on the terrace. Groupings of backpack-wearing mannequins slid around the tracks in a repeating pattern. On one side, whips cracked from static, demonic statues and flayed them as they passed.

"What are we looking at here? Not that it matters. If it's not trying to kill us, I am out of fucks," Roz said, gesturing with a hand and wincing at the motion. Every movement hurt. It hurt to breathe, let alone move. "But these things are in our way."

Audrey stared at the figures clacking by. They were moving too fast to stop safely. An area next to the swinging whips drew her eye. A small generator.

"I wonder if there's a—" Roz began. But Audrey had already slammed her spear into the chain mechanism. Sparks erupted, and the generator whined in a high pitch. She pulled the spear out with a smile.

"Control panel," Roz finished, as he gestured at the panel.

Audrey undid a backpack from one of the mannequins. "Looks like they're all the same." Inside each pack was a hazmat suit, complete with full face hood with a scrubber canister.

"The tenth *malebolge* was supposed to have plague elements," Audrey said.

They each grabbed a pack and moved forward now that the path was clear.

Diogenes scampered along, tongue lolling. Ever the irrepressible optimist, the hopeless romantic.

After crossing the last footbridge, they found a greenhouse-like dome, its interior obscured by mist. To the right lay the medical stairs. Roz tried them. Locked.

At the dome, they suited up in front of an airlock. "Dio can stay here until we figure this out," Roz said. The hound wasn't happy to be separated from the pair, but he patiently sat and watched as they sealed the airlock from the inside. Within the dome, a dim light strobed in the mist, and the whine of electronics filled the air. They moved in. A keypad stood on a pole at the center of the dome, the source of the flashing light.

"Another code. What do we think the number is?" Roz asked in a muffled voice.

"Dante was a fan of 2, 3, 5, 7, and 10. It's likely some combination of those," Audrey answered.

"But how many, and what order?" He peered at the keypad, looking for something, anything, that could help them figure it out.

"And what happens if we get them wrong?"

"My vote is for a *Goonies*-style scenario where the floor falls out, one bit at a time."

"What's a Goonie?"

Roz shook his head at her in weary disappointment. "I won't even dignify that with a response."

Audrey got to work. She tried a six-digit combo, but the screen reset after three numbers. She tried two other combinations before the one that caused the airlock doors to hiss open. "Three, seven, nine." Her voice was muffled and distorted by the mask and hood. "He was obsessed with trinities of things, seven for seven deadly sins, and nine for nine levels of Hell. Easy."

Roz stared, gave a slow clap. A compressor kicked on under the floor. The mist sucked into vents at their feet. As it cleared, a stone, ten-foot-wide hand became visible on the floor.

The dome slowly retracted downward. The air seemed fine, and he prayed that the venting had done whatever it needed to do. Dio scampered in, happy to be reunited. They shucked out of the suits.

"The hand of *Antaeus*. Supposed to bring Dante and Virgil to the Ninth Circle in the palm of his hand."

"So, talk to the hand?"

Audrey grimaced. "Is there a point of delirium where you will stop making these sorts of comments?"

Roz considered soberly. "The delirium actually improves them."

They climbed onto the hand.

CHAPTER 28

Roz—Easter Sunday, 12:30 AM

If I had rhymes as harsh and horrible as the hard fact of that final dismal hole

which bears the weight of all the steeps of Hell,

I might more fully press the sap and substance from my conception;

but since I must do without them, I begin with some reluctance.

For it is no easy undertaking, I say, to describe the bottom of the Universe;

nor is it for tongues that only babble child's play.

But may those Ladies of the Heavenly Spring who helped Amphion wall Thebes,

assist my verse, that the word may be the mirror of the thing.

O most miscreant rabble, you who keep the stations of that place whose name is pain,

better had you been born as goats or sheep!

Inferno, Canto XXXII

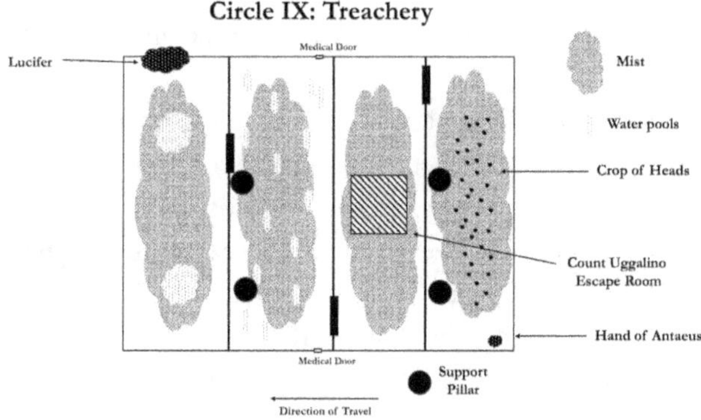

THE TITAN'S PAW CLANKED UPWARD.

Up, up, up.

Toward the last level.

Treachery.

Roz ached in a dozen spots—from fighting the dogs, wolves, falling off the wall, deathtraps, demons, fires, cold, drones, more demons, and general exhaustion.

Audrey put her head on his shoulder. She smelled vaguely of a flowery soap. Clean, even after the ordeals.

He put an arm around her.

They didn't speak for a while, content to linger in the moment as the hand ascended.

Toward whatever waited for them there.

"I'm sorry about Hark," she said finally.

Roz nodded. He patted the hound's head with his other hand, stroked the bedraggled fur. They felt the air change. Colder. Their breath plumed in front of them in the dim light, revealing itself as ephemeral white wisps before vanishing.

A wide expanse opened on either side, and the hand ground to a stop. The final level of selection was perhaps four stories in height. A chill mist drifted on the floor.

"Four rounds in the Ninth Circle," Audrey said. "Four different flavors of traitors. Against kin, country, guests, and master."

The immediate area was bare, save the mist. It lay on the floor like a soft carpet, obscuring everything below their knees. Diogenes snorted, pawing his nose.

"I'm gonna say, we go there?" Roz pointed toward an opening on the far side of the chamber.

Audrey nodded, shivering in the chilly air.

Roz dug out a beanie from his pack, gave it to her. "Always have a beanie. One of my life mottos."

"Thanks," she replied with a grateful yet puzzled expression. "That's a weird thing to have a motto about."

"Oh, this is not just any sort of beanie. It has a handcuff key and a straight razor sewn into the lining."

"Have you ever used it?"

"No."

"Has anyone you know ever used it?"

"Not yet."

"Seems excessive, but somehow on brand for you."

"It only takes once." Roz's foot brushed against something, and he peered down. He kicked to clear the fog and flinched when the clear air revealed a human head. As he looked closer, he realized it wasn't real. It certainly looked and felt the part. The eyes blinked, and the mouth opened and closed in a motorized fashion. He showed it to Audrey, and they discovered they were among a field of the heads, spread out toward the entrance to the next section of the level.

"Disturbing," Audrey said.

"Yeah."

Dio sniffed at them but was otherwise unbothered. By exploring left and right, they found an open path that wound through the field of heads, curving slowly to the opening.

The next section of the level was similarly blanketed in mist, but with no heads. No macabre harvest.

They were halfway through the next section when it happened.

Steel bars shrieked into the air from beneath the mist, trapping the three of them.

When the bars reached well above their heads, a large section of the floor rose beneath them. As the bars reached the ceiling of the circle, a trapdoor in the floor opened, and they plunged into a chamber below.

The door closed smoothly with a pneumatic hiss, sealing them inside.

A combination lock on the inside of the trapdoor kept them from opening it, and the material was too fortified to pry open. They found themselves in a study. A gas fire blazed in a stone hearth, ringed by sitting chairs. Bookshelves ringed the walls, and a writing desk squatted in the corner, next to a full-size bust of an ancient figure, clad in clothing, hat, and glasses. Several mannequins in eerie likenesses of dead humans lay on the floor. Bar-filled windows revealed they were at least two stories in the air, above the misty floor.

"'Welcome to my parlor,' said the spider to the fly. It's so nice to see you again, Rozzy." The voice seemed to come out of the walls.

Milena.

They put themselves back-to-back and examined the room. Dio sniffed at the mannequins, snorted in what had to be canine disgust.

"No doubt you are familiar with the tragic story of Count Uggalino of Pisa. Locked in his tower with several of his sons, for political miscalculation. He backed the wrong horse. A tale as old as time. And here we think cancel culture is bad today... With no food, they starved to death. In *The*

Inferno, Dante hints Uggalino ate some of his sons before finally starving himself."

Roz moved a chair to stand on and examined the lock on the trapdoor.

"Now, now, Rozzy, let's not get ahead of ourselves. Let me explain the rules, start the countdown."

Audrey and Roz exchanged glances. Dio moved over to the bookshelf, got low. His hair stuck up, and a low growl came out of his throat.

"I'll be square with you—you figure out the clues, I'll let you get out. I won't mess with that. Keep it like old Saint Nicky B. wanted it."

"I wondered when we were going to hear from you." Roz fiddled with his watch.

"Sticks and stones. Is it nice to hear from an old friend?"

"All my friends are gone."

"Ah yes. My condolences for Hark. He went down swinging. Literally. Didn't look good, last time I saw him. But Ms. Zhou seems like a delightful new acquaintance."

"What's the matter, Milena? Can't find good help these days? Your idiot brigade couldn't get me the first two times you sent them for me. Maybe you should see if there's any other task force folks on the open market."

Silence. "What are you talking about? I did no such thing."

"You know, the ones that followed me and attacked me. Attacked us at Hark's. Your assistant put them on my scent."

Silence.

He paused. "Are you serious? You expect me to believe Grace did that without telling you? What about murdering the other selectees? Are you going to deny that, too?"

Longer pause. Finally: "We only approached selectees with job offers, like we gave Audrey. No hit squads. Apparently with the exception of the one Grace sent against you."

Roz exhaled heavily, stared up at the camera mounted in

a ceiling corner. "Whatever. You mentioned rules? And a countdown."

"All business this fine Sunday morning, are we? Fine. There are a series of clues, hidden in the items inside sad Count Uggalino's chamber. Think of it as a fun date night for the two of you. Ten minutes and counting, before the tower goes under the floor again. If you get out, great. Bully for you. If you don't, the room will become your tomb. I mean, you could eat the dog first, then contemplate eating each other. Probably run out of water first. Your call. Either way, it should be fun to watch. May the odds ever be in your favor, Rozzy Bear."

Audrey made a face at him as the tower shuddered slowly down at a glacial yet constant pace. "Your adulterous ex-lover seems nice."

"*Murderous* and adulterous." The carpeted floor shook with vibration. He looked around. Pictures on the walls. Shelves filled with old tomes. Writing desk. Sofa.

So much to go through.

Too much.

"Okay, 'Rey, you're the Dante expert. What do you think?"

"No idea."

Roz looked at the statue. "Who is this?"

Audrey stared at it, then her eyes widened in recognition. "That's Dante himself. I didn't recognize him because he's never depicted with glasses."

Roz pulled the glasses off the statue. In the flickering light, they had a pinkish hue. He put them on. Roz walked around the room, looking at various objects with them on and off.

"Whoa," he murmured. "Check it out." He held out the glasses.

Audrey took them and looked where he gestured. A

picture of a man in red, in between a hellish tower and an old city. "This is Dante in Florence," she murmured. "But his book... There are details here that differ from the normal painting. The letters in his book are different when you look through the glasses. It says...*ombre della prima opera*. Shadows of the First Work."

"First work, first work... Like first book, like the bible?"

Audrey shook her head. "No, the Gutenberg bible wasn't until the 1450s. Inferno was written in 1300 or so."

Roz looked out the window, gauging the pace of their descent. "What do we know about his other stuff, besides the *Divine Comedy*?"

She told him the title, and they both spent a minute poring through the bookshelves. "Here!" she exclaimed triumphantly. "*La Vitta Nuova*. This was the first thing he published." She turned it over and over in her hand. "His first work."

Roz stood over by one of the flickering fake torches. "Toss it here." The tower ground down, down, down. The floor of the Treachery level was nearly even with the windows.

He held the book up to the light, swiveling the musty volume in all directions. When he had its spine towards the light, he found that two letters cast out onto the wall, in flickering dark patterns. "B P."

"B P, B P, B P..." Audrey murmured. "Beatrice Portinari! His love!"

"Over here," Roz said, pointing to a painting of three women and a man, standing next to a canal in a medieval city.

Without a word, Audrey felt the painting, fingers stopping at something. She dug her fingers into the center woman's midsection, where she held a flower. Roz watched with amazement as she pulled out a bracelet with a small charm on it. She looked closer at it.

"Ruggeri!"

He jumped up onto the chair and entered the name on the keypad. The trap door clicked open.

Boom.

From the bookcase came a pounding sound.

Boom.

Roz boosted Diogenes through the opening.

BOOM!

The bookcase splintered apart. A golem-like figure stood in the wreckage.

"Heeere's Johnny!" Milena's sardonic tones clearly came through a speaker on the robot. This one was made up to look like a ghoulish medieval noble.

"Count Uggalino," Audrey whispered as it shambled toward them. Roz boosted her up, then jumped himself. He was almost out when a stiff hand enclosed his calf in a vise-like grip.

"Another few pounds of pressure and I can pulveri—" Milena began, but she broke off her taunting when Diogenes leapt onto the Count's chest, knocking the robot backwards. The golem lost its grip on Roz's leg and Audrey pulled him all the way out. Before he could climb back in, the trap door slid shut in his face, trapping Diogenes inside. Roz pounded frantically, searching for a way to open it from the outside. The door was flush with the floor and offered nothing to find purchase on.

"Help me!" he called out, voice taut with panic riding just under the surface. Audrey didn't answer, her posture still.

Roz looked up.

A stone-faced Tau loomed above him. Behind his slab of muscles, Gabrielle smirked and aimed a pistol his way.

FROM HIS PARKING SPOT ON THE STREET, Barrett surveyed the west face of the Plek building. He watched the crowd gather in the physical world, even as he tracked their progress in the virtual one. On social media, the various strands of Gabrielle's following coalesced around the consensus she was held against her will and needed the help of her fandom. Close enough to the truth, the lifeblood of any good propaganda. Her primary audience was the nexus of upper-class yoga devotees and those sucked too deeply down the rabbit holes surrounding the wellness movement. Academics used the term "conspiritual"—a combination of conspiracy prone and spiritual. Tonight, they were out in force, ready to support one of their favorite influencers.

The sect of QAnon Barrett wormed his way into was here as well. The two groups had a surprising amount of overlap in beliefs, although it didn't seem obvious on the surface. Both groups were frustrated, mildly confused, and, above all else, angry.

Angry at the system that had failed them, in a myriad of different ways.

And all those emotions demanded a relief valve.

A *Rene Girardian* scapegoat for the rage.

Right now, society was an overpressured system, stressed far beyond the manufacturers' suggested ratings.

Barrett knew at the first sign of trouble, the foundation likely contacted the SFPD. Police cruisers circled the periphery, orbiting the buildings like sharks amid a chum field. A few uniformed units at first. But in short order, they realized the crowd was growing faster than they could contain with available units on duty. Holiday weekend, Easter Sunday, and all that. Barrett was certain that an urgent call went out to bring off-duty officers in from quiet nights with families. The younger, more boisterous ones from outings with friends and dating app connections. At least they'd get overtime, he mused, sipping coffee.

A rap on his window pulled him from his thoughts, slammed him back into the here and now with the abruptness of a splash of cold water. Uniformed policeman, beat cop, one hand resting loosely on his belt. Close enough to his holster. Barrett felt the tension roil up and down his body, fought the urge to go for his own pistol. He inhaled deeply, grinned, rolled his window down. Kept his hands frozen on the steering wheel. Can't make them feel threatened. Lost more than a few friends growing up that way. "Can I help you, officer?"

Nothing to see here, just an upwardly mobile African American businessman waiting for a sales call. At ten PM. On a Saturday night. 24-7 grinding. You know how we do.

"Good evening," the officer responded, sizing Barrett up. "Are you aware you are illegally parked?"

Barrett adjusted his wire-rimmed glasses and affected an embarrassed demeanor. "No, I was not, officer—my deepest apologies. Thank you for bringing that to my attention. I'll move right away."

"Parking garage three blocks that way, if you're interested." The cop gestured vaguely to the south down the street. "Could be a little hazardous out here tonight. Lots of crazies out. Whole world seems like it's gone mad."

"That it does, officer, that it does. Thank you, I appreciate the concern. I'll head toward the parking garage. Have a great night." Barrett beamed a grin at the man one last time, with just a touch of chastised ruefulness thrown in for good measure.

But the policeman was already moving on, canvassing the street.

Barrett turned his attention back to the crowd.

There it was.

The first real altercation went down beyond the posturing and stabbed fingers. An overweight white woman and a rail-thin Black man wearing an enormous cowboy hat began to tussle, hissing venom and slapping one another. The man grabbed the woman's protest sign. A skirmish broke out in earnest between several factions. No doubt the livestreams and video posts would receive massive interaction. That would fan the flames, like a bellows to a blacksmith's forge. He watched both the police and the QAnon folks throw tear gas. Even with an augmented security force and an outer perimeter of law enforcement, it wouldn't be enough. There was no hope of matching the growing intensity and zeal of the mob, a rising river that would shortly crest the levee. The rioters spread out, like water seeking the lowest level. Searching for the most unprotected places in the security perimeter to gain entry to the Plek Foundation building. With a footprint as large as it had, someone was bound to get through. And when they did, they would suck up much of the bandwidth of both Plek's security teams and the police.

A glow blossomed in the early morning light.

Someone had thrown a homemade incendiary device.

He looked back down at his laptop, watching as his supporting assets came online. Barrett had courted the services of several enterprising individuals, each seeking to augment their incomes with a side hustle. You have to love the gig economy. He forwarded them the links to several promising social media feeds. His very own troll farm. The youths would amplify and direct hashtags, trends, and engagement metrics through the use of sock puppet accounts, bots, and virally harnessed vitriol. Already the QAnon threads and vitriolic corners of the internet were having a field day with the event. Videos circulated through the social media ecosystem faster than content monitors could remove them. Besides, why remove them unless they forced you to?

These sock puppets drove the almighty *engagement*—a metric sometimes known as "Time on Site." Eyeballs, comments, likes, shares—the lifeblood of the profit model for these companies.

Good for business, all that stirred-up fear and rage.

Like scratching poison ivy.

It felt so good.

But you ended up in worse shape than when you started.

Off in the distance, he would hear the sweet tones of approaching sirens. A vain attempt to bring order back from the chaos unleashed. Barrett could see a law enforcement command post getting established down the street, where an ambulance and a fire truck backed into an alley to stage. They would earn their money tonight. If Gabrielle made it to the end, none of this would be necessary.

Some wrote books.

Others sculpted.

This, *this* was his art.

His calling.

The canvas where he painted with humans, reveling in the chaos.

Tonight was shaping up to be a great night.

He flicked the window shut and pulled out onto the street.

CHAPTER 29

Roz—Easter Sunday, 1:30 AM

ROZ AND AUDREY TRUDGED IN FRONT OF TAU. After taking their shield and spear, Gabrielle let them keep their packs. She forced them to walk in front through the portal into the next section of Treachery.

"I need some guinea pigs," Gabrielle said as she gestured with the pistol for them to move. "Lab rats to run the remaining parts of this absurd maze. You're it."

Tau said nothing. Held his silence.

"How did you figure out the medical stairs from the eighth level?" Audrey asked.

Gabrielle shrugged. "The gods provided."

It remained freezing in the third round of the Treachery Level. More of the low fog at their feet. After studying the area for long moments, Roz pushed into it, working his way down the wall lengthwise. The entrance to the final section was in the opposite corner.

"That way," Gabrielle ordered, sending Audrey toward the center of the chamber. Roz moved to catch up, and Gabrielle paused to give him some space, gun held in a relaxed but precise posture.

Definite training with that thing.

He gazed down at yet another ghastly sight. Roz wasn't sure why this seemed more bizarre than the mixture of other things they'd encountered over the last thirty hours. Before them, in some sort of hideous crop, were row after row of what appeared to be human bodies, frozen to the floor up to their waists. An eerie chittering flowed across the cavernous space like the fog pooling around their legs. A foulness filled the air, decay, and waste. Years ago, he'd done a "crossing the line" ceremony on a Naval ship, a tradition reserved for crossing the equator for the first time. As part of the process, he'd had to crawl through various trash-filled tunnels and a vat of odious smelling water. The place smelled very similar, a rancid foulness that turned his empty stomach. The wailing rose and fell at an irregular pace. Here and there, there were openings in the frigid floor that revealed water below. The Ninth Circle was supposed to be one large frozen body of water, but Roz doubted the entire thing was water underneath. Maybe the holes were small pools for dramatic effect.

"And here I thought the suicide trees were bad," Audrey murmured. As they watched, some of the figures came to life, articulating their arms in an inhuman fashion. Getting through untouched by the figures would be tricky.

"Alright, this will not get any better the longer we wait." Roz took her hand and together, they walked into the orchard of corpses. He did his best to pick a path through that kept the things from touching them, but sometimes it couldn't be avoided. The exit was just ahead. What could be seen of the final section was shrouded in shadows. Fog swirled out of vents in the walls. It oozed and puddled on the floor, floating languidly in unseen currents. The chittering grew louder as they approached.

"That's far enough, Mehran," Gabrielle called.

Roz was waiting for this.

He knew eventually the benefit of having both of them as trap-sniffers would exceed the risk. Made sense to get rid of him first. There was a small opening in the floor in front of him, a pool rimmed with an icy frost.

"You understand the situation from my vantage point, yes?"

He stared back and slowly nodded. Roz looked down at the water, then up at Gabrielle. Her gun was rock steady, extended. Hammer cocked back so there was even less pressure required to pull the trigger. It wasn't pointed at him, but at Audrey.

"We can finish together, Gabrielle. There's no need to do this. I can still be of use to you."

Gabrielle smiled thinly, licking her lips. "Maybe. But I'm not taking any chances. Look at it this way—you can be reunited with your canine companion earlier than you expected."

Roz turned to Audrey, giving a rueful smile. "Catch you on the flip side."

Audrey glared at Gabrielle, and when she turned to him, her gaze softened. She spoke in low tones. "They implant gills in you guys, don't they?"

"Some of us, yeah. Only the SEAL Delivery Vehicle Team guys. It's an industry secret."

Roz looked at Gabrielle. "What did my tarot card say again?"

Gabrielle smiled. "Chaos and distress, making room for something new. It's one of the few—"

Roz burst into motion. He launched into the air and speared his body down into the watery hole

She cursed and snapped a hastily aimed round.

Roz felt the pain of the bullet impact, and his blood spattered the concrete floor before he disappeared into the frigid, inky water.

JUSTINE DIPPED THE TEA BAG IN AND OUT of the faded porcelain cup. It had a mural of a Mandelbrot set on the side—the fractal, chaotic patterns, and a small chip that was rather sharp if you caught your lip on it. She stayed away from that part. Problem solved. If only her other problems were so simple. The cup was her mother's, one of the few items she had left from a life long gone.

Burned away by hard choices.

The capricious steam coming off the liquid was comforting in its irregularity, as she stared at the camera feeds in the center of the room. They all depicted unrest of varying intensities. One of her people shifted the camera angle on the left, to take in a wider view of the situation. You could see Feroz and Audrey moving ahead of Gabrielle and Tau, who slunk through the fog in the last circle of the tower.

On the middle monitor, real-time social media comments

and posts flew by, as individual accounts spread word of the event to their networks.

The chaos on the right screen was the more troubling one. It was hard to tell from the drone feed, but it appeared to be a crowd of at least several hundred. And it was growing. The police showed little inclination to use force to suppress them. An angry group had a perverse psychology of its own, an emergent overmind. The aggregation of the assembled individuals—what some called an *Egregore*, a non-physical entity that arises from the collective thoughts of a group.

"Ma'am, our internal security forces are launching tear gas," Hazel reported tersely, as they watched the crowd probe the temporary fencing and various barricades. There was a large burst of light, and the crowd scattered back. Even the police retreated as a fire broke out near a section of neatly organized construction equipment.

"Molotov cocktail, thrown by this guy," Rena said, rewinding the feed on her iPad and capturing the frame after enlarging it. "Dark hoodie, mask, backpack."

"This is moving beyond where we can control it," Hazel said, looking back at her. "If they breach these fence lines, we'll have to clear the entire building manually. We may need to think about ending selection early."

Justine sipped the tea. "And what is the status of our security forces?"

"The primary units are deployed, and the reserves are staged and ready, Ma'am. We have an overwatch position in our building two floors up—that's where we're controlling the drones. Another team is staged on the helicopter, waiting on our call to recover the selectees. The medical bay is manned and ready as well. Harkness has been safely evacuated to San Francisco General, and they just took him into the operating room in the ICU."

Justine took it all in, tapping her fingers on the table. They were so close. For a moment, she let herself think about talking to the lawyers. To see if she could end the contest early, considering the imminent threat. She dismissed it, banished it from her mind. They were committed now.

Until the end.

For Nicky.

"Call Reinholm. Let's see what pull he has with the riot squad. We need to break this up before it escalates further."

She glanced at her computer screen, where a chat message popped up. Dmitri. The guy curating the selectee experience. Or at least he was, until control of the process was wrested from their hands.

Need to talk. In private.

She looked down at him. He made eye contact briefly, under the brim of that ridiculous trucker cap, then he smoothly rolled his wheelchair past the other staffers, engrossed in their screens. Out into the hallway.

Justine stood and followed. Kathy fell into step, a pace behind her.

She trailed Dmitri's receding chair to a side corridor, out of sight of the normal pedestrian traffic flows around the ops center.

"What is that symbol on your hat?" Justine asked as she walked up.

"It's a Gracie triangle. Brazilian jiujitsu. Mind, body, spirit. When it's in 3-D—a pyramid, it's meant to symbolize stability. Like a cat, you always land on something steady." He eyed Kathy. "Does she need to be here?"

"She has my trust and confidence to hear whatever you have to say."

"Fine. Your funeral."

"I hope it doesn't come to that." Kathy stood behind silently.

"Anyhoooo. I have an idea about how to deal with our mole situation. I want to send you an internal message, telling you I've identified them by name. You will acknowledge, and then I will talk about the plans to detain them. The mole has admin rights—root access to the system, and they'll be able to see the message."

"Who do you think it is? The mole," Justine asked.

Dmitri wheeled his chair absently back and forth, balanced in mid-air. It must take some core strength to pull that off. "I have some suspicions, but I'd rather confirm them first."

Justine nodded. "Fair enough. Do it."

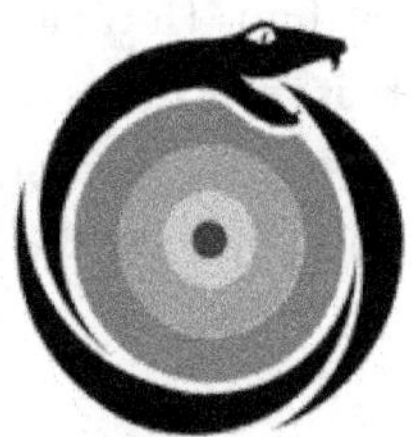

AUDREY FELT THE PROD OF THE PISTOL at her back and picked up her pace. She couldn't believe Roz was gone. Although she'd only known him for a brief period, she felt a connection all out of proportion to the brief time they'd spent together. Audrey had already mentally rehearsed introducing him to her mother, and dealing with the ensuing raised eyebrow it would bring.

So much communicated in that one little movement.

The final round of the Ninth Level was one long room. Totally barren. The fog was higher here—waist-high, making it seem as though they sloshed through water as they walked.

Dominating the space was an enormous statue, easily thirty feet high.

Satan.

Three heads, each mouth filled with a twisting and writhing corpse shape, cries of pain and despair to accompany the sight.

A perverse, shadowed inversion of the Christian trinity.

The wings of the statue were easily the size of automobiles, and beat in slow, ponderous motion. They kept a constant stream of frigid air in motion in the space. Tau walked at the back of the group, club at the ready.

"And did you read the passage on this part of Hell, Ms. Zhou?" Gabrielle gazed up at the statue.

"Anything in particular you want to know?"

"Who do you think those are corpses supposed to be? The ones up in the mouths."

Audrey pursed her lips. "The final round of Treachery is reserved for traitors to their leaders. Each of Satan's mouths holds a human embodying that sin. The far mouth holds Judas Iscariot, who betrayed Christ, while the others contain Brutus and Cassius, both of whom betrayed Caesar."

"Huh. Bunch of dead white guys."

"I suppose. If you consider Jesus white. Most scholars don't."

"So, how do we get out of here—I don't see an exit. Don't make me devote any more attention to this stupid book than I already have."

"Not enough Zeus in it for you?"

Gabrielle laughed, surprised by the comment. "There is never enough Zeus."

"In the book, Dante and Virgil climbed Satan's back. Somewhere along the way, gravity is supposed to reverse, and they end up climbing downward. Depart Hell on the other side of the world."

"Huh." She paused, coming to a stop as they came to the base of the statue. More pools of water here. "Come out, Mehran. I know you're there." Silence. Nothing. Gabrielle sighed theatrically and pointed the gun at Audrey's chest.

From the far side of the Satan statue, Roz slid into view. Wet, covered in grimy filth, and parts of his clothing frozen.

Blood oozed from his left shoulder, staining his flannel shirt.

He looked amazing.

A crooked grin stole over his features as he stared at Audrey.

"Well, well, well. I guess you do have gills, Mehran."

"Why are you doing this? You can't share leadership of the foundation with either of us? You're that greedy?" Roz held his shield. He must have circled around and grabbed it. Audrey's eyes fell on the base of the Satan statue, where her spear leaned.

Gabrielle laughed. "Well, I *am* greedy, full disclosure. Unfortunately, neither of you signed with my employer. Ms. Zhou had a chance and declined." She made a rueful face. "Your loss."

"Hey, Tau, what are you doing with her? You know she's gonna drop you like a sack of potatoes as soon as she gets what she wants. You really think she's going to share stewardship with you?"

The New Zealander regarded him, then stared at Gabrielle. "That is the agreement, yes?"

She looked back at him and gave him a reassuring smile. "Of course, baby."

"What's wrong, big boy? Starting to doubt her word?"

Tau cracked his neck ominously and stepped forward. "I think you should stop talking."

Roz smiled. "Okay, tubs, you can shut me up right now.

I'm ready. Unless you'd rather she does it for you." He looked at Gabrielle, then back to Tau. "What's wrong, sausage neck? Don't like your chances?"

Tau put out a hand to stay Gabrielle. He wagged his tongue in the air and slapped his club with his massive free hand.

Roz grinned. "That's more like it."

The two circled each other. Tau didn't wait long. The big New Zealander hammered at Roz with his *wahaika*. He took the hits on the shield, and the powerful impacts knocked him from his feet. He got up heavily, shook himself off like a dog. "Come to papa, big man." He set the Aegis down and gestured with one hand toward Tau. As Tau closed the distance and swung the club, Roz ducked under it and hugged one of the man's tree-trunk-sized thighs. He spun in a circle in a move that tripped the larger man. The pair fell into a water hole. Tau struggled to the surface, arms flailing. Then they both disappeared.

After a minute, Gabrielle sighed. "Fine." She looked at Audrey. "Well, this is awkward."

They stood, watching the faux corpses in Satan's mouths, listening to moans carried by the winds.

"It's disappointing that a woman wasn't one of the top three worst traitors in history, according to Dante. It's a problematic critique, if you ask me."

"Are you auditioning?"

Gabrielle laughed, a full body shiver extending from her belly. "Who said professors had no sense of humor?"

With a great sucking gasp, Roz burst to the surface. He towed an unconscious Tau. Roz levered himself up onto the floor, then dragged the big man out.

Gabrielle and Audrey gawked, both too surprised for words.

Roz slapped Tau's face several times, and after long moments, the big man spurted water from his mouth and turned on his side. It took him a moment to regain his senses.

"Why…why save me?" He stared at Roz.

Roz had a nasty black eye forming from one of Tau's strikes. "I never thought you were with her." He pointed up to Gabrielle. "Figured you were along for the ride, looking for an exit the entire time."

Gabrielle gestured with the pistol. "This is cute, really it is, but—"

Tau lurched to his feet, cutting Gabrielle off. "Enough. Enough of the killing. There is room for all of us. We four can share the stewardship." He held up a hand and advanced a step toward Gabrielle.

"No. No, we can't," she answered calmly, firing two shots. A pair of holes appeared in the New Zealander's forehead.

Tau fell to his knees, then to the ground.

Gabrielle backed up a few steps, staring at the two of them. She shrugged. "Well, we were going to part company at some point. Dawn is coming."

Audrey looked over Gabrielle's shoulder. She watched the fog slowly part in the distance, disturbed by some unseen cause. "I have one last thing I want to say."

Gabrielle looked bored. "Sure, I'll bite."

"Oh, no," Audrey replied. "He'll bite."

Diogenes sprang at full speed in a long leap, jaws locking onto Gabrielle's right forearm. Audrey sprinted for the spear as she heard the pistol go off. Turning, she saw Gabrielle had lost the gun and had a wicked-looking knife in her left hand, slashing at Dio.

Audrey took several steps and launched the spear. It lanced into Gabrielle, erupting from her back. Her stabs grew weaker and weaker, until at last, she slumped to the ground.

Diogenes seemed to sense when she expired, and he came off on his own. He scampered to Audrey, teeth red, tongue lolling.

She caressed his head. "Good boy." She turned to Roz. "Two things. One, are you going to explain why you thought challenging a guy twice your size to a fight was a good idea?"

He squinted in the glare of the lights above. "I figured it was a better play than getting shot? Shot again, I mean."

"Hmm. Foolish. Bold. But mainly foolish. Two, did I hear you call him 'sausage neck'?"

Roz gazed back sheepishly. "I was running out of body-shaming insults. Did I hear you say, 'He'll bite?'"

"Let me look at you." She did a head-to-toe check of his body, the way the trainers taught her. She'd gotten basic first-responder training as a member of the embassy staff and the other tours she'd done for the government.

"It's a through and through," Roz husked through closed teeth.

She regarded the wound. "One sec." Audrey used the last bit of her tape to plug the entry and exit wounds of Roz's gunshot wound. "Okay, you're going to live."

"Easy for you to say." They checked out Dio, doing what they could for his injuries, which were mostly small knife wounds. Nothing life-threatening.

Roz took the lead, limping around the curve of the statue. On the backside, it looked like any rock wall you'd find in a climbing gym—multicolored handholds ascending upward. He'd hidden Hark's pack there.

Thankfully, the ascent was a forgiving one, and Satan's backside had ample holds for even a novice climber. Thick strands of ebony rope dotted the devil's hindquarters. Dio's tactical harness doubled as a climbing harness, and Roz clipped it to his belt. He winced at the lancing pain in his side as he ascended. His ribs needed a long vacation. The ledge at the top led to a surprisingly normal-looking white door. Roz opened it, and they limped inside.

CHAPTER 30

Roz—Easter Sunday, 2 AM

THEY STUMBLED FORWARD, INTO DARKNESS.

As their eyes adjusted, the contours of the room took shape. The floor was soft and springy—a damp earthen mix. A greenhouse of sorts, filled with plants. Birds chirped, and several flitted in the leafy plants. Sitting incongruously in the middle were three leather chairs, with what looked like hair salon drying machines behind them, with wide armrests filled with wires and machinery. A flatscreen television stood mounted on one wall, and at the far end of the greenhouse, a closed door.

The pair looked at each other.

"Any thoughts?" Audrey asked softly. She looked beautiful in the light.

He took her hands in his, staring down into her eyes. "Oh,

I have lots of thoughts, about all kinds of things." He leaned down, softly kissed her on the lips.

"What was that for?" she asked.

"I've been wanting to do that for a while now."

She leaned forward and kissed him hard on the mouth.

He looked at her with a wry grin. "That one was better." He brushed the hair out of her eyes with callused fingers. "I'm glad we made it."

"How did you survive, anyway?"

"Gabrielle grazed me in the arm as I dove into the water. I pulled Hark's HEEDs bottle out and used that to calm down and catch my breath."

"What the hell is a HEEDs bottle?"

"Helicopter Emergency Egress Device. Basically, a small canister of air, gives you a few dozen breaths, enough to escape a sinking helo."

Her eyes widened. "That's handy."

"Don't tell the Texan, or he'll never let me live it down. Anyway, I found out that there was a channel of water under there that connected two or three of the open holes. They were only five feet deep or so. I swam down to the next opening and took a peek. Then it was a matter of waiting for you three to get out of earshot. Once you did, I hauled my freezing ass out and ran back to the beginning of the circle."

"Remarkable foresight, bringing a bottle like that."

Roz smiled and nodded. "Hark. That old mustached bastard thought of everything. Don't tell him, or he'll become a complete diva. The running helped warm me up. I triggered the tower trap again. Once it came up, I got Dio out. Then I crawled under the fog to get close, and Dio stayed put so he could make his grand entrance later."

"How did she know you were there? I had no clue."

"That woman had some superb instincts. I don't know."

On the wall, the monitor powered on.

Berenger, sitting in a room full of books. "Congratulations," he began. "You have finished your journey through Hell. It's easy for me to say from the comfort of the past, but I had to be sure about the stewards of the foundation. There is too much riding on it. More than I can say now."

Roz sat down in one of the reclining chairs, a touch woozy from the blood loss.

Berenger continued. "You are now, or you will be shortly after all the paperwork is complete, the controlling figures for all that I have created. The work of a lifetime. It's up to you, now, to carry the promise of Plek into the future. There is much to tell you, and little time to do it. Humanity stands at a crossroads, beset with at least a dozen interlocking crises, paralyzing our ability to understand and act. Our old ways, the traditions and institutions that built the modern world, are failing. Decaying. Entropy is an implacable physical constant that enacts its toll on everything. The dominant thinking of the day in media and academia has offered much in the way of critique and new perspectives. But it does little to generate constructive solutions. We've forgotten so much of our Indigenous and traditional faith wisdom that the little we do remember seems to be more akin to fairy tales than anything truly helpful. A system built on an infinite growth model cannot long endure on a planet with finite physical and attentional resources. There are many ways for humankind to progress into the future. Some paths end in darkness, and others muddle through in bleak, unhappy trails. But there are different ways of being in the world. As you were born anew in the Inferno, so too can the world be born anew.

Berenger's face grew hard. "But it won't be easy. The old world will not die a quick and painless death. There's a reason why scientific paradigms don't shift until the adherents of the old one pass on. As Ursula Le Guin said, '*We live in capitalism. Its power seems inescapable. So did the divine right of kings. Any human power can be resisted and changed by human beings.'* The universe moves inexorably toward greater forms of complexity. From inorganic matter to single-cell organisms, and finally to humanity itself, this complexity is reaching a critical mass. Pierre Teilhard de Chardin framed this progression as the *Geosphere*—the physical environment, the *Biosphere*—the living creatures within it, and the *Noosphere*—the local collective consciousness now blooming into being. The internet and social media have sped up the development of this *Noosphere*. The foundation is intended to be a midwife to that new world."

"Was *not* expecting a college lecture," Roz remarked. He munched on a protein bar, splitting half and handing it to Audrey.

On the screen, Nicholas continued. "But our intentions are not without detractors. Many view it as an unacceptable loss of control and will resist. At times violently. Plek's research efforts have yielded revolutionary breakthroughs in unlocking the power of human perception. This perception shapes our reality—*'I am what I attend to,'* as psychologist William James said. The road to our future as a species begins with improving our individual ability to make sense of the world, to come to consensus on collective action, and to work in concert with one another toward meeting them. It won't take some sort of mass conversion of humans to make this happen. A phase shift can occur with as little as three percent of a population. Through the work of an engaged minority, significant change can come about. In the words of Margaret Mead, *'Never deny the power of a small group of committed individuals to change the world. Indeed, that is the only thing that ever has.'* This is what the foundation has been called to do. To midwife the new world."

Back in the past, Berenger took a sip of his beverage,

which Roz estimated was a very expensive tumbler of whiskey. "I'll have more to say later on, but for now, congratulations." The grey-haired man lifted the drink in salute. The screen faded to black.

The far door opened, and an ebony woman in a long dress walked out. Her eyes shone with a sense of peace that radiated. "I am Teela Phillips. Chief of neurobiology for Plek. I'm glad that you made it. And hello, Diogenes—I'm glad you made it." She squatted down and gave the hound some love. "I will guide you through the rest of the process."

"The rest?" Roz asked, stuffing the bar wrapper into his pocket. This didn't seem like a place to litter. Sacred, almost.

"We have already exposed you to some psycho-active elements as part of the selection process. Less than you probably think you were, because human imaginations are so powerful."

Teela adjusted the plaits in her hair. "There are three components to this process. The first is bio-chemical, the second is neurological, and the third is ritualistic."

"What if we say no?" Audrey asked. "What if we don't choose to partake?"

Teela nodded. "Consent is important. We have no desire to force anything, whether the administration of this protocol or ideas upon the world. This change must be voluntary for the participants, or it will fail. If you elect not to take part, Justine informed me you will receive the sum of ten million dollars for your participation. This process is necessary to assume stewardship of the foundation."

Roz looked at her and shrugged. "In for a penny, in for a pound."

Audrey sighed. "Agreed."

Teela smiled. "When you're ready, please take your seats. Before I discuss the biological, let me tell you about the final component. The ritual part. You won't train for the ritual until a later date—there's a good deal involved in the preparation. There are long histories of ancient rites, used by cultures across the world, with entheogenic compounds. In dozens of tongues, words of power that can alter conscious states. A greater union and connection to a mystery beyond normal sensory comprehension. This sounds very 'woo.' I get it. When I began my research here, I thought the same thing. But the results speak for themselves. I ask that you approach the ritual portion with a modicum of humility and curiosity about what the process might bring. Once you get to the island, we have trained personnel who will guide you deeper through this. Now then, the chemical element. Several years ago, our historians discovered a reference to a tree. A very specific tree. A long-lost variant of *Tabernanthe iboga,* found in Central Africa. Indigenous tribes used it ritually, to commune with their ancestors and the divine." She finished with Audrey, moved on to Roz. "I won't bore you with the molecular names. Recent clearcutting has brought some of these ancient mysteries closer to the modern world, one tragic silver lining to the colonization and rape of the earth. Our pharmacology team refined the chemical composition and delivery of this rainforest shrub." She handed them each a half-filled pewter mug, intricately carved runes on the sides. "I could give it to you in a plastic cup, but this is a little better, don't you think?"

They drank the mixture, a confluence of sour and sweet that he couldn't quite place. "Excellent. Now, for the mechanical element. The device now lowering to your heads is a Plek proprietary device, developed in house as a joint project between several of our research teams. It combines elements of trans-cranial stimulation, virtual-reality optical and audio interfaces, and an interactive software program driven by an artificial generalized intelligence. It will modulate your experience based on brain pattern feedback to curate the optimal experience for the user."

Teela came to a stop in front of them. She smelled like some sort of soap. Maybe sandalwood. "I promise this process will be unlike anything you've ever experienced. Please adjust and tighten the eye cups and insert the earphones. When you are ready, we can continue. As I was saying, this element involves high-volume knowledge dissemination through optical and auditory sensory modalities, besides modulating neural pathways. This delivery process, while rapid, takes the human mind a period to process and integrate.

Try to relax."

He heard Audrey laugh nervously next to him. "Easy for you to say."

"Oh!" The ebony woman pointed upward. "I forgot to mention. After you finish, take the stairs to the roof. Justine will send someone to collect you there."

"Why can't we just go down the stairs?"

Teela shrugged. "Part of Berenger's directives. *The Inferno* ends—"

"With Dante and Virgil watching the sunrise. Got it." Audrey finished for her.

"Enjoy the ride," Teela said with a slight tilt of her head.

Slowly, the goggles brightened, coalescing into shapes and characters of an unfamiliar alphabet. He heard sounds, not words or music, necessarily—various types of tones, a sonic whispering that built in volume. It alternated between ears, sometimes left, sometimes right, and sometimes both. Images flickered between the characters and shapes, coming across in milliseconds. The images and sound sluiced over them in a deluge. It was difficult to process the information consciously, which, in the dim recesses of his cognition, he realized was the point.

Roz's head ached from the firehose of sensory input. More than anything, he wanted to rip the goggles and earbuds from his face. Images, video, sound. Swirling patterns of dots, swarming and flocking like a murmuration of birds. Patterns, icons, charts, maps. Every time he tried to hold on to something, the cycle moved on to new content. It was too much. There was just too much. It hurt. He went to a place where he wasn't conscious anymore, at least not how he understood it. Roz lost all sense of time, and then he lost all sense of everything. The Void claimed him.

At some unknown point after that, Roz felt himself ascending toward consciousness, riding in a disembodied form on unseen currents. His focus followed a low beeping tone. Once he came to, he stripped off the goggles and earbuds. Pulled the needle out. Killer headache—migraine on steroids. Audrey stirred, and he helped her get unhooked and attuned to the situation.

"That was wild," she mumbled with unfocused eyes.

The two of them watched the smoke rise from the equipment.

"Looks like something internal just fried everything when we disconnected from the system."

"Weird. How long were we out?"

Roz glanced at his watch. "Whoa. Four hours."

Audrey raised an eyebrow. "Felt like a lifetime, though."

"Yeah. Let's get out of here." He extended a hand, and she grasped it.

They walked up the stairs, hand in hand.

CHAPTER 31

***Justine**—Easter Sunday, 6 AM*

JUSTINE ATTENDED TO THE RHYTHM of the operations center.

The slow murmuring of side conversations, the hiss of a Keurig coffee maker as it spat out yet another steaming cup of single-serving coffee.

The squawk of communications headsets, the smell of microwaved takeout. A never-ending stream of social media feeds on a side-screen infinite scroll. Camera shots from building walls and the circling unmanned drones. The nervous system of a superorganism with one overriding goal. To uncover those worthy to become stewards. Since they'd locked down all wireless and cellular transmissions, they didn't have access to the other camera angles inside, save the overhead shots of the Ninth Circle. The last several hours had been intense. None of the predictive models expected the outcome. The staff was elated Zhou and Mehran were going to be the stewards and had prevailed against such long odds. A jubilant confidence wafted around in the air.

Hazel broke her from her musing. "Ma'am, the tear gas is having its desired effect. The assembled groups are dispersing." On the main screen, they could see the crowds spreading out and dissipating. Whatever fever possessed them had broken.

"Thank you. Let's get a damage report when able, figure out if any of these folks are still inside the perimeter. We have enough legal issues as it is."

Hazel shared a glance and a smile with Dmitri. "Understood, Ma'am. We just got word from Teela—the selectees are on their way to the roof." She turned to the rest of the group. "Alright, people, the helicopter is airborne in five minutes, to collect the selectees and get them looked at in medical. Let's finish this thing."

Justine was ready to put it all behind.

To move on.

She didn't think she'd ever get over losing Nicky, but at least she could complete his last request, in accordance with his directives. Then she could figure out what she was going to do with the rest of her life.

She watched Dmitri wheel himself to the operations center main exit, stopping and turning to face the circle of workstations. Blocking the door. *What was he doing?* Justine saw Manbuns move to the only other exit. Then Jarvis got up, slung his messenger bag over his shoulder, and moved toward the door.

"Going somewhere, J-bone?" Dmitri said softly.

"Bathroom. Can I get through?" Jarvis shifted from side to side, scratched his neck. "It's a little urgent, if you get my drift."

"Why are you taking your bag, though?"

"Personal. Medical stuff. I don't need to tell you about it.

Get out of my way." So far, no one else had noticed the exchange. Manbuns crept up slowly, sliding around the circle.

"No." Dmitri turned his ball cap backwards, the Gracie triangle facing the exit to the room. "Why'd you do it, J-bone? Was the pay not good enough?"

"I don't have to explain myself to you. You wouldn't understand, hipster."

Dmitri wagged a finger at him. "I'm not a hipster. I'm *sincerely ironic*."

Jarvis made his move then, dodging to one side, then shouldering the wheelchair roughly. Dmitri got one hand on him and used it to lever himself upward as the chair crashed to the floor, onto Jarvis's back. His legs dangled in a boneless flop on Jarvis's side as he clung to the man. People looked up finally, to see what the commotion was. Dmitri reached with one hand and got a hold of Jarvis's collar. The man elbowed and tried to shrug Dmitri off, but he held onto Jarvis's back like a lamprey eel. By the time they got to the door, Dmitri had both his arms around his neck.

After a few seconds, Jarvis went down. He crashed into their coffee station. Sugar packets and disposable cups exploded into the air. Napkins fluttered gently down. The fight had the full attention of the room, but no one understood what they'd seen.

Manbuns came over and brought Dmitri his wheelchair, gave him a fist bump. Another guard applied restraints to a disoriented Jarvis.

"Nice work," Justine said. "I had no idea about your hidden talents."

Dmitri smiled sheepishly. "Purple belt. Five tournaments so far. They never see me coming."

THEY WATCHED DAWN STEAL OVER THE CITY, hands clasped as one.

Even with the light pollution, the stars still shimmered until well after daybreak. When they'd walked up the last set of stairs, a vault-like door had boomed shut behind them, locking with a weighty click. Hark's absence cast a long shadow in the dawn light. Roz wouldn't be here without him. He hoped he could live up to what the Texan had seen in him. Whatever it was. Roz felt the enchanted state of the last few hours slowly leaving him. The soreness, aches, and pains came to the fore once again.

Roz looked over at her. He never tired of looking at her. Of drinking in her beauty. "Happy Easter."

She traced figure-eights on his hand with a slender finger. "Christ is risen, indeed."

Roz looked down, momentarily losing himself in the whorls of his hand. The patterns were so clear. He thanked the universe that she stood next to him on the roof. He was hopeful again. "What are you going to do?" They shared beef jerky and the last of Audrey's water. Breakfast of champions. He had to be imagining it, but he thought he smelled hot coffee and breakfast food from the streets below, as well as exhaust from the building systems. He found himself estimating the location of vehicles on the street below from the sounds reflecting from the skyscrapers. The noise bounced and reflected like sets of surf in the ocean from different directions.

She looked out toward the harbor. "My mother. See if I can convince her to fight the cancer. One last time. If she won't, then I'll figure out hospice." Audrey looked at him, and something rough and ragged broke loose.

She *saw* him.

Saw the pain and failure and heartache and imperfections, and she didn't look away.

He promised himself he wouldn't look away, either.

"What about you? What are you going to do?" she asked.

"What I don't want to do, but what I think I'm supposed to do, if that makes any sense."

She laughed, and Dio threw her a quizzical glance. "After what we just went through, I'm not sure 'makes sense' is a super relevant metric."

"Probably right. There are some things past words. Past reason. Hey, this is a weird question, but are you feeling at all…different?" He watched her face, fascinated by the play of emotions across her features.

Audrey gazed back, considering. "It's hard to tell. I think I'm noticing more things. Things about the environment. My sense of smell is off the charts right now—I swear I can smell a street vendor's food. Which is ridiculous. And…" She looked at him and then her eyes widened. "Microexpressions. On the order of forty to two hundred milliseconds. Basically, between one-twenty-fifth and a fifth of a second."

"I wondered if that was happening. Guess we're in the processing and integrating phase Teela mentioned."

"I guess so. What do you think the steward gig will be like?"

He considered. "Do you remember when you started—started as a Foreign Service officer? That sense of optimism, purpose. Duty, country, all that."

Audrey smiled. "I remember that girl, yes."

"And then remember how you felt after your attack. Dark. Bleak. Jaded."

She swallowed and nodded. "That too." She fed Dio a piece of beef jerky.

He watched her neck, the pulse of her carotid on porcelain skin. "We're supposed to get over all that. To realize it's not going to be perfect. Hell, it's not even going to be pretty, most of the time. But we have to keep moving forward. Keep trying to do our best. Even in the face of all the tragedies. To get past them. The only way out is through."

She stared at him. "The world according to Roz?"

Roz grinned. "I probably stole that from one of the *Rocky* movies."

"Which one?"

"*Rocky Four*, of course. The only *Rocky*."

Audrey laughed, a joyous tinkle of sound. Over the soft hum of the city, Roz heard the jagged strop of a helicopter blade cut through the marine layer. A line from an old Army marching song came unbidden to Roz from a course he'd attended early in his career.

The sound of the rotors was loud and cold.

There was a weird wobble to the engine. A subcomponent of sound he picked out from the other noises generated from the bird. Must be reflecting from the other buildings. They watched the craft slide through the skyscrapers toward them from the east.

Small pebbles and other loose items flew at high velocity as the machine settled on the roof. Two helmeted and masked security types waved them forward, flanking either side of the exposed passenger cabin door.

They limped towards the helo, eyes squinted against the spray of debris. They shuddered to a stop. Too late, Roz's eyes reached into the cabin, saw the woman and the Mona

Lisa smile on her lips. On either side of them, the men triggered tasers in tandem. He felt the world blank out for a moment when the barbs hit his chest. It felt like hornets crawled into his skin, set up shop, made themselves comfortable. Someone rolled him to his side, cuffed him, and pulled him roughly to his feet. His legs were woozy, but the guard manhandled him into a seat in the passenger cabin, buckling him in for good measure. The other did the same for Audrey and Diogenes, whom they'd shot with several tranquilizer darts.

"Rozzy," Milena said sweetly.

THE CRAFT LIFTED OFF SMOOTHLY, pressing Roz into the cream leather seat, creased from years of use. His shoulder ached from getting thrown in, and the gunshot wound oozed—broken open again. From the seat, he'd watched Milena's henchmen run downstairs and return, defeated by the massive door. He stared at her across the passenger compartment. The years since he'd seen her added new lines to her face, and she looked exhausted. Like her soul was worn thin, the old Stone Temple Pilots song lyric. He couldn't believe he'd destroyed his marriage for this woman.

"Well done. I knew you had it in you." Something beneath the plastered-on haughtiness. Something unsettled.

She's afraid. "Doesn't this violate the terms of my restraining order?"

"Consider it an exception. I won't tell if you won't."

His eyes flicked left. Audrey, hands cuffed as well. Diogenes, strapped to the seat next to her. Unconscious, but heart fluttering his fur at a manageable rate. One guard in the passenger compartment, a muscular black man, waved a pistol, clad in 5.11 chic. The woman filling the final seat had to be Grace, the new girl. She held a conversation on one phone while texting furiously on another. Her facial expressions morphed between fear and anger, depending on whether she was focused on the phone call or the text. Large black eye on her face. The purpling shape seemed to faintly ripple in the early morning light. The other guard would be up in the front, with the pilot. He looked at Milena. "What do you want?"

Milena leaned forward, put her hand on his jaw. "What I want is in your head, and coursing through your veins. Plek is at least three years ahead of their competitors. Maybe five. I should know—I'm one of those competitors. Giving our nation's special operators heightened sensory processing should be a goal you can get behind." Her glacial-hued eyes dilated as she spoke. "I just need access. See what's under the hood. I can make it worth your while."

Audrey shifted in the seat next to him. "How so?" he asked. Behind his back, his fingers hit the record button on his watch for the harness camera.

"I can get your dishonorable discharge upgraded to a general. Hell, I might even be able to pull an honorable, depending on what new friends I make on the HASC and SASC. I'm already working on an upgrade for Barrett here." Milena gestured at 5.11 guy, who shrugged.

"HASC? SASC?" Roz asked.

Audrey leaned over and rested her head on his shoulder.

It was getting stuffy inside the cabin, with all six of them in there. The flight path swung over the bay, banked left. Heading north. "Armed Service Committees. House and Senate," Audrey answered, never taking her eyes off Milena.

"Aww. You two are so cute. I don't think I ever mentioned that Phillip Winston, Colleen's father, is an old family friend, did I? Went to Yale with my dad in '72. I can get this all turned around, Rozzy." Milena leaned forward, staring at him with a beguiling intensity. "I know Phillip hates your guts—that won't change. But he owes me. I can get you visitation rights. Who knows, maybe you could come work for me again. Get that old magic back."

Grace murmured in her ear, and Milena looked down at the screen she held up.

While that was happening, Roz felt Audrey nuzzle her head on his shoulder, like a cat. Something warm and dry fell onto his fingers. *The beanie.* He clasped it in his fingers, pulled it closer, and watched 5.11 guy for any reaction. Nothing.

"When we were in the Uggalino murder room, you said you didn't send anyone after me. What about the other murders of selectees?"

Milena glared to her right, at Grace, who looked out the window into the distance. "Some of my staff felt the need to *violate my trust,* take matters into their own hands to keep you from participating. Unfortunate. But we weren't behind the other murders of selectees."

"Then who was?"

Milena rolled her eyes. "How should I know? I don't *care,* Rozzy."

"You hung me out to dry. For a murder I didn't even commit. So, if you don't mind me asking, who actually killed Vanders?"

Milena shrugged. "Does it really matter, at this point? You

were convicted. *The Uniform Code of Military Justice* says it was you."

"It matters to me. And if you want me to help you, it matters to you."

"Fine. I called in some favors with a contracting company I knew. Invictus Outcomes. You probably know some of their contractors. Old SOF guys." *There it was.*

He shook his head. "You didn't think twice, did you? Throwing me away. Did it give you pause, at all? I was *loyal* to you. More than loyal." Roz fiddled with the beanie behind his back, pulling the handcuff key from its hiding spot.

Milena nodded solemnly. "You were indeed. Believe me, if there was any other way. You understand Rozzy, the mission comes first. Before anything else. Even my personal desires." She straightened in her seat. "And now, it's about protecting America from what's coming over the next ridgeline. I know you want that, too."

"We might disagree on exactly how to do that," he shrugged. "Did your husband know about us?"

Milena pursed her lips. "Tim and I reached an understanding, early in our marriage. We had a very…French interpretation of marital boundaries."

Roz squinted and cocked his head to the side. "So, he's good being a cuck?"

Milena's lips curled into a frown, as though she'd bitten into something rotten. "He wouldn't use that word, per se."

"What's a cuck?" Audrey asked.

"Are you serious?" Roz and Milena said in unison as they looked at her. Grace stared at her as well, and so did 5.11 guy.

Which is why no one was ready for what Roz did next.

CHAPTER 32

Roz—Easter Sunday, 7:30 AM

HE PULLED UNCUFFED HANDS FROM HIS BACK, the unexpected yet inevitable reveal of a magic trick. Roz smoothly unbuckled the seat belt and pulled the Benchmade pen from his pocket.

Callused fingers curled around the filigreed Damascus steel, like bro-hugging an old deployment mate you hadn't seen in years.

5.11 guy's pistol indexed upward at a pedestrian pace. Roz found himself reading the serial number on the firearm as he leaned forward. *Glock 17, light scratching on the left part of the slide.*

Roz stuck the pen into his eye, deep enough that his pinky rested on his orbital socket.

The man roared.

With his other hand, Roz redirected the pistol upward as the guard jerked the trigger and fired the magazine dry.

The rounds blasted into the ceiling of the compartment, high-decibel roars that had nowhere to go but their ears in the confined space.

Grace screamed as blood squirted onto her face, a morbid Jackson Pollock brought to life.

After a moment, a viscous spray of searing oil spritzed them like a demonic rain. Roz grabbed a loose strap and looped it around the man's head. He used that as leverage, as the helicopter shuddered. Roz strangled him with the strap, fighting off 5.11 guy's attempts to free himself.

Roz had never killed someone at such close range.

It was a different animal.

The helicopter lurched upward for a moment, then began a rapid descent.

"We're going down—I'm heading for the closest land!" The pilot yelled through the slit between the passenger compartment and cockpit.

Face dotted in blood, he shook his head at Milena. "It's over." He pulled the pen out of the still twitching body.

She scowled through the blaring of an alarm. "Nothing is over."

Roz handed Audrey the handcuff key and checked on Diogenes. Still out. But breathing. He watched the land grow closer and closer out the window as the helicopter spun in a lazy downward arc. Not clear at all if they were going to make it. In his mind he extended vectors, estimated velocities and descent angles. *Fifty-fifty shot.*

"No, no, no," Grace keened over and over again, eyes closed.

Roz put his seat harness back on.

WHEN THE BIRD FINALLY CAME DOWN, it was more of a hard landing than a crash. Roz had been in worse.

The craft settled into a Tokyo-drift-style shimmy on faded asphalt. Then the rotor broke apart in a moan of metal and sparks as the blades struck a small shed. The helicopter canted to the side and slowly settled into an exhausted slump.

Roz opened the sliding door, pulled Audrey out.

Went back for Diogenes.

Pulse thready. Still breathing, though.

Roz felt Milena's eyes on him as he hoisted Dio onto his shoulder like a potato sack. "Follow me," he murmured, and they raced up a faded asphalt access road. His entire body was one big sore. Thursday of Hell Week vibes. And the hallucinations to go with it. Someone would notice the helo crash and come to investigate. They just had to hold out. Wind blew from the northeast, perhaps twelve miles an hour intermittently. The smell of the vehicles on the bridge above them was noxious, as was the mechanical buzzing of the engines. The sound and smell combined to produce a deep unease, and something approaching nausea. Audrey used the spear like a walking stick as they hurried up the cracked and broken road.

A round snapped past, and Roz watched the bullet trace smack into the side of the Nimitz house. They scurried behind an old wooden building. "Whoa. Did you see that?"

"What?"

"I could see the round pulse through the air. I've only ever been able to see that on glass behind a sniper."

"You saw the bullet?"

Roz peeked from behind the shelter. Not much of a head start. Milena and the last guard jogged up the road. It appeared the pilot stayed with the helo. Probably not in his contract description to pursue fleeing kidnappees on foot. Roz doubted Grace would be of help to Milena, either. "I think so."

"Hmmph. Sounds like a problem for future Roz and Audrey to wonder about if they live through the next ten minutes. I assume you have some semblance of a plan?"

"As a matter of fact, I do. I know we just started hanging out, but is it too early to bring you home?" He led her between a set of white wooden buildings. Old officer housing.

"You have a house?"

"Sort of."

The Coast Guard had locked the front door with a heavy chain, so Roz took her to the ladder. Once in the attic, Roz led them down to the master bedroom. "I used to sleep here sometimes, make a fire in the hearth when I had something to cook." The fireplace was massive—easily six feet wide. An enormous pile of ashes and half-burned driftwood sat inside. He set Diogenes down gingerly in the master bathroom tub. "We have less than ten minutes to get ready to host."

THEY GOT FIVE.

Gunfire.

Splintering crash on the first floor.

Long seconds. From his position, Roz heard their shuffling feet on the ancient flooring, estimated their pathway.

Finally, a pistol barrel poked in the door to the master bedroom.

The other security guard, Milena lurking behind. The pair moved into the bedroom.

Milena threw open the bathroom door and found Audrey, Diogenes in her lap. "Where's Feroz?"

"He left us here and ran off."

"Bullshit. Start talking or I'll put one in the dog."

The guard went to the open window, looked out at the back yard.

Phut phut phut phut.

He convulsed as bullets slammed into his face and neck. He dropped. Milena whirled, saw Roz's arm, covered in ash, a silenced pistol extended from the pile of wood in the fireplace. He could kill her now. It would be easy. She deserved it, for the hell she'd put him through. Something gave him pause. An intuition, from somewhere deep inside, a place he couldn't name, bid him to let her live. He didn't understand it. He realized he wasn't supposed to understand it. "Hands, Milena."

She hesitated, calculating. "Where'd you get that pistol?"

Roz winced as he extricated himself from the ashes. "Funny story. You probably paid for it."

FLASHING LIGHTS WAITED OUTSIDE. They held their hands in the air. Coast Guard security from nearby Treasure Island. By the time they arrived, an ambulance and an SFPD car joined the cruiser. Roz set Dio down gently. Audrey held Milena at gunpoint, arms secured by some old drapery rope. EMTs came over, checked out their injuries.

A wiry man with a nervous energy approached. "Ms. Zhou. Mr. Mehran. I'm Detective Reinholm. I've been in close contact with Ms. Lipton at Plek. As I understand the situation, the occupants of that helicopter took you against your will." The mid-thirties woman in plainclothes showed them a badge.

Roz squinted at her as an EMT applied a dressing to his shoulder.

"We're arresting Janek for kidnapping, based on Ms. Lipton's report. What will be her side of the story?" Reinholm asked.

Audrey chuckled. "Whatever it is, it'll be good."

"We have something better," Roz said with a lopsided grin. "Audio and video."

CHAPTER 33

Roz—Easter Sunday, 10 AM

ROZ AND AUDREY LAY ON HOSPITAL BEDS. The ambulance deposited them at San Francisco General. Reinholm sweet-talked the staff to allow Diogenes to accompany them and finagled a joint room. The hound lay on a patchwork quilt a nurse had thoughtfully set down, next to a makeshift water bowl. He munched on a cow hoof. The antiseptic smell in the room was fierce, covering a moldering stench of decay. He'd jammed Kleenex into his nostrils and sweet-talked earplugs and sunglasses for the two of them from the floor nurse. Too much. It was overwhelming. Hark was out cold, heavily sedated in the room across the hall.

The surgeons needed to amputate his left hand, but he was still alive. That was the important thing. Over ten units of blood replaced so far. What a miracle. Sophie was over there, keeping a solitary vigil. For the last hour, Roz and Audrey had digitally and physically signed a succession of documents. More than he'd ever had to sign to close on a house, or join the military, which he guessed came with the territory for leadership of a multi-billion-dollar entity. A mousy man scurried back and forth between their beds, pointing out where to sign and where to initial. A pair of Plek employees and a uniformed SFPD officer stood guard outside.

The door opened and Justine entered, Kathy close on her heels. Justine smiled at them, her features showing a mix of sadness and peace. "Congratulations, you two. Well done. The actual test was signing all the documents, and you passed with flying colors."

Roz nodded and gestured with a hand languidly, IV-line dangling from it. "Mind telling us what happened in there?"

The brightness of her smile dimmed a fraction. "There are some rather malign actors who sought to disrupt the process. Through nefarious means, they smuggled in the weapons which were used to injure you, Mr. Mehran, as well as the telephone that Gabrielle employed to summon the mob of protestors. For that, I am very sorry. The doctor tells me you should recover from your wound quickly, given adequate rest."

"Not the first time. No hard feelings."

"The video recording you took with Diogenes' camera is going to keep General Janek tied up in legal wrangling for some time. My sources indicate her board has grown weary of her. But Janek and Laughlin Carmichael—they're only one of the factions seeking to disrupt our efforts. The bottom line is that there is an array of aggressive multinational corporations, as well as a few ideologically centered groups focused on acquiring our insights through any means. We've fought them in courts for years and physically defended our facilities against their incursions. Most likely, they were behind the sabotage of Nicholas's plane. They had at least the

Corsteads on their payroll, possibly others within the final selectees. They attempted to recruit more, and when that failed, they eliminated potential candidates. It turns out that Laughlin Carmichael wasn't behind the deaths of the selectees—at least, before they got into the tower. Another group was responsible for that."

"Who?" Audrey asked.

"Have you ever heard of the Hopf Collective?" Justine replied.

Roz looked at her. "Hopf... They did the pipeline bombing in Wyoming a few years back."

"That's the one. They're an anarchic organization currently on the FBI's radar for a string of minor vandalism incidents, besides various online postings. Hopf is a loose, decentralized constellation of environmental, social justice activists, and academics. They had representation both at the TAZ in Seattle and some of the most violent parts of Minneapolis."

"Dad!" Bella ran into the room and threw herself on the bed, hugging him. She had the Ahura Mazda pendant around her neck.

He winced and turned it into a smile. "Hey, peapod."

Colleen stood stiffly in the doorway, arms crossed. "The cat with nine lives." Her normal contempt was leavened with a touch of guarded concern.

Roz grinned. "More like a bad penny. Thanks, Coll. Good to see you, too."

"I didn't wish you a happy birthday. The other day."

"It's okay."

She walked over and stared out the window at the bay. Finally, she spoke. "Did you get a lawyer yet? I'm sure now you have the ability to keep us tied up in court for years."

"I'll sign the papers, Colleen."

"What?" She swiveled her head to regard him.

"Got 'em on you?"

He could see her breathing change and watched the carotid artery pulse in her neck quicken. These changes were going to take some time to deal with. At least the headaches seemed to have subsided.

She rummaged in her handbag, pulling out a folder. She looked for something to write with, but he held up the Benchmade pen. His eyes passed over traces of 5.11's blood, drying black in the grooves of the Damasteel patterning.

After glancing through, he signed at the spots indicated by the sticky tabs and handed them back.

Colleen received them awkwardly, spilling a few in the process. "I, uh, yeah, so. Thanks." She was silent for long moments. Wiped a tear. "What made you change your mind?"

Roz scratched at the bandage on his shoulder. "It's clear—painfully clear, I need to work on some things. Sort some stuff out. Before I can be a good dad. Before I can be the father that Bella *deserves*. In the meantime, the best way to know if I can trust someone is to trust them. Taylor Swift said that. I have to trust that you will do what's best for our daughter while I figure things out." He stared up at her. "For what it's worth, I'm sorry. I'm sorry that I couldn't hold up my end of our marriage. I'm sorry for all the pain I caused you. You didn't deserve any of it. You're a good woman, and a great mother."

"Wow." Colleen leaned back. Saw him with new eyes. "I was not expecting to hear that from you. Thanks. It means a lot. But I'm pretty sure Taylor Swift didn't—"

But Roz was already talking to Bella, holding her close. "You mean the world to me. *You,* my love, are the best thing that I was ever a part of. The best thing I've ever done. You can come see me whenever you want."

She hugged him tighter and tighter until he winced and laughed.

"Hey. Easy on the ribs."

Colleen nodded, gave him a wistful smile. "See you around, Feroz." She took Bella's hand, and together they walked out.

Roz exhaled, wiped tears of his own from his eyes. "So, what's next, Ms. Lipton? After we sleep at least a week. Maybe two."

Justine looked at Audrey, then at him. "You both need training, to master the changes from the Berenger Blend. When you're ready, we can talk about the next step."

Roz stared at Audrey, who met his glance with a mischievous grin that matched his own. A glimmering promise of things to come.

Roz glanced at Diogenes, who kept his own counsel. He always did.

Roz looked back at Justine. "Let's go."

CHAPTER 33.3

Kathy

SHE EXCUSED HERSELF TO USE THE BATHROOM, flicking the phone menu as she walked.

She dodged orderlies pushing patients through the hall. She only had a minute. By the time Kathy made it to the bathroom stall, she logged into the anonymous message board, after tunneling through a virtual private network, and using a second SIM card built into her phone.

Tell the Collective all is well.

Be ready to move on my word.

Soon.

THE END

ACKNOWLEDGMENTS

If you made it this far, I would appreciate it if you could drop a review on Amazon—it really helps. This QR code leads to the Amazon page for review:

This novel has been a long work in progress. Over the years I have been fortunate to have had feedback and encouragement from a long list of people. Thank you to all of the following:

To my early readers—particularly the ones I inflicted *way* too early drafts on—I can't thank you enough. That's a rookie mistake I shan't be making moving forward.

To the SEAL Writing Group—thank you for all the evisceration (in the most loving way) of submitted work. Long Live the Brotherhood.

To my Story Grid group—Mark, Christine, Eva, Margo,

Johne, and Moneet—thank you for the hours of great discussion and critique. I'm grateful to know each of you.

To my Nerdfest crew—thank you for years of laughter and collective storytelling. I love you guys.

The Story Ninjas—Randy and Laura—did my first round of developmental editing. They gave me a comprehensive, actionable report that took me in the right direction.

Chris Morgan did my second round of developmental editing and helped simplify and outline the final bits.

Matthew Revert did the cover and delivered the Art Deco vibe I wanted while being amazing to work with.

Deirdre Stoelzle provided expert copy-editing and found errors I never would have.

Kristin McTiernan did a final proofread, so if you find typos, hit her up ;).

Jamal West did an amazing job on the audiobook.

Thank you to my extended family for the years of encouragement and support—I am lucky to have you all!

To my three beautiful and brilliant children—thank you for sharing me with this novel.

To my mother Rebecca—thank you for reading *Clan of the Cave Bear* to me in the bathtub when I was a kid, instilling a love of reading that will stick until I shuffle off this mortal coil. Love you mom!

Lastly, my wife Christine has endured the travails of being the spouse of a Frogman and a Writer—doubly-cursed. Thank you for understanding, and when you couldn't understand, letting me be. I love you.

Subscribe to my newsletter for essays and writing updates.

https://www.adamkaraoguz.com

https://adamkaraoguz.substack.com

www.ingramcontent.com/pod-product-compliance
Lightning Source LLC
LaVergne TN
LVHW010640110826
845149LV00014B/2897

* 9 7 9 8 9 9 3 6 7 8 2 0 7 *